Letting Go

DONNA LYNN LITO

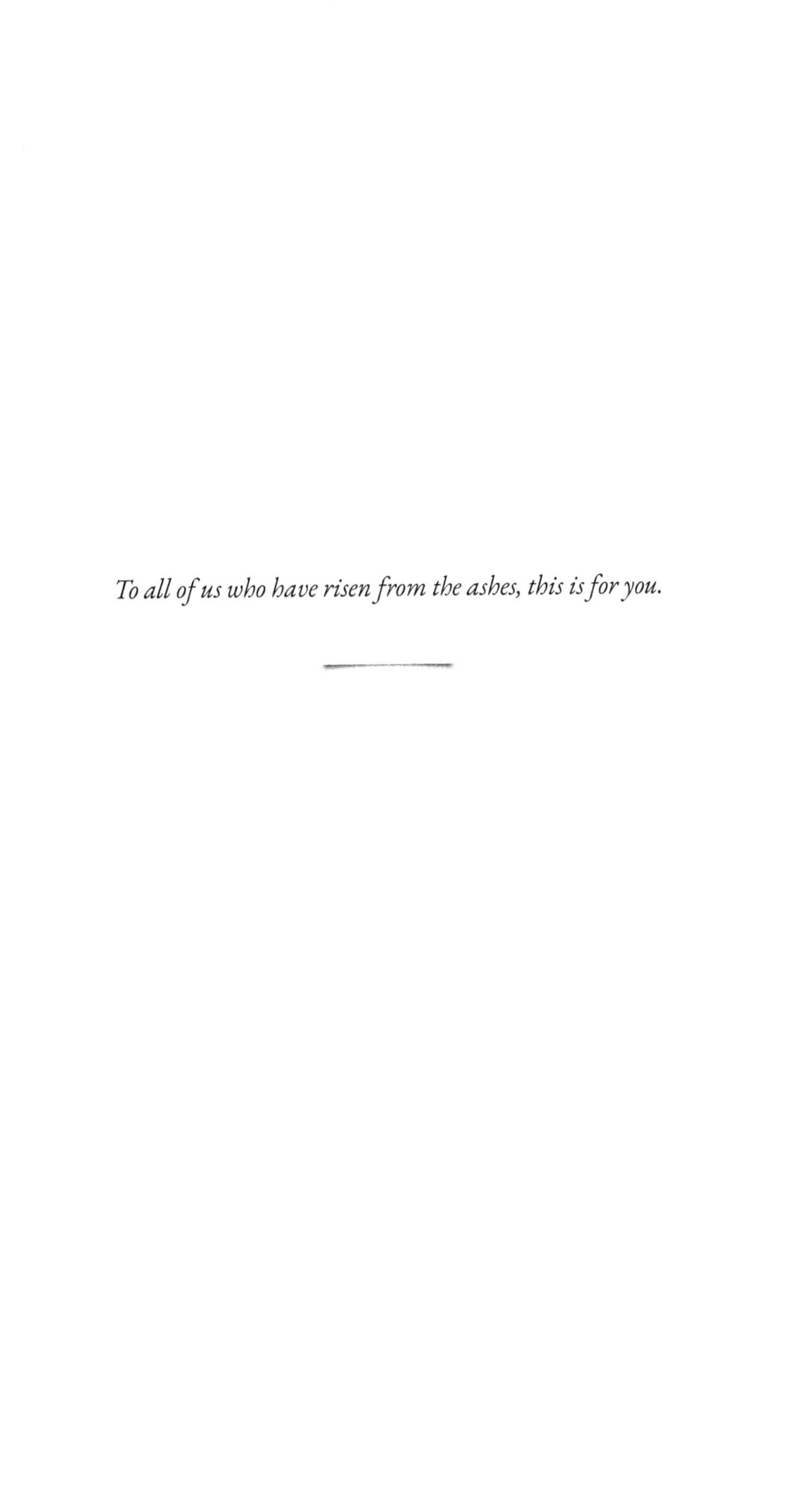

To all of us who have risen from the ashes, this is for you.

Chapter 1

"I'm a chameleon," he said as her lean legs rubbed against his long limbs under an oak tree. Jacob surprised her with a picnic on a late April afternoon.

The weather was unseasonably warm in New Hampshire, and as they lay on the grassy field on a polka dot blanket, she found his words charming.

"What do you mean?" she inquired.

"I can change into many forms to fit my surroundings," Jacob explained.

Mae was mesmerized by this boy who seemed to have all the right answers for a college student. Boys in college were usually looking to get laid, but not Jacob.

He had been looking for a serious relationship from the start.

A butterfly came flying along, tickling Mae's head. She watched in wonder as the yellow wings flapped among the surroundings with no apparent destination; the creature seemed to be just content aimlessly exploring the grass surrounding the picnic blanket until it grew bored.

Then, it flew off in another direction.

"I'm like a butterfly," Mae announced.

Jacob's eyes narrowed.

"I like to be free, explore, and enjoy the beauty around me."

Jacob's lips curled as he studied Mae, looking off into the distance.

Her hair flowed to the middle of her back, and she wore no makeup, sitting comfortably in loose jeans and a slightly stained white t-shirt.

As simple as Mae was, she had a radiant natural beauty. Jacob wondered what it was like to be Mae, not caring what others thought and being comfortable in her skin.

He hadn't been raised to be self-indulgent in this way.

Despite her free spirit, Jacob could sense that there was more to Mae, a side she kept hidden. She would get lost in her thoughts and there would be a faraway look in her eyes when she thought no one was watching. Even her dependence on her mother's approval contradicted how Mae presented herself. It puzzled Jacob while also intriguing him to learn more about Mae.

Jacob had always been a problem solver, and Mae was a project that helped him focus on something other than his mother's overbearing, impossible personality.

Jacob filtered that relationship by being an overachiever who displayed confidence, though deep within, he was insecure and anxious.

"You know, Mae, most butterflies only live a few weeks. It might be prudent to be something more than a glorified moth."

Mae laughed at his analogy. "Why are you always so serious, my friend?"

"Friends? Is that what we are?" Jacob said now with a serious tone.

"Who needs a label? Let's just enjoy the day," Mae said as ants gathered up the crumbs that had fallen on the picnic blanket.

Jacob's eyes furrowed, and Mae could sense a tension between them. Confrontation was uncomfortable for Mae, so she quickly added, "I like being friends with you. I've never met anyone like you."

"I can say the same," Jacob replied.

Even though she enjoyed his companionship, Jacob would make kind gestures for Mae, indicating he wanted more. Their differences in life views were evident. However, Mae didn't take this as a warning sign at the time but rather as a romantic gesture from a mature student who cared for her and always seemed to have the right answers.

Jacob also wasn't like the kids she had known at school. He was focused, serious, and had a plan. And despite her utterly opposite approach to life, she was part of it, a notch on his belt and another obstacle to overcome, except she didn't know that at the time.

They walked the path lined with the beginning budding flowers.

Hints of spring were all around as the tulips bloomed, their vibrant colors exaggerated by sunny blue skies. Jacob took her hand and nonchalantly announced, "Stick with me, and you'll have the ride of your life."

How exciting, she thought. Jacob had already proved to be responsible, always on time, had a job he attended after his classes ended, and was academically at the top of the class.

Mae, on the other hand, had different plans, and having a steady job was never part of them. She wanted to travel the world after school, helping others in third-world countries.

She'd even researched overseas retreats to aid in young, underprivileged education, hoping to make a difference. Life was about the journey for her, not the destination.

There was no timeline or plan to follow, and she also did not want one.

She was just a young, mildly naïve optimist who knew she didn't want to live a suburban life and end up like her mother, someone she deemed boring and predictable.

Just as for many parents of that time, life consisted of work, a family meal, and an evening passed by on the couch, watching sitcoms. Mae did not know her biological father, so Kevin was the only father figure she had known. She'd cringe at the sight of her mother's seemingly dull existence, vowing never to let that life become her own, nor would she accept anything similar.

No, she craved a life of adventure, dreaming of meeting people around the world, becoming a nomad, and, like many young women of the time, having the freedom to live life on her terms.

She never particularly subscribed to the life of her ancestors.

Mother, wife, and caretaker, basically trapped in their minds, ensnared in a gender role she was unsure she could fit into or endure its demands.

She wasn't up for the challenge, nor did she want to fit into a box laid out for her even before she was born. Not only did she think outside the box, but also, there was no box in Mae's world.

There was only an open space where she could live her truth in a world of authenticity.

It worked for her. While many of her friends set out to impress boys, Mae had little interest in impressing anyone. She was committed to embracing her quirks and walking through life on her individual path, even if that meant she walked alone. Alone didn't frighten her.

She was rather used to it and quite preferred the solitude of knowing that the emotional walls built around her would protect her from hurt.

She was particular about who she let into her life, too; she didn't want to waste time, and if you came with baggage and weren't willing to unpack it, Mae had no interest.

Jacob, however, was persistent. Although Mae preferred no strings attached, Jacob had already set his sights on her. Perhaps it was the challenge of her dismissiveness of him or the blatant declaration that she had her mind set on changing the world.

Either way, Jacob wanted Mae … and he always got what he wanted.

Mae stopped for a moment to admire a dragonfly gliding across the tulips. The large wings spread out like a biplane before taking flight. She noticed its hesitation, lured by the aroma of wildflowers nearby. It lingered for another moment, taking in the smell of the honeysuckle. Mae waited anxiously, hoping to watch it soar through the garden. Instead, it stayed immobile longer than it should have until eventually taking flight. Mae watched in amazement as the dragonfly freely graced the sky, only stopping momentarily before finding another place to land.

Trying again to connect with Jacob, Mae said, "I will never tire of watching nature. It fascinates me. I admire the inconsistency of it all and the freedom it represents."

His eyes narrowed once again, considering her statement.

Jacob looked at Mae with intrigue and concern.

"So, you want to fly around aimlessly," he asked.

"I can't imagine living any other way," Mae declared. "Can you?"

Jacob smiled momentarily, took Mae's hand, and said, "Being zany is cute."

Jacob found Mae charming and immature, which ordinarily he would have found annoying in other girls. But with Mae, she had a certain innocence that allowed him to impress her and ensure that he remained in control.

They continued to walk the path in silence.

In the distance, the birds chirped with delight, the rhythm offering a good distraction from the awkward silence between the two. He reached for her hand, and Mae felt her jaw tighten.

His grasp, too, tightened as she slightly pulled away.

If Jacob noticed, he hadn't indicated that he'd felt her hesitation with his physical touch.

Mae thought of Jacob calling her zany; was it supposed to be a compliment or an underlying insult? His sense of humor tended toward putting others down.

Mae never found it funny but laughed anyway, ensuring her easygoing reputation would not be challenged. It infuriated her that she forced a laugh to accommodate the male ego. His condescending remarks annoyed her, but she always forced a giggle to ease his easily hurt pride.

Why did she internally care so much about what others thought, anyway?

By nature, she was easy to please and eager to make others smile. She knew what she wanted for her life but felt unworthy of achieving all she set out to do. Her tenacity and determination helped guide her through those emotions, though her immense guilt and shame for desiring more than she deserved were often overwhelming. She wondered, *why must women feel the need to take up less space in the world? When were we conditioned to do this? Why have we allowed it?*

Mae dreamed of setting her expectations high but felt confined by the restraints of her gender.

The insecurity of being abandoned by her biological father made her eager to be approachable. Nonetheless, she found Jacob interesting, kind, caring, and maybe even a little fun, but she did not intend to be part of his planned life. Despite his best efforts, Mae wasn't interested in a committed relationship, though she enjoyed their time together.

"Let's go skip rocks by the river," she said. "I'll race you."

Mae ran freely, feeling the warmth of the sun and the softness of the grass beneath her feet.

As she approached the river, she looked to see Jacob walking steadily behind, watching her in amusement. "C'mon, slowpoke, I bet I can skip more rocks than you!" said Mae.

Jacob approached her, smiling.

"You are beautiful and fun, and one day, I'm going to marry you," he said.

"Well, I don't know about that," Mae said, laughing. "But for today, I'm going to beat you in rock skipping." The two skipped rocks for hours. Mae determined with her pile of stones to get each one across the river. "I did it!" she announced when she noticed she was the first to complete the game. Elated, she looked at Jacob, who was now sulking.

"Who cares about this stupid game? Do you even know the origin of skipping rocks?"

He looked disgusted but quickly smiled again.

"Let's go, love," he said. "Let's take a ride before I have to get back for class."

Mae was distracted by his green eyes, trying to insist they had plenty of time to frolic.

"Mae, you know how I hate to be late. Let's go," said Jacob.

"Okay, okay, I'm coming," Mae said as she gathered the blanket and took another bite of her half-eaten apple.

Light rain began to fall as the two gathered the rest of their picnic and put it into the car.

The droplets were hitting Mae's tongue as she stretched her arms to the sky; with a bent neck, her tongue sought to catch the falling raindrops, making her smile.

She heard the squeaking of Jacob's wet shoes, and he impatiently stuffed the rest of the damp belongings into the car trunk. He slammed it down harder than necessary, growing rapidly impatient with Mae's appreciation of the rain.

Jacob's pinched mouth relaxed when Mae started singing, though she was wet through.

He shook his head, laughing to himself, and Mae unapologetically enjoyed the feel of the wetness on her skin and the sound of the drops surrounding her.

The ride back to campus in Jacob's black jeep through the hills made them both feel free.

The wind in their hair as she grabbed his hand made her feel safe, something she didn't often experience. She remembered her days living in North Carolina with her mother and the oppressive heat. Now, she embraced how the crisp New Hampshire air felt on her cool skin, which she had gotten used to living up North. Before her mother married Kevin, it was just Mae and her mother, Judy, living in a small house and scraping by for money.

By the time Kevin was in the picture, Mae had already finished her junior year of high school.

The New Hampshire streets, lined with large oak trees, winding roads, and open spaces, reminded her of home. As they drove, a Jimmy Buffet song came on the radio, and the two sang 'Cheeseburger in Paradise' together.

Jacob grabbed his wallet and keys as they pulled onto campus.

Then, he was off to class in a hurry. "I'll call you later," he shouted as he went down the hill to the economics building classrooms.

In no rush to return to her dorm, Mae stopped on the way to the cafeteria to grab an ice cream. While enjoying her sweet treat, a sign caught her eye: '**WANTED: Students to volunteer in Guatemala this summer and aid in the reform of the eco-agriculture culture project while assisting impoverished children.**'

Mae took down the information, excited about the possible opportunity.

She had researched other programs, but many entailed paying the airfare to the country.

This particular program was government-sponsored and accessible to any student who qualified. Mae knew the only way to get overseas was through a program that helped facilitate the accommodations. She certainly couldn't ask her mother for help, as she was just getting back on her feet from a bout of breast cancer. It had been touch and go for a while, and she didn't want her mother to feel obligated to come up with the money for such a frivolous trip.

While Kevin would have helped, he had recently been laid off, and money was tight.

As it was, her mother helped pay for her books and living expenses, and she was grateful that she could get scholarships to attend college for practically nothing. Mae worked hard in high school to ensure she could pick the school of her choice, and her hard work paid off.

Now, she had her eyes set on spending the summer overseas doing something good for the world, her way of giving back since she had gotten so much from other generous people.

The meeting was set for two weeks from Thursday, and as Mae jotted down all of the information, she stuffed the remaining vanilla ice cream cone down her throat. Her sticky hands stuck the paper into the back pocket of her jeans as she smiled warmly at a rainbow overhead near the courtyard.

Chapter 2

After class, Jacob went to the library to get some extra study time. He preferred the third floor where it was quiet and overlooked the common area where many students played hacky sack and frisbee. Today, he was tutoring another student in math, to make extra money.

He had already been waiting for fifteen minutes and was slowly getting agitated. "No wonder this idiot is failing math. She can't even tell the time." He groaned silently.

Jacob looked out the window to kill time, soon noticing sweet Mae in the courtyard.

He watched her long legs run for the frisbee that was quickly getting away from her.

She laughed, unaware the other students were noticing how easily she moved about the lawn.

There was an air about her that intrigued Jacob. He was used to other girlfriends falling over themselves to be with him. Not Mae, though. She was content being herself, with very little regard for Jacob. The challenge of getting her attention was what kept him most interested.

She was different from other girls, and he was absorbed in her strong sense of self and confidence. He was also a little jealous of her free spirit; he wished he could live life on his own terms.

As he sat alone waiting, he reflected on his mother, Jane, a minister in a small church in Maine. The rules had been clear to Jacob from a young age; he would need to behave in a way that would allow her to reflect within the congregation as a mother with an intact family.

Jane had inherited her father's fortune and had only become a minister to preach for her own self-interest. Though Jane never let on that she was in a loveless marriage of her own, she judged the families who attended service each Sunday.

"Did you see how her seven-year-old was dressed?" she would complain to Jacob later that day. "And the nerve to show up late with their three toddlers like that! When I had you and your brother, we were always on time, and I had you dressed perfectly. Not once did we show up late!" Jane had a way of being judgmental of everyone around, probably to avoid thinking about the life she believed she portrayed herself, one which was drastically different from reality.

Still, she showed up to the bake sale every Sunday, noticing other volunteers' lack of skill and sometimes even calling them lazy. She displayed her pies and cookies as if they were prize-winning, and in her mind, no one else could bake as well as she could.

She played with her white pearl necklace as she watched the congregation devouring her tasty treats, happily encouraging and absorbing every compliment coming her way.

It was not lost on Jacob his attraction toward Mae. As he continued watching her in the courtyard Jacob understood his attraction to Mae was because she was different from his mother. Perhaps his flare of rebellion made her alluring because he knew Jane would never approve of women like Mae. Jacob longed to make decisions without his mother's approval, and Mae was a bold way to show his independence. He wore her like a banner, proclaiming his uniqueness.

But he did worry. What would Jane think of Mae when they eventually met?

She wasn't one to withhold her thoughts and he feared she would ruin his chance of keeping Mae in his life. He had planned to introduce them next week, but was worried about how Jane would react to Mae and her outspoken ways. Mae had strong opinions about politics, religion, and life, and Jacob was unsure how his mother would receive her perspectives.

Nor was Mae one to shy away from debate; she could be outspoken about it.

Jane, on the other hand, believed politics should never be discussed, though she made plenty of passive-aggressive comments she would mutter about "those people," never divulging to whom she was referring. Jane was complicated, portraying herself a certain way on the surface, though she was intimidating and controlling behind closed doors.

Later that week, when Jacob went home for a visit, Jane was having yet another meltdown. "It wouldn't be Christian to speak ill of people," she said incredulously. Though she often did exactly that; if there had been a prize for excelling at it, she would have won the trophy hands down. For example, Jacob's brother Charlie struggled with drugs and alcohol. He had gotten thrown out of college when he'd shown up to class belligerent, carrying on conspiracy theories about the government. Charlie had already been arrested for drunk driving, disorderly conduct, and shoplifting. As part of the family dynamic, Charlie was never held accountable.

With a few phone calls and charitable contributions to the university, Charlie had been allowed back to complete his education. The family solved problems by paying people off, intimidating them, and using their family name, which was known throughout the community.

It was easier for establishments to look the other way than to take on the wrath of the family's power in the community. Despite some of the problems Charlie encountered, he was a good brother to Jacob; the two boys had come to rely on one another to escape their mother's unattainable expectations and their father's lack of protection.

"The pressure of Mom's expectations is too much for me to handle, bro," Charlie would complain. "She expects us to live within the guidelines of her holier-than-thou image, when behind closed doors, we are all miserable, and she is doing all the same things she complains of."

Unlike Jacob, Charlie couldn't stay within the perimeter of his mother's restraints.

Even as a child, the boy felt suffocated by her non-negotiable expectations. It was partly why he acted out and often was cruel to his brother.

Strangely, Jane never laid out her expectations, just assuming her boys would behave and conduct themselves the way she deemed fit, though no one really knew what that meant.

As a result, her unwritten expectations were confusing and toxic.

Charlie, therefore, had little patience for his mother and preferred dealing with his father.

Jim struggled with alcohol too, but was kind, reasonable, and supportive. He also knew to stay well away from Jane, hiding in his garage to escape her constant nagging and judgment.

Jacob joined his father in the garage when the men had enough of Jane's unrelenting criticism. Charlie and Jim, exasperated by Jane's latest outburst, disappeared into the back of the garage, where they had set up tables, chairs, and a small mini fridge of snacks and beers. As Charle relaxed with a cold beer, he complained that Jacob was his mother's puppet and that their relationship had become most irritating.

"They are codependent on one another," Charlie complained.

Jim took a long breath and said, "I think your mother has a peculiar relationship with your brother. She has always expected too much from that boy. One day, he is going to snap."

"I don't know how he does it."

"Me either, but it gets us both off the hook," Jim said, patting Charlie on the back. "Enjoy it while you can." Within moments, Jacob, who rarely went to the garage, appeared. Jane was on yet another rampage over politicians, and Jacob felt the weight of his mother's demands and needed an outlet. His shoulders slumped as he appeared defeated. It was apparent he was bothered by something.

"Dad, aren't you her husband? Why must I be dragged around to all her church obligations?"

"Fuck, Jake, say no, dammit," Charlie said, rolling his eyes.

"You know how she is. There will be tears and the silent treatment for days if I don't go to the women's knitting group tonight."

"This is fucking nuts," Charlie said, taking another swig from his secret stash of bourbon.

Jim gave Jacob a small smile and looked sympathetically at his son. "I'll go offer to escort her to one of her silly church meetings, son."

Jim walked away, only looking back at his boys for a moment.

Today, he was only mildly intoxicated.

"Jake, we need to get out of this house. She's passive-aggressive and controlling. At least with me, she doesn't expect as much, but man, she has her claws into you and won't let go," said Charlie.

"It's not so bad. She's proud of us."

"You. She is proud of you," Charlie interrupted.

"She's proud of you too, Charlie. You just make it a bit more difficult," Jacob said with a half-smile.

"Seriously, you need to get out of here. Otherwise, you'll be taking care of her for the rest of your life." Charlie's voice was earnest now. He looked at his brother sincerely.

"Aren't you dating that girl pretty seriously now, anyway?"

"Well, I'm trying," Jacob quipped. "I like her, but I'm afraid to bring her around just yet. I don't want to scare her off. Anyway, she's different. She isn't much into formalities and structure. But I'm working on it."

"Mom will love her," Charlie said sarcastically, rolling his eyes.

Jacob chuckled, but inside, he was nervous, knowing that Mae would not blend well with his mother. Perhaps that was why he was so attracted to her.

Charlie rebelled by breaking the rules in the most obvious ways, but Jacob was more subtle with his rebellion, having not even told his mother about his relationship with Mae for fear of her reaction. Many of the girls from church had crushes on Jacob, and each time, Jane would comment on how he could do better.

In the end, Jacob never really liked those girls, finding them boring and desperate.

Mae though, she was like no one he had ever met.

Bright, beautiful, sassy, and nothing at all like his mother.

"Let's get out of here before Mom comes looking for us," suggested Jacob.

"Ok, mama's boy. We don't want her to come looking for her number one son," quipped Charlie.

That evening, with the conversation with Charlie still fresh in his mind, Jacob began searching for apartments. He was aware that he needed to forge his own path away from his mother and her control. He needed to leave his parents' house for his sanity and the chance to stay with Mae.

Jacob meticulously planned out the next six months of his life.

If his plan worked, he would get the job he'd recently applied for, which would bring him closer to work. Then, he would be able to convince Mae to move in and settle down.

Jacob was skillful in manipulating to get what he wanted. He'd had plenty of practice.

Mae would be better off with him, and he was determined to protect and take care of her so she could see a life with him as a great benefit. He felt certain he had much to offer and wanted Mae to be a part of the life he was envisioning for them both. He was persistent in his quest to win Mae over, despite her unwillingness to acquiesce to societal pressure.

Once he fully captured her heart, he could escape his mother's control and be free to start his own life.

Chapter 3

Jacob made the grievous error of talking about Mae in front of his mother. She immediately insisted on meeting her, but Jacob made a plethora of excuses.

"Mom, I'm not ready for you to meet her. It's a new thing. And I'm not even sure she likes me like that,"

"How could she not? I expect to meet her soon."

Every day for two weeks, Jane would call Jacob, asking about Mae.

"We're free to meet her anytime."

"Mom," Jacob would groan.

The inquiries didn't stop until Jacob finally surrendered to his mother's demands; otherwise, she was threatening to force herself into their lives.

"I think it is appropriate for me to meet the person you've spent so much time with," Jane complained. "Don't you think so? You're my son."

"Mom, I'm not ready to introduce her to everyone. Give us time."

"Let me be clear," Jane said as she took a homemade apple pie from the oven. "You have a week for us to meet, or I will go to that campus and knock on her door myself."

Jacob knew this was not an idle threat. He was fully aware of what his mother was capable of and that she would persist until she got her way.

He sighed, reluctantly succumbing to his mother's demand, mostly because he knew how brutal she could be. Conceding was easier.

"I'll see when Mae is available."

"Well, if she is as wonderful as you proclaim, we are the ones who should be setting the date for it. I'm certain she'll make the time," Jane retorted.

Jacob regretted ever telling his family about his new relationship.

He should have known his mom would find a way to ruin it.

Jacob got up the nerve two days later to tell Mae about his conversation with his mother. "My mother insists on meeting you. I tried to defer it till much later, but she's having none of it."

"Don't you think this is a little bit too soon?"

"I do, but Mae, she insists. This is important to me. I'd really like you to meet them, and they're excited to meet the woman I'm always talking about."

Mae looked up from her phone, noticing his worried look for the first time.

She wasn't thrilled with the idea but figured it was the least she could do for Jacob. The thought of meeting his parents while in a relationship she didn't take seriously made her uneasy, but she didn't want to be rude. She put down her phone and fiddled with her hair.

Though reluctant to say yes, his pleading eyes made her feel bad. "Okay, I'll do it. But Jacob, please, let's take things slow. I'm really not interested in a serious relationship. I told you that."

Jacob's shoulders relaxed momentarily, and the panic on his face became sullen instead. "Mae, I really like you. I want to be in a committed relationship with you. I'll try to take things slow, but I know what I want, and it's you."

Embarrassed, Mae felt a rush of blood come to her face. She had never had someone interested so intently in her, and while it was flattering, it was also terrifying.

He only ever spoke about what *he* wanted. What about her own desires in this; didn't her wishes even count? Did he think he could take ownership of her like a possession?

The following week, Jacob and Mae had plans to meet for coffee. Jacob, constantly aware of the time, arrived five minutes before one o'clock and saved a table. He hadn't spent much time with Mae since their picnic by the lake, and she hadn't called him back in days.

They had made plans to meet today, and he could only hope she hadn't forgotten.

He'd even left a note in her dorm room, reminding her last night. Jacob wondered where she'd been but dismissed those thoughts, knowing she often took time to be alone.

He waited another half-hour, slowly getting more agitated as the minutes passed.

How dare she leave me waiting for her? he thought.

Unaccustomed to chasing or waiting around for anyone, he looked about, embarrassed, wondering if anyone noticed that he'd been stood up.

He hated looking stupid, and the thought of anyone thinking he was a fool only enraged him.

Appearances mattered; what other people thought of him was important, and he had a reputation for being an 'in control' kind of guy.

He certainly didn't want some girl to change that perception around campus. This was his senior year, and he'd already been applying for jobs across the city.

He refused to be distracted from his plan and grew tired of Mae being inconsiderate. Just as he was about to leave, she rushed in with a big smile.

Gosh, is she beautiful, thought Jacob. With that, all his annoyance melted away.

"Hey, hey," she said, casually brushing past him.

She hadn't noticed the time or mentioned where she'd been and said, "So glad we could meet up. I'm going to grab a coffee. Want anything?"

Jacob stared, not answering for a moment, giving a weak, "I'm okay."

If Mae noticed the time or her tardiness, she showed no sign of regret.

He thought about mentioning it to her but didn't want to ruin the mood, so he was grateful that she had come at all. He knew physically she was out of his league and felt a sense of pride as they walked through campus with her on his arm.

Mae didn't notice the looks other students gave them when they were together.

She returned to the table and said, "So, what's new?"

Jacob was still lost in his thoughts, wondering why she was late and where she had been the past couple of days.

"Hello, Earth to Jacob. I asked what's new?"

"Oh, sorry," Jacob said sheepishly. "I was just thinking about something."

Mae looked at him and smiled. "It's a beautiful day out. You should take time to enjoy it."

"I've been having interviews for jobs, Mae. We graduate in three months. Have you considered looking for a job yet?" he asked.

"Actually, funny you should say that," Mae said slowly. "I'm planning on going to Guatemala to help underprivileged kids. It's a volunteer role."

Jacob glared at her, waiting for the punchline that never came.

After a moment's silence, he said, "Wait, you're serious? Mae, have you lost your mind? Why would you want to do that? You need to get a paying job and work out what you plan to do with your life! It's time to grow up. We're graduating soon."

Mae started to giggle, thinking Jacob surely had to be joking.

His cheeks were flushed, and he was sweating a little.

"Relax, it will be an adventure! I've always wanted to help others, and it's a great opportunity to put something cool on my resume," Mae said.

She had always been so nonchalant about life and any 'concrete' plans, a trait that both amused and infuriated Jacob.

Softer now, he asked, "Mae, what about us?"

"What about us? I'll come back, and we'll see what happens when I return."

Mae could brush off uncomfortable conversations in a flash.

Jacob was visibly upset, but her tactic was avoidance.

I hate conflict, she thought.

They walked back to campus in silence.

Mae made up an excuse that she had to meet someone just to ease the tension between them. Jacob was taking their relationship far more seriously than she did.

Hadn't she often mentioned to him that she didn't consider them exclusive and wanted the freedom to figure out life on her own? Jacob couldn't accept that, assuming she'd eventually come around if he just waited for her to mature a bit.

Mae gave no indication that would be the case, but he had no intention of giving up on her. He had his eyes set on her, remaining persistent.

The following day, Mae attended the meeting about her trip to Guatemala.

She gathered the information and filled out the paperwork, excited for the journey that would take place two weeks after graduation. She began preparing and packing, unsure what she'd do when she returned to the States after the six weeks were up.

She thought she would find an apartment to rent or maybe stay on one of her friends' couches for a bit. Jacob had mentioned getting an apartment together, but Mae had no interest in living as a couple like that; she wasn't even sure she wanted to date him for much longer.

He was great in many ways, but where was the connection with him that she was supposed to have? Two people in love were supposed to feel far more than this, weren't they?

He was simply her safety net. At times, she depended on him out of convenience, but she mostly avoided him because of his controlling ways. He was focused and mature, but he also spoiled the good things about him by trying to change her and getting upset when she didn't follow his plans.

She'd ignored it for months but figured that once she returned home, she'd break the news—for a second or even third time—that she wasn't ready for any serious commitment. *I hope he'll lose interest due to the distance in the meantime; then, we can both move on with our lives.*

The last two months at college went by fast. Mae was busy with graduation and planning her trip. Her passport was up to date, and she put all the paperwork and passport in a box at the back of her closet. She was set. The only thing left to do was to wait. Mae was excited about the trip, and although she would miss her college life, she was ready to explore the world.

Jacob came over to spend time with her and asked her something surprising: Would she consider moving in with him when she returned from overseas?

"Jacob, that's a big step. I'm not even thinking about anything but my trip."

"Just think about it. Please."

She hesitated, then said, "I'll think about it," though she didn't intend to.

She didn't want to leave Jacob on bad terms, and as it was, she was starting to feel the pressure over where she would live once she returned home from Guatemala. Her friend Jill already had a cousin coming to stay with her for the next six months, and she didn't have the room to host both of them. So, for now, at least, Mae didn't want to burn any bridges with Jacob in case she needed a place to crash. He would take her in, even temporarily.

It wasn't nice to think she was using Jacob, but he was eager to help, always wanting to do things to make her life easier. Mae didn't want to upset him, benefiting from his eagerness to please. This seemed to be a win-win situation, and she'd deal with the emotional things later.

For now, she was too busy getting ready for the trip of a lifetime.

"At least think about moving in when you return from your trip," Jacob insisted.

"It's a long plane ride, so I'll certainly give it some thought," Mae said.

"In the meantime, remember when I told you about meeting my family? Well, I've told them so much about you, and they'd love to meet the woman I brag about," Jacob said.

Before Mae could respond, he continued, "I've made dinner reservations for tomorrow night at seven. My mom and dad will meet us there."

Mae smiled in agreement, but inside, her head was screaming that this relationship was going way too fast, making her uncomfortable.

Jacob went to pick up Mae at four-thirty, but as anticipated, she wasn't quite ready. He hid his impatience, deploring the thought of being late.

When she finally emerged from the bedroom at four forty-five, he was nervous; what would his mother say about them arriving this late to the reservation?

They planned to meet halfway, which would take nearly two hours without traffic.

They arrived at the restaurant at seven-fifteen, and Jacob immediately saw his mother pacing about the small waiting area like a caged beast.

His father was casually sitting at the bar, having a drink and chatting with a fellow patron. He looked relaxed, but Jane was not. Her eyes were piercing, and she looked extremely annoyed.

"Oh, you finally showed up," Jane said, glaring at Mae. "Very gracious of you both."

"Sorry, we're late. There was traffic," Jacob said, embarrassed.

Jane spat, "Jacob, don't give me that. There is always traffic on all the roads. It would be very strange if we had a huge road network and no traffic on it, wouldn't it? The point is, we plan to accommodate these things. Only bad planners and indolent people ever arrive late to an appointment; imagine if this were a job interview! You kids need to get serious about life."

"Hi, I'm Mae. So nice to meet you," Mae said timidly.

She extended a hand to Jane, but there was no reciprocation.

It was as though the unpleasant woman saw right through her. Mae had become a specter, a ghost. Jane's eyes wouldn't notice her, at least not in a good way.

"I think our table's ready. We should go sit before they give away our reservation," Jane said, striding away to meet the hostess. Jane seemed so cold and aloof, unfriendly.

If Jacob thought that meeting his parents could entice Mae to want to join their family someday, then he would have to think again. Meeting the stand-offish Jane was so far a major deterrent to seeing Jacob, on even a casual basis. But no wonder Jacob had turned out so pushy and insistent; these were also his mother's ways, and they oozed from her.

Dinner was tense, Mae staying quiet for most of it as Jane talked directly to Jacob.

Every once in a while, however, Jane looked at her with disdain, through cold gray eyes.

However, Jacob's father, Jim, at least tried to converse with Mae, asking her about her hobbies, hometown, and family and siblings.

Mae was grateful for the interaction, having a last-ditch attempt to impress Jacob's parents, though she wondered why she was bothering if what she had with Jacob didn't matter to her.

"Well, I love to run and just competed in a marathon about a month ago," Mae said.

She would have continued but Jane interrupted. "If more women minded their homes and families instead of being so damn vain about their physical appearances, this world would be a far better place." Mae looked down, trying not to make eye contact with anyone at the table. Her stomach turned, and her cheeks flushed with anger and embarrassment.

Jacob didn't mention his parents much, and Mae hadn't asked.

She was completely caught off guard by how judgmental Jane was.

And she thought, *why has he put me in this awkward position?*

When dinner was over, and Jacob and Mae were driving home, he took Mae's hand, but she pulled it away and stared out the window.

"What the fuck was that?" he barked. "Didn't you have a nice time?"

"I actually didn't, no. Your mom clearly can't stand me. I honestly can't work out why you would subject me to this; you must've known that was how she'd behave."

"Mae, please, I'm sorry. I actually had no idea she'd behave that way. We were late, and that set her off. She's always been like this, and it's nothing personal, nothing against you. That's just how Mom is. Overprotective and a little controlling," Jacob tried to explain.

"A little?" Mae said, her voice rising. "And you thought it was a good idea for me to meet her? That's just weird, Jacob. It's ridiculous."

"I promise I'll talk to her. She'll warm up to you, don't worry. We were very close when I was in high school, and I think she's having difficulty letting go. She still thinks I'm her baby."

"Well, you're an adult. She needs to get over it," Mae said. "She behaved like a kid herself. I kept thinking she was about to throw a tantrum."

"She's my mother. You're out of line saying that," Jacob said in a faint voice. "So rude."

"Rude! You dare to call me rude after that woman stared at me all evening and could barely say a word to me! She even gave your dad filthy looks each time he spoke to me. So, don't dare come to me, telling me I'm rude. She was rudeness personified! Even refused to shake hands."

For the rest of the drive, Mae stared out the window, tears burning her eyes. She was embarrassed, angry, and upset that Jacob had not protected her from his mother.

He'd let her down for the first time, and his insensitivity toward her feelings hurt her, making her feel unworthy and lacking in self-esteem.

It was something she normally wouldn't suffer from, but all her confidence had fled.

Mae sought to brush off the negativity. *It's just Jacob's mistake and a one-time deal.*

Jacob was usually kind and considerate, and this situation had put her on guard, that's all. Thoughts raced through her mind, reminding her that Jacob was pushing this relationship too fast. From the beginning, Mae had only wanted to be free, and slowly, she was feeling trapped.

No, to be specific, *he* was trapping her, and willingly. Envisioning the butterfly from the park aimlessly flying, she imagined Jane chasing her with a huge pair of scissors to clip her wings.

Then, she imagined Jacob had handed her the scissors. The image made her wince.

"Look, Jacob," Mae said, interrupting the silence. "You are such an interesting guy, and I enjoy our time together, but I never wanted a committed relationship. I still don't."

Before Mae could continue, Jacob cut her off. "Mae. No!" His voice was stern and panicked. "Please. I am begging you," he said, enunciating each word. "I regret taking you to see my parents so soon but please, don't let this come between us. We have so much together."

His desperation not to lose her was surprising.

Jacob had a lot to offer. So, why was he so hung up on her?

"It's just that I'm leaving soon anyway. I have a lot I want to do with my life, and a relationship isn't something I've considered, especially long-term or long-distance."

The tires of the car screeched as Jacob pulled over to the side.

Mae gasped, afraid of his sudden dark mood.

"Mae, you listen to me. I'm not willing to lose you. I can't. You are everything I dreamed of, and I promise I will make a good life for us. I refuse to let you go."

His voice was sincere and desperate. He had much stronger feelings for her than she had ever thought. His boldness and willingness to fight to continue their relationship was almost scary.

But whatever—her mind was made up, and she was leaving.

"I just need some time," Mae explained. Tonight was a lot."

"My mother is a lot," quipped Jacob. "I agree."

Mae laughed, softening the mood. Jacob smiled, wiping a tear from his eye.

"Please, Mae. I want to be with you. I know we are young, but I want us to be together."

Mae had seen this declaration of love in the movies, but could such a thing ever happen in real life? His feelings of being enamored were clear; Jacob adored Mae.

Mae considered this before saying, "Okay, Jacob. We can continue spending time together and see where this goes until I leave for Guatemala."

"That's all I could ask," replied Jacob. With a sly smile, he glanced at Mae. "But before then, I'll make you fall in love with me. Then you will know we were meant to be together."

Smiling, she said, "We will see about that, big guy."

Jacob pulled into the street and continued driving at a slower speed.

During the drive, he apologized relentlessly. "You have to see that my family is odd but that should not worry you, Mae. I'm nothing like my mother."

Mae ignored that comment, instead asking, "Tell me all about Charlie?"

Jacob oddly described his brother as the family's black sheep.

"You know what they say about black sheep? They're always the ones telling the truth," Mae said.

Jacob didn't respond and just continued driving, increasing the volume on the radio.

She was right, but he didn't want Mae to realize that Charlie was both aware of and vocal about the dysfunctional nature of Jacob and their mother's relationship.

By the following day, Mae had recovered from the night before, and when Jacob apologized again, Mae replied, "No worries. It's kind of funny how different you are from your mom!"

"Thanks for understanding," said Jacob.

"Your dad is great, though," Mae offered.

"He is, but let's stop talking about my family and grab some lunch."

"Good idea, I'm starving," Mae said.

Jacob never mentioned his family again and never invited Mae to another family gathering. All of which was more than okay by Mae.

Chapter 4

Although Jacob didn't get the management position he'd been aiming for, after knowing it had been a long shot, he happily became employed as an entry-level assistant to a financial advisor.

The job at JR Financial Services would start after graduation. The opportunity to work at one of the largest financial groups was exciting, and Jacob couldn't wait to make his way up the ranks. He had dreamed of eventually managing a team of investors, and being placed in a competitive field satisfied him. He wasn't afraid of hard work, envisioning for himself a life of wealth and status. Graduation was three weeks away, and he was meeting with a real estate agent to sign a lease for a studio apartment overlooking a lake.

The windows made the apartment seem so much larger, and the view of the lake gave a comforting sense of home. Jacob had worked every summer, saving his money to afford the modest apartment, not wanting to be like other kids his age, moving into their parents' basement after graduation. Besides, he'd meticulously planned for life after college.

He had enough money to afford the rented place, and now, with his earnings from his new job, he was on the right track.

As he looked around the cozy property, he saw possibilities.

This would be the start of his independence and the life he had spent so much time planning. He reached into his bag and pulled out his notebook, flipping through the pages until he found what he was looking for.

Jacob had written out a list of goals for himself with timelines and specific objectives.

He put a large checkmark next to his listed items: APARTMENT and JOB. Under these was the word MARRIAGE. Overly organized and goal-driven, he put a lot of pressure on himself to succeed, at least in terms of what he thought his mother considered success.

Happiness wasn't part of his plan, only his image. A positive image would gain his mother's approval, achieving happiness for him and his mom. He longed for her affection and thought he would eventually get his mother's respect if he achieved certain milestones.

In his youth, he had often been denied love, attention, and sometimes even food if he didn't meet those essential goals set for him.

The thought of his childhood filled Jacob with anxiety, and although he was now a young man, he never wanted to return to a place of his mother's disapproval. Sometimes, even now, he felt as though he had metamorphosed into that helpless child again, the vulnerable, scared boy.

As a child, if he didn't meet Jane's standards, she'd point her finger at his little face and whisper sternly, "You are a bad boy. No one will ever love you if you continue acting like this."

Jacob's eyes would fill with tears.

Jane's eyes would only narrow as she hated emotions, especially crying. Then, she would grab him harshly by the arm and say, "You stop your crying, you weak, pathetic child."

She could be cruel. She had little patience for small children and was appalled at the slightest sign of what she deemed poor behavior. As Jacob grew, he wanted to please Jane to avoid reprimands. He learned what made his mother happy and abided within those guidelines.

Sometimes, it exhausted him, but Jacob wanted her acceptance. It was easier to obey her unwritten rules of perfection than to endure the constant stress of her endless harsh words.

He wished he could be more like Charlie, who didn't care, and her words meant nothing to him. No matter how often Jane tried to break him, Charlie would simply walk away seemingly unscathed, then he'd carry on. It puzzled Jacob how little Charlie cared about their mother's opinion, and in his teenage years, Charlie began teasing Jacob about him being a mama's boy.

Admittedly, Jacob was terrified of Jane. For one thing, she expected more from him than she ever did from Charlie. When Charlie wasn't around, she was more aggressive toward Jacob.

"Listen here. Don't you go crying to your brother about this, or you'll be sorry," she'd growl.

Jacob could never figure out what he'd done wrong, knowing only that Jane was always upset about something. From not standing up straight to touching the walls as he raced down the stairs, to not having a smile on his face, she always found plenty of things he wasn't doing right.

Jacob focused back on the phone, noticing his hands had a slight shake.

As he pressed each digit, the anxiety built. The phone rang as Jacob exhaled loudly, knowing he needed to change his demeanor to appease his mother even over the phone.

"Hi, Jacob." He heard the voice on the other end of the line.

"Mom, guess what? I got the job!" Before his mother could react, Jacob continued before he lost his nerve, "And I just signed a lease to rent an apartment."

There was silence on the other end.

"Mom?"

"Oh, yes, I'm here. Well, this is sudden. I thought you'd move home after graduation. We discussed renovating your room. I told the church community they would get help with many events once you moved back. Now, I have to disappoint everyone because of your whims."

Her voice was strained.

Jane could no longer criticize and put fear into Jacob the way she had done in his youth. Now, the silent disappointment in her voice did all the damage.

"Mom, I'll still help. I won't be too far away. This is just such a great opportunity," he continued. "I thought you would be happy, maybe even proud. I haven't even graduated from college and already have a job. Most of my friends—"

Jane cut him off. "Since when do I care about what your friends are doing?" she said. "Let me guess, you told that little twat about the job, and I'm sure she's thrilled to know that she can use you for your money."

Jacob tried to control his rage. Jane had already done enough damage between him and Mae, and now she had crossed the line. "Leave Mae out of it."

"Excuse me? You don't care what I think about her?"

Jacob knew better than to reply. Quickly changing the subject and hiding his defeat, he said, "It's my first real job, and I thought you'd celebrate it. I misjudged."

"Well, Jacob, it sounds like you've made up your mind without discussing it with your mother. Congratulations, then. I hope it makes you happy."

She hung up the phone quickly as Jacob stood there, his heart beating feverishly.

He took a long exhale, feeling the drain of the conversation. He'd known even before making the call that she'd be disappointed. He pushed off the thoughts of guilt and gathered his papers, looking around once more at the place he would soon call home.

Driving back to campus, he thought about Mae and her upcoming trip to Guatemala. He wondered if she had really thought this decision through, her impulsive nature often not planning for unexpected circumstances. "I don't think she should go," he mumbled. If he were to tell her that, though, she'd laugh at his worries, and he hated looking like an overprotective fool.

What if she gets hurt or contracts a disease?

Why doesn't she think of the ramifications of her actions?

Later that day, Jacob agreed to help Mae move her college belongings into storage until she returned from her trip.

"Looks like you have everything packed and ready to go," he said.

"Yeah, I think so, at least. Whatever I've forgotten, I guess I don't need it too bad," Mae said with a quiet giggle.

How could she not have a list of necessary supplies? Thought Jacob.

"I wrote a list of things you might want to take. And picked up some first-aid supplies in case something happens," said Jacob.

"You are so thoughtful. And prepared," Mae added.

Mae and Jacob packed up his car with the boxes as Mae hummed, carefree, to the radio. While she was outside loading a box of clothes into his trunk, Jacob noticed her passport in the back of her closet, sitting just inside an open box. Without thinking, he grabbed it and stuffed it in his pocket before she returned. He immediately regretted it, but it was too late to replace it. This was his chance to keep her here and not risk her being whisked away to a faraway country.

"You are the best. Thank you for helping me. I don't know what I'd do without you," she said, kissing his cheek softly.

Jacob flushed with shame. What had he done? Should he just put the passport back?

Instead, he offered, "Looks like we got everything packed up. Let's grab some dinner before we load everything into the storage unit."

"I'm going to miss you, Jacob. You've been good to me," offered Mae.

He grinned broadly. "You see, we're good together. I told you so."

At that moment, Jacob knew he was making the right decision by taking her passport. She needed him and his reasonability, and she would thank him later for his quick thinking and prudence, he was sure. Not that he would ever tell her what he'd done, and he hoped she would never find out. Eventually, she would get over losing her passport and forget about the trip when she got herself a job and started making money. Besides, Mae was to leave in three days, and he still had a chance to change his mind about taking the passport. He could pretend that it had fallen out of one of the boxes and he'd found it between the seats of his car. He wondered when she would notice when it was missing. Knowing Mae, she would only discover the issue when leaving for the airport. She waited until the last minute for everything. That was Mae.

Jacob was quiet while the two enjoyed their pizza.

"So, I guess this is goodbye for now," said Mae. When I get back, let's talk like you said."

Jacob looked at her, unsure what to say.

A pang of overwhelming guilt consumed him, but he'd taken the passport for her own good.

"That would be great," he said.

After leaving the pizza shop, the two embraced. Jacob held onto her a bit longer than Mae felt comfortable. He knew how distraught she would be when she realized she wouldn't be going on that trip after all. While it was terrible to be causing her harm, he found solace in the fact that she would come running to him for comfort.

They parted ways, Jacob knowing this wasn't the last he'd be hearing from her this week.

Two days later, Jacob's phone rang at four-thirty in the morning. Still in slumber, it took three rings for him to pick up. "Hello," he said, half awake.

On the other end of the line was a hysterical Mae who could barely get out the words.

"Jacob, I can't find my passport."

She was breathing heavily. Jacob could tell she'd been crying.

"Calm down, Mae. Are you sure it isn't in one of your bags? Maybe it fell out."

"No, I'm positive. I put it in a box at the back of my closet. When we moved my stuff into storage, I took that box with me, but now my passport's missing," Mae said frantically.

"Hey, we can sort this," he said, pretending to be the rock she could lean on.

"I'm supposed to leave," she wailed, her voice cracking. "I looked everywhere and can't find it."

"Ugh, that is terrible. I'm so sorry. What are you going to do now?"

"I don't know. I have no place to stay, no job, nothing!"

"Don't worry, Mae. I'll get you, and we'll figure something out."

Jacob sprang from his bed and opened the top drawer of his dresser, glancing at the passport.

He thought momentarily before tossing it in the garbage, grabbing his keys, and heading out to get Mae. When he pulled onto the street of Mae's friend's apartment, a group of people stood on the corner, gathered around. They were the rest of the volunteer group, ready to leave by bus.

They were comforting Mae as she tearfully said goodbye. Jacob waited in the car, giving her time with her fellow would-be volunteers, and when she approached, he got out to greet her with a warm embrace. She held on to him, squeezing him tight as she sobbed into his shirt.

"I just don't know what could have happened to my passport," she cried.

"I know, love. I'm so sorry." Jacob's voice was strained as he inhaled the sweet smell of her hair. He vowed to himself to make things right for Mae. "Are you sure you've looked everywhere? Is there anything I can do?"

She sighed, saying, "I've been searching for hours, going over and over the same things."

"I'll take care of you. Don't worry," he mumbled as her cries became heavy sobs.

The drive back to Jacob's apartment was quiet, Mae staring out the window in defeat as Jacob held tightly to the steering wheel. Getting closer to his apartment, Jacob said, "I think you will like my apartment. Stay as long as you need. It has a beautiful view of a lake."

Mae nodded and gave a slight smile.

Once inside, Jacob showed her to his bedroom, bringing an extra blanket.

"I'll take the couch. Get some sleep."

He lay restless all night. The guilt began to consume his consciousness.

What have I done? he thought. He was comforted knowing that Mae was with him now, where he could protect and show her how much he cared.

The following day, Mae didn't wake until half past noon. Jacob was preparing her pancakes as she emerged from his bedroom, still sleepy. He loved the feeling of being here with her, waking in the same place. Surely, this would encourage her to move in with him.

He would spoil her and give her so much attention that she'd feel she couldn't live without him at her side. "Good morning, love. Pancakes are ready, coffee's brewing, and you, my dear, look as beautiful as ever."

Her piercing blue eyes were swollen, but her smile was soft with gratitude.

"You are a lifesaver, Jacob. What would I do without you?"

"Hopefully, you'll never have to find out," Jacob said, giggling as he tickled her side.

A week passed, and as Jacob suspected, Mae's mood slowly lifted.

She quickly overcame the disappointment and said, "I guess it wasn't meant to be."

Jacob admired her ability to see the bright side.

Mae started looking for jobs in the legal field.

Two weeks later, she landed a legal secretary position at a small law firm. Although she wasn't sure what to do with her communications degree, this position would provide her with stability and steady pay.

Halfway through college, she'd considered law school once she graduated, so she'd begun researching how to apply. Her advisors had suggested she could attend regardless of her undergraduate major, but she'd stay in the communications major to avoid falling behind.

Specifically, immigration law attracted her since she was constantly feeling sad about the stories of so many migrants fleeing countries in search of refuge. The point of the lesson had been about communication, but when a lawyer came in to speak, Mae found herself rapt.

"I think I'm going to look into law school," Mae said one rainy Saturday as Jacob surfed the internet.

He looked up briefly, then refocused on an article he was reading.

"Jacob, did you hear me? I'm thinking about applying to law school."

"I heard you, Mae." He didn't look up again from his computer, which irritated Mae.

"Well, what do you think?" she asked.

"I think it will cost too much and will be too stressful," he said with a deflating tone. "Why put yourself through it? What's the point?"

Mae considered Jacob's words.

They sounded harsh, and Mae wondered if *he meant to be this insensitive.*

Out of the forced proximity, they'd grown closer, Mae out of desperation, but she surely hadn't appreciated Jacob's judgment.

"Ouch!"

"It's true, Mae. You still owe one student loan. I know your family doesn't have the money to help you. And well, don't you think it's selfish to take on more debt for us? Or worse, to have your mother feel responsible for them." His voice began to soften now. "Look, Mae, we both know your mother will want to take on the burden of your education. She's getting older and still recovering from cancer, and as you've mentioned, she's worked multiple jobs to pay for your college. Do you think she'd stop work, knowing you were absorbing the cost of law school?

"It doesn't seem fair to put that kind of burden on her when she's aging and unwell."

He had a point, of course.

What Mae had noticed, though, was when he'd mentioned *taking on more debt for us.*

Us ... There was no 'us' as far as Mae was concerned. She thought they got along well, but she was not thinking of becoming such a close couple that they pooled money or shared their debts.

Mae felt the air come out of her chest. He was right, but she still wanted to apply for law school. She had been thinking about it for years.

"Why don't you settle into life a bit, save money, and consider it when you have more money saved?" Jacob offered.

Jacob had a way of being too practical, changing the way Mae began to think. His compelling arguments made her doubt herself and rely on his opinion more than her own.

Chapter 5

By now, most of Mae's college friends had gone their separate ways. Even Jill was almost an hour north, and getting together when they had such busy work schedules was difficult.

Mae had been unprepared for this kind of life after college, an enormous adjustment since she'd been planning to go overseas.

Life now seemed dull for Mae too; she was still longing for excitement. She was also still troubled about her passport and was applying for another one, hoping to go overseas with a different program. "It would be great if we could vacation somewhere in Europe. Maybe France, Greece, Italy," he proposed. "Maybe we should save up money and have a vacation fund so that we can plan for it."

Mae looked at Jacob perplexed. It was as if they spoke two different languages.

An exotic vacation with Jacob couldn't have been further from her mind; she didn't want a vacation. What she yearned for was to experience a third-world country and help improve it.

"I don't know," said Mae softly. "I thought I could help others and experience life more organically."

"What? And miss out on all the delicious wine and food?"

"Well, yeah, but that wasn't the point of my planned trip."

"Oh, sweetie, you are so good. But stick with me, and I'll show you how to live. Besides, I'd hardly say your trip was planned."

She eyed him quizzically, not understanding.

"If you'd actually sat down and planned it, there's no way you'd have lost your passport."

That was hurtful, and her mouth turned down. Why did he have to criticize her?

Jacob chuckled under his breath, not realizing Mae was watching him closely.

"What's so funny?" she snapped.

"I was just thinking what my mother would say if I told her I was going to Guatemala. Trust me, it's better for everyone if we just visit Europe and bring her back a nice bottle of wine and a box of chocolates." Jacob was amused at the thought as Mae was seething inside.

She felt as if he was mocking her ideas and dismissing her wants. It was becoming a habit with him, and she was starting to feel intimidated to share her thoughts.

Jacob got up off the couch.

He nuzzled his chin into her neck, saying, "I love how zany you are. It's so cute."

This wasn't the first time Jacob had referred to her as zany, and it would bother her more and more each time. She began to feel as if what had drawn her to him was now disparaging.

Later that night, Mae secretly started looking into apartments, though when she saw the cost, she realized she was stuck living with Jacob for some time. It wasn't that she didn't want to be with him, but specific attributes concerned her, and she needed space to be on her own. She decided to make the best of the situation and see where the relationship led.

Jacob and Mae settled in as a couple, and the old comfort of the two was something they both needed. Jacob was happy to have Mae staying with him and hoped it would soon be permanent, while Mae was grateful to have a place to stay and felt safe with Jacob. Before she knew it, she had become dependent upon him, and her free spirit had slowly faded.

Jacob was planned and organized, and Mae began to adjust to his rigid ways, starting to enjoy the monotony of his lifestyle. Though she missed spontaneity, Jacob made life both consistent and safe. They spent their weekends hiking, exploring new towns, and trying new recipes at home. Mae's feelings for him strengthened as she found solace in his protection and stability. After six months of living together, the pair officially became a couple and began making long-term plans. Sometimes, Mae would suggest something more spontaneous, such as backpacking across New England, but Jacob always found a reason they couldn't.

"C'mon, Jacob, let's go do something fun!" Mae said.

"Wanna go house hunting, Mae?" Jacob replied.

"What, No! I don't want that responsibility. Let's travel or go on an adventure," Mae quipped.

"Whatever happened to our trip to Europe? You said that we would plan something. Let's do it!"

Mae had been waiting for the right time to ask Jacob about it and decided it was time.

She was bored with life and wanted adventure.

"Oh yeah, I forgot about that," he lied. "Let's figure out a time to discuss it, and we can plan something soon."

Jacob seemed happy enough to discuss plans but never followed through with what Mae wanted. Instead, he would find a way to divert her desires and replace them with his own.

Only rarely would he agree to do something she had suggested.

"How about taking a ride to the mountains? It's not too far, and it's a wonderful day to ski," Mae asked one time.

Reluctantly, and to her surprise, he agreed, and they drove to the mountains for the day.

Mae felt peace within as she glided down the hills.

The feeling of freedom reminded Mae of life before they'd met. *No rules, no rigid schedule to maintain, and a sense of release from life's stress,* she thought as she jumped the moguls.

Despite their efforts of spontaneity, a nagging feeling of confinement continued deep within Mae.

Jacob was kind, considerate, and generous, and she felt selfish to complain.

Most would appreciate his attentiveness and focus, but it felt overwhelmingly suffocating.

Something else was unsettling, too, something she couldn't quite put a finger on, which made her uneasy. Most of the time, she thought she was being too sensitive and ignored her feelings, but she never could completely trust Jacob and didn't know why.

Anyway, for now, she had no opportunity to think about it; they had to get home to prepare for the arrival of her mother. She was excited to see her mom again, missing her dearly.

"Jacob, do we have enough pillows for Mom? I want her to be comfortable. Her health isn't the greatest with her high blood pressure, so I want her to be as stress-free as possible. It's a long ride and—"

Jacob interrupted.

"Mae, I set up everything last week. It will be great, and she'll be fine. I promise."

"I'm just worried. Kevin passed away recently, and I know she's still so sad."

"All the more reason," Jacob assured her.

Mae thought about it and decided Jacob was right.

Judy was to arrive the following evening, and Mae was excited for her to meet Jacob in person. When she arrived, she was immediately drawn to him, encouraging her daughter to consider settling down seriously.

After Jacob went to bed, Mae and her mother sat at the kitchen table to spend time alone.

"Ice cream?" Mae asked.

"That sounds lovely," Judy said as she took two large bowls from the cupboard. "Honey, he is so mature for his age."

"I guess," Mae said, more interested in choosing her ice cream flavor as her mother continued to pry about her intentions.

"Do you think you'll marry him?"

"Mom! Marriage! Jeez, I haven't even thought of it."

Judy took a breath. "Sweetie, take it from me, there aren't a lot of men like Jacob. I'd hate for you to miss out on such a great guy with a bright future."

Judy hugged Mae from behind before continuing. "It's just that I don't want you to end up like me. Struggling with money, having no financial security. Being alone, it's not easy."

Her voice trailed. "It would be nice to know that you are secure and taken care of, that's all."

It hadn't occurred to Mae that she even needed to be 'taken care of.'

She thought for a moment, letting her mother's words sink in. "Mom, I can take care of myself. Don't you think so?" Mae felt her cheeks flush as the words spewed out of her mouth. "I know you can, but why should you when you have someone eager to look after you? He really loves you, and he's good to you, so what's the hesitation all about?"

Mae couldn't answer that.

She didn't know why she was scared to let Jacob in fully. Could she ever be vulnerable with a man? Jacob was perfect on paper, but she didn't have the feelings for him she thought she should. Still, as her mother pointed out, she didn't want to let a good guy slip away. She thought she could grow to love him, but somehow, something didn't sit right, and she couldn't pinpoint what made her so uncomfortable around him.

Judy looked at her young daughter lovingly, hoping her words would resonate with her and she would consider their discussion. Jacob had revealed to Judy his plan to ask Mae to marry him.

He wanted Judy to feel Mae out, to help convince her they would have a great life together if she only gave him a chance.

"Do you want chocolate or vanilla?" Mae asked, trying to change the subject.

"Both!" replied Judy.

Mae spoke about her plans to get another passport and reapply for the volunteer internship.

"What about Jacob? How does he fit in?" said Judy.

"I don't know if he does, Mom, to be honest," replied Mae. "Why is marriage so important to everyone anyway? Why is everyone so obsessed with structure?"

Judy could see Mae breathing heavily, and the pressure of societal expectations of adulthood weighed on her. She had to proceed gently. "Sweetie, there's nothing wrong with any of that. Most women your age are starting to think about settling down, though. You are twenty-four, after all, and it's just a part of the growing process."

Mae fiddled with her long brown hair, twirling it around her finger. She would do that when she was younger and was feeling anxious.

"I'm really glad you're here, Mom. I've missed you."

The two embraced, taking long breaths between tight squeezes.

It was nice to be reunited, even for just the night.

Judy was to leave for a cruise with her book club the following day and couldn't see Mae until after the holidays. Jacob had surprised her with the generous gift, and Judy was excited.

"I can't believe your boyfriend would go to all this trouble for me," she enthused. "Mae, you're so fortunate. He's one in a million. So sweet and generous."

"Hmm, okay. I hope you enjoy the cruise." Mae hid her shock about not knowing Jacob provided the funds for the cruise.

It was clear that as Judy hadn't been on a cruise before, she was dazzled by the idea.

In secret, Mae was highly cross with Jacob.

When finally alone with Jacob, Mae couldn't keep her dismay silent any longer. Irritated, she said, "Why wouldn't you tell me you did this? It's way too much. You could have consulted with me first; she is *my* mother."

Jacob looked hurt at Mae's sternness but quickly shifted his demeanor. "I'm sorry, love. I thought it was a nice gesture. With Kevin's passing, I thought it would be a good distraction."

Mae felt foolish for her sharp tone. "Look, I'm so happy for my mother, but you should talk to me before making big decisions, especially when it has to do with my mom."

Her voice softened, and she approached Jacob. "I've never been without my mother for the holidays, and I guess I'll just miss her," she said.

Jacob took her hand, stroking it softly. "You have me, Mae, and that's all you need," he said, kissing the tip of her nose.

Mae returned to the living room, where her mother sat leafing through the pamphlet.

Judy's face was bright and excited.

"This is too much," she said. "It's far too big a gift. Jacob, let me pay half at least."

"I wouldn't dream of it. You are worth it. Judy, go and enjoy your trip," he said with a smile.

"I'll miss you both," she said, stroking her daughter's face.

Mae secretly seethed. *She will miss us both? She's only met him once! For goodness' sake!*

"I'll miss you too, Mom, but like Jacob says, go enjoy yourself," Mae responded.

Jacob looked so smug, so self-satisfied.

Mae lay with her mother in the spare bedroom as they drifted to sleep, both dozing that night with a heart full of love and the comfort of knowing they would always have one another.

Chapter 6

The winter was colder than usual, the snowfall exceeding the years prior. After work, Mae would cozy up with a warm cup of soup, spending her nights reading.

Jacob worked late almost every night, and Mae didn't seem to mind being alone. He had already expressed his desire to move up the ladder at the firm, and she could not hold him back.

He was persistent and focused on his career, making clear that he also wanted Mae to benefit from his achievements.

But Mae thought *I seem to be your co-star, not your equal. And it seems that's how you want it.* At first, this bothered her, wanting more from life, but Jacob insisted she was pivotal to everything, that he needed her there to support his dreams, and later, it would be her turn.

Mae counted on that, though she didn't understand his resistance to her getting her law degree in the meantime. Regardless, she continued working as a secretary but was considering applying for law school again. She'd thought about it often, but only recently had she decided it was the career path she would pursue. This time, she kept it quiet, never revealing that she'd applied.

An acceptance letter came, and she was elated.

Now, she could apply for a school loan, but she knew she would have to depend on Jacob to financially support her for a couple of years until she graduated. She finally broached the subject.

"You see, I'm made for this career; they accepted me so easily, and I really want to give it a go. I promise to pay you back as soon as I land a job."

"Sweetie, I'm not worried about the money, but we should hold off on getting your degree. Right now, I'm trying to make partner, and with both of us having demanding careers, I'm afraid it will be too much for our relationship. It can't handle two of us with demanding days."

"But Jacob," she continued. "I don't want to be a secretary. What better time to do this than now? I want this so much; you know I do. But I need your help."

Jacob was pensive.

"How about we talk about this in a month once my annual review is completed at work? I'll have some time to think about it, and we'll make a plan," he said.

"Deal," Mae said with confidence.

Later that night, as they were getting ready for bed, Mae walked into the living room, where two glasses of Prosecco, candles, and soft music graced the room.

"What's this?" she asked.

"I want to celebrate us," Jacob said.

They sat in bed nibbling on crackers, sipping on the sweet taste of the imported Prosecco. Every time Mae's glass was halfway empty, Jacob refilled it generously.

"I'm getting tipsy," Mae said, giggling.

"Enjoy and let loose," Jacob said with a smile as he poured the remainder into her glass.

As she took the last sip of her drink, she looked at Jacob with a bright smile. Clumsily, she stumbled toward the bedroom door, and he began kissing her softly.

His hands slowly caressed her soft skin, and she let out a groan, her breathing beginning to quicken. The touch of his hands on her breasts was electrifying.

He teased her with his tongue as her body pressed up against his groin. She felt the hardness in his pants and unbuttoned his blue jeans, quickly pulling down the zipper.

Jacob grabbed her hands and laid her down on the bed more aggressively than he intended.

He continued to kiss her more gently, caressing her, inhaling the scent of her skin, drunk on her essence for a moment. He loved her, and the way her body ignited his passion was erotic.

Slowly, Jacob undressed Mae and made his way past her belly, licking between her thighs. He would hesitate for a moment between each touch, waiting for her to desire him even more.

He continued to feel his way around her body until she couldn't resist him anymore.

She removed his clothes as their mouths opened, and their tongues collided with deep, passionate kissing. Jacob climbed on top of Mae, slowly inserting himself.

She groaned with pleasure as he eased himself deeper inside her.

The screams of pleasure continued as Jacob's breath became heavier until finally, he lay limp inside her satisfied body. Both lay there for some time, drifting in and out of sleep.

When Mae woke up hours later, her head spun slightly from indulging the evening before. She soon realized the candles were still burning and their clothes lay scattered throughout the room. A wet drip rolled down her legs as she moved toward the bathroom, and Mae gasped.

"Jacob, wake up!"

Jacob's messy, thick hair rolled closer to Mae. He began kissing her gently.

"Good morning to you, love," he said groggily.

"Jacob, we didn't use protection last night." Her voice was strained.

"We didn't? I'm sure it's fine," he said.

"How do you know?" Mae asked frantically.

"Mae, quit worrying. A baby wouldn't be the worst thing in the world. And we only did it once; it's not like we've been having sex for weeks unprotected."

He pulled her closer and fell back to sleep. Mae stared at the ceiling, considering his thoughts. They weren't married, and she was nowhere near ready to have a child.

What was he thinking? she thought, feeling he had taken advantage of her incapacity.

She was planning to attend law school and had little interest in marriage or children. After fifteen minutes, she dismissed the notion; the chances were slim, just as he'd said. She had just had her period ten days prior, and the odds were surely in their favor.

She wasn't even sure if he'd fully completed inside of her. She barely remembered the night.

Mae fell asleep and didn't wake until eleven in the morning, forgetting all about her concerns when she opened her eyes to Jacob sitting beside her with a suitcase packed.

"Let's go, Mae," he said. "We're going on an adventure."

"What do you mean?" she inquired. "You're kidding, right?"

Her curiosity was piqued. It wasn't at all like Jacob to plan anything resembling a surprise. God knew she'd been asking him to try new things for long enough, and he'd always said no.

"It's a surprise. You have a half hour to pack your bags and get ready. Our flight leaves in a couple of hours."

Flight? she thought. *We are flying? Wow! Jacob, this truly is a surprise!*

She adored spontaneity, and it made her happy that Jacob had at last listened to her needs.

"Pack enough for seven days on a beach," Jacob called out as he left her to get ready.

A beach! Oh, my God! I am the luckiest girl!

She quickly grabbed her suitcase and began throwing outfits together.

On the plane heading to Mexico, it was at moments like this that Mae fell deeper in love with this man. His potential to live unprompted also gave her so much more hope than expected.

Perhaps they could build a life together where they would both feel satisfied!

The week was filled with romantic gestures, laughing moments, sunshine, and contentment. In the evenings, they would walk the beach holding hands, talking about life and their future.

"I'm excited about the opportunity to go law school," Mae said. "I just need your support."

Jacob was quiet for a moment.

He looked out to the ocean, then up to the stars. The night breeze felt good on his skin. He grabbed Mae and said, "I want to make all your dreams come true."

He took her hands, and by the time she knew it, he was down on one knee.

"Mae, will you be my wife?" His eyes glowed with anticipation. Mae's mouth was agape, speechless at this unexpected gesture. Her mind was racing, thinking of so many reasons why she should say no, but Jacob looked so genuine and happy. She replied, "Yes, yes, I will."

He placed the ring on her finger as she gazed at the beautiful solitaire diamond with delight.

"You have made me the happiest man on earth," Jacob said tearfully.

They embraced under the moonlight, holding onto the moment.

Mae listened to Jacob's breath beside her as she lay awake after a long night of lovemaking.

The night's eerie sound and Mexico's warmth had conspired to leave her sleepless.

A nagging feeling consumed her as she contemplated her engagement.

Mae had been clear with Jacob, hadn't she? Didn't she recall saying that she had no intentions of getting married? If she was being honest, she appreciated what Jacob represented but didn't want the constraints, at least not until she'd earned her law degree.

Mae tossed her body to get comfortable, thinking of her mother.

Judy wanted Mae settled because she had never felt financially secure herself; she tended to think with her head and never her heart due to her own limited life experiences.

As a child, Mae could recall her saying, "Find a man to take care of you, and an easy life you will enjoy."

She'd worked three jobs and was often tired.

Mae wished her father hadn't walked out on them both. Where had he gone, and did he ever think of her? Would he someday return?

Whenever Mae asked her mother about it, she would simply say, "A coward walks out on their family. I have no time for cowards."

Seeing her mother struggle made Mae want to avoid heartbreak, not run toward it. She couldn't understand for the life of her why her mother thought marriage was the answer to financial struggles when she'd had her own problems *because of* marriage. It perplexed Mae the way her mother thought, but she always gave her the respect she deserved.

Mae was scared of love from anyone. Now, lying next to Jacob, she was wondering how she had gotten herself into this position. When Jacob had proposed, her gut had been screaming to say no. She'd even considered ending their relationship many times but enjoyed his taste for the finer things, though she found it all over the top. A part of Jacob also frightened her, though she couldn't quite understand it. Her body tensed when he touched her.

She felt he could see through her, desperately finding herself trying to hide her feelings.

She suspected he didn't care about her hesitation toward him either, always reminding her that he had strong enough feelings for both of them.

For hours, Mae thought about ways to break it off with Jacob without breaking her mother's heart or his. She didn't want to be the villain in the story others had written for her, but this relationship was wrong. A feeling of urgency rushed through her veins as she got out of bed and gathered her belongings. She didn't know where she was headed but she'd flee before Jacob awoke. She threw her dress from the night before—retrieving it from the floor—into the suitcase, then swiftly grabbed her cosmetics and shoes, shoving them hastily into her bag.

She was quietly beginning to wheel her large pink suitcase toward the door when she felt the buzz of her cell phone. She looked down. It was a text from her mother, held up due to lousy WiFi.

'Congratulations, my dear daughter. I have worked hard and waited a long time for this day. I couldn't be happier to know that you will never have to live a life as hard as mine. All of my efforts have paid off. I love you.'

Mae's heart sank as she reread the message, then shoved her phone back into her pocket. She went into the bathroom and quietly wept. Mae's mother had already sacrificed her life for her daughter, and the thought of disappointing her left Mae sobbing into her hands.

She considered her alternatives, struggling in both scenarios.

If she left Jacob, both her mother and he would be crushed.

She would have no place to live and little money to support herself.

Mae didn't make much at her current job since she had no experience. But her efforts would pay off over time, and she could seek better employment.

She had to give it a little time before making her move. She could have confided in her mother, but Judy had already sacrificed financially for

Mae to finish school, and it would be too much to ask her to support her until she found better-paying employment.

Mae took a long, deep breath, knowing the choice had already been made.

Jacob is a good man, she thought. *Why walk away from him, to struggle alone and disappoint my mother?*

She shook her head, wiped the tears from her eyes, washed her face, and climbed back into bed with Jacob.

He started to stir as she moved closer.

"Where have you been, love?" he said in a sleepy voice.

"Sorry to wake you. Go back to sleep," Mae said, quickly burying her face in the pillow so Jacob could not see the redness in her eyes if he put on the light.

Mae acquiesced for the rest of the week, and the two enjoyed celebrating their engagement.

It was a magical time for the pair, and when it was time to return home, they left with new motivations and goals.

Three weeks after returning home, Mae woke up feeling drained. Her stomach was turning as if she had just exited a carnival ride, and her throat was moist with a dreaded taste of bile. She was devoid of energy too. Had she caught a bug? Should she call out sick from work?

That day, she lay in bed, unable to eat, and slept for hours.

When Jacob arrived home, she was dehydrated and could barely move.

Jacob smiled, taking her hand and glancing at the round diamond sparkling back.

"Could you be pregnant?" he asked.

"No, definitely not," Mae said insistently. "We used protection the entire time we were away. I think I caught some dreadful bug," she said, barely moving.

"Let me get you some soup from the deli down the road," he offered. Fifteen minutes later, Jacob returned home with a large container of chicken soup, a freshly baked loaf of Italian bread, and herbal tea. He sat on the bed beside Mae and spoon-fed her some broth.

"You need to eat. Just take a couple of spoons of it."

Jacob was a great caretaker, wanting to ensure that Mae always felt loved and protected.

"Get some rest, and hopefully, you'll feel better in the morning. I'll sleep on the couch so I don't disturb you," he offered.

Mae lay under the covers, trying to be comfortable until she vomited. She ran to the bathroom, barely making it as she hovered over the toilet bowl.

Jacob sat by her side, holding her hair and using a warm washcloth to clean her up.

The following day, she was feeling a bit better but still had the feeling of nausea threatening to unleash at any time. She managed to make it through the workday by drinking water and snacking on dry crackers. The day seemed to drag on forever, and she couldn't wait to get home and crawl right back into bed. She felt tired and drained walking home from the train station, wanting to find the nearest bench and sit down.

Whatever this is, it's kicking my ass, she thought.

It had been six days by now, and Mae was still having bouts of sickness.

She hadn't felt well all week and suddenly remembered many bills were due by the weekend.

She grabbed the small calendar from the refrigerator door and sat, paying everything that was due. She noticed the date. She'd missed her period.

It was over three weeks late, and she hadn't even noticed. Mae sighed nervously.

This can't be, she thought. A part of her didn't want to know the answer.

She was too scared to find out the truth, though it was becoming painfully obvious.

Mae prayed that her period was simply late and that her not feeling well had nothing to do with it. It took her another three days to finally purchase a pregnancy test at the drugstore.

She sat on her bed, staring at the package. "Please be negative," she pleaded out loud.

She hadn't mentioned anything to Jacob, unsure she was ready for his reaction.

He would be elated, which wasn't good news for her.

It was an hour before Mae could muster the courage to take the test. Within a minute, the pink plus sign glared back, Mae's eyes welling with tears. "Fuck!" she exclaimed.

The tears now flowed more steadily down her cheeks. Mae hadn't considered being a mother, certainly not so soon, so young. She was just settling into being engaged. If she was being honest, she didn't want to be married either and had been swept away in the moment with Jacob.

"Fuck," she said again. She put her hands to her face, now sobbing uncontrollably.

Now, all her dreams of attending law school would have to be put on hold. Her plans to volunteer overseas would also have to wait for another time. The more Mae considered all that would be lost by having her baby, the more she resented the idea of being a mother.

She googled abortion clinics, considering her options. She needed time to think; her head was spinning, and the constant feeling of nausea was causing anxiety.

She needed to escape. Without thought, she packed a bag and scribbled a note to Jacob.

'Please don't worry; I'll be back in the morning.'

She called her friend Jill, who lived two hours away, and asked if she could stay the night.

"Oh, Mae, are you okay?" Jill said.

"No, I'm anything but okay. I'm pregnant," said Mae.

Jill noticed the ring on Mae's finger and looked at her curiously. "Are you engaged?"

"Ugh, yes. Sorry, I didn't tell you. It was unexpected and happened in Mexico. Everything's happening so quickly," Mae complained. "I wish I could turn back the clock, Jill."

"Mae, you don't have to do any of this," Jill offered.

"I know I don't, but I feel obligated. Now, with the baby ..." Her voice trailed off. "I was planning to start law school. I even got accepted."

"Why can't you still go? Plenty of women manage careers and motherhood."

"Jacob will never go for it."

"So, do it without him. Mae, why have you become so submissive? Whatever happened to that carefree, give-no-fucks girl?"

"She got pregnant," Mae said flatly.

"Whatever you decide, I'm here. You have options, you know that, right?" said Jill.

Mae was quiet, considering Jill's words. She didn't want to talk about it or even think about it anymore. "Let's go get burgers," Mae said.

Mae and Jill spent the rest of the night catching up on their lives, not mentioning Mae's predicament again. They had some laughs and reminisced about their college days.

"Don't you miss the feeling of freedom?" Mae said.

"You still have it," Jill replied.

"Adulting sucks," Mae said with a laugh.

"I'll drink to that," Jill said as the two gulped down soft drinks, chomping their burgers.

Mae left the following morning, refreshed and settled.

She hadn't made any decisions but was grateful to have received an honest and valued conversation about her feelings before sharing them with Jacob.

She arrived home early in the afternoon, finding Jacob waiting in the living room. She had expected him to be at work, but no ... She saw him pacing the living room.

He rushed toward her as she opened the door.

"I've been worried sick, Mae; where the fuck have you been?"

"I told you I'd be back today," Mae said. "I went to a friend's."

"Well, you didn't mention where, and I've been worried," Jacob said tersely. "I tried to call, and you didn't answer. This is incredibly thoughtless."

His expression seemed to say, *and selfish.* But he didn't dare vocalize it.

Mae glanced at Jacob and saw the worry she had caused him, now feeling terrible about not being more specific about her whereabouts. Past him, she noticed the empty pregnancy box sitting on the coffee table beside a bottle of Champagne.

Mae was so overwhelmed by discovering her pregnancy that she'd stupidly forgotten to hide the test pack. She had tossed it on the top of the trash when she'd left, failing to bring out the garbage. "Shit," she mumbled under her breath.

She wasn't ready to have this conversation and had been seriously considering terminating the pregnancy, never revealing to Jacob that she had been pregnant at all.

She could still do as Jill said, still be independent.

She could find herself again and either choose a termination or become a single mom. Being single, if the old Mae came back, she would still be able to achieve all her dreams.

"I'm just glad you're home and safe," said Jacob.

Mae began, "Listen, Jacob, we need to talk."

Her voice was quiet, and she wasn't sure what she would say next, still needing time to process the pregnancy.

Maybe I won't tell him after all.

Then Jacob said, "Mae, you do realize I know about the pregnancy! I saw the test and I'm so excited. I guess you fled because you thought I'd be angry; well, I'm not, far from it! I couldn't be more delighted, and I called my folks, who are very happy as well. Your mother couldn't believe it; she was crying happy tears. I figured you'd left the packaging there for me to find, so then I looked in the trash, and there was the positive test! This is so unreal!"

"Wait, you told my mother? Jacob, we hadn't even discussed it between us."

Mae was visibly irritated.

"I know, I know; please don't be mad. I was just so excited, and you weren't here, and I couldn't wait to start celebrating with someone," said Jacob. "So, I guess I reached out ... Anyway, no harm done. Everyone's so excited for us. My Mom can't wait to plan the wedding. She insists we get married before the baby is due though, and I agree."

Jacob continued rambling as Mae's heart sank.

What about what I want? she thought but didn't dare say the words out loud.

Mae stood with her hands by her side, defeated, her mouth agape but no words emerging. Tears started to form again, and before she could stop them, Jacob was by her side.

"I read pregnant women are overly emotional," he said, not ever considering how condescending he sounded. "Let's rest and let me take care of you."

Mae was in a state of shock; all she could do was obey his instruction.

She lay down on the couch as Jacob called his friends, telling them he was getting married and was going to be a father, and wasn't this so incredible?

Mae slept through the night and most of the next day.

It wouldn't be until late Sunday afternoon when she emerged from her bedroom to find Jacob scrolling through homes for sale in the area.

"Jacob, what's this?" She felt unsteady on her feet.

She shifted her body to lean up against the wall. The smell of morning coffee nauseated her as Jacob consumed large gulps, smacking his lips before responding.

"We can't possibly stay in such close quarters," he said, smiling at her. "I found some great properties for sale that I think we can afford if we're careful." Jacob was scribbling numbers on the notepad beside him, not noticing the sheer panic on Mae's face.

"Jacob, don't you think this is all a little too fast? I still intend on attending law school."

"Too fast? Mae, we're having a baby. Babies need a home. I want to have a home with you and our kid. Anyway, law school can wait."

Jacob rose from his chair and gently caressed Mae's back. He enunciated the word "baby" as he touched her belly. Mae winced at his touch but smiled weakly.

The urge to run from the mounting pressure was building, but Mae was careful with her words and actions. Confusion swirled through her mind, and feeling out of control overtook her nervous system. Before she could react or say something she would later regret, she said, "I'm going to get dressed." Once in the bathroom, she stared at her reflection.

She hated herself for thinking so but only wanted to escape this situation and forget about marriage, babies, and sharing a home with Jacob.

"Maybe this is just hormones," she reasoned. She looked down at her belly, making a reluctant decision. She stared again in the mirror, talking to herself, trying to convince the image that stared back. *Grow up, and stop evading responsibility,* screamed the voice inside.

Her heart sank at her words, wishing the reflection would have the answer. She got on her knees and prayed for the first time in a long while. She wasn't even sure for what—for clarity, calmness, a way out? She wasn't sure. She felt alone and desperate, ensnared in someone else's life.

This was not what she had imagined or wanted. How had she got here, and why?

She could not come up with an answer.

She said softly to herself, "Do the right thing, Mae. You got this."

Mae spent most of her time in bed, pretending to be tired but mostly shutting out the world. She avoided Jacob, blaming her absence on tiredness because she would much prefer sitting in the dark than dealing with the reality of her life.

By the end of the following weekend, without discussion, Jacob had signed a contract on a small ranch home with a large yard three blocks from his office. The house needed little work, but Jacob thought they should paint the place before leaving their old apartment.

"We're moving? Mae asked. "Don't you think we should have discussed this and gone together looking for homes? Mae felt heat rising to her cheeks.

Jacob had the habit of making decisions without her, but this was a big one.

"You've been sick, and I didn't want to give you another thing to worry about," Jacob said, his eyes showing a trace of hurt. "I thought I was doing a nice thing for you."

"Moving is going to be overwhelming right now. Can't we wait a couple of months?" Mae complained. "Anyway, I like it here."

Jacob moved slowly toward her, taking her hand and kissing it. "I know this is a lot for you, but I'm setting us up for our future. Don't you worry about a thing. I will handle this, and you handle growing our baby." His words rang condescending, but she didn't say more.

She put her head down and resisted the tears threatening her eyes.

Jacob hired painters who needed to come into the new home before they moved to eliminate Mae's inhalation of the fresh paint smell. It seemed like a good idea, and Mae suggested, "Could we paint it bright blue? Like cornflowers. The color makes me feel happy."

His face lit up, seeming relieved that she was at last taking part in their forthcoming move.

She showed him samples of the paint color, and he nodded. "It's a restful color," he said.

Moving day was uneventful, as Jacob had hired a moving company to transfer most of their stuff.

The house was in an unfamiliar neighborhood, temporarily satisfying Mae's sense of adventure. Big, ancient oak trees with vast branches lined the streets, and there was a sense of community in the suburban town, making it a friendly place.

Mae watched children ride bikes, and parents walk behind them, contentedly taking in the scenery of the blooming flowers. In all honesty, she couldn't deny it was a good place to live.

As she entered the home, she noticed the foyer was painted a creamy ivory, making the space bright but bland. There was no sign of her cornflower blue.

She looked at him and said, "Cream," just looking at the walls.

He nodded. "Looks fresh and cool, don't you think?"

She didn't have the energy to argue over paint colors and anyway, maybe he'd forgotten.

It also seemed smaller than she had imagined, with no space to escape one another.

"I know it isn't much, but we can move to a bigger home in a couple of years," he offered.

Mae hid her disappointment but appreciated his efforts. Since Jacob paid most of the bills, what right did she have to insert her opinion? Silently wishing she had more input on the big decisions, she'd come to accept Jacob's control for an easier life. She reasoned he had good intentions, though she hated the feeling of being dismissed. Mae pushed her resentment aside as her belly grew and the morning sickness subsided.

Lately, she had even been warming up to the idea of motherhood, knowing that whether she was ready to accept it or not, the due date would be coming soon.

Jane appeared unexpectedly at the door early on a Saturday morning, knocking.

Mae said to herself, *who would come at this time?* It was awkward and embarrassing since she was still in her old pajamas. And she hated seeing Jane anyway, fearing yet more judgment.

"Jane, oh, hi," Mae said as she pulled her robe tighter. "What brings you here so early?"

"Jacob didn't tell you?" she said with a strained smile.

Mae looked at Jacob emerging from the bathroom, dressed in a blue button-down shirt and khakis.

"Mother, good morning," he greeted her warmly.

Confused, Mae looked to Jacob for an explanation.

"Mom is planning our wedding. We thought it would be nice to have a simple backyard one. Just a few people, nothing big or flashy. Mae loves simplicity and—"

He may as well not have bothered.

"You'll have an elegant one," Jane interrupted. "I hired a wedding planner who should be here any minute to transform this place into a romantic, elegant venue for your nuptials."

"Upcoming nuptials?" Mae said, holding back her shock. "What do you mean?"

"Sweetheart, you don't want to walk down the aisle showing, do you? That would be an embarrassment. In your condition, we must take care of this wedding very early, before the baby comes close to arriving. This hasn't given me a lot of time to prepare, but I think we can make it work," she said, peering out the window to the backyard. "It's very messy out there, Mae," she commented. "I'd have thought with you at home so much, you could have tidied it."

"We just moved in, Mother," Jacob said in an attempt to defend Mae for a change.

Mae tried to steady herself and calm the increasing rage that was building.

Jacob glared at Mae, noticing her discomfort, and quickly suggested, "Why don't you put on something more comfortable while Mother and I discuss plans?"

Inside the bedroom, Mae paced with exasperation.

Once again, Jacob had created a situation that left her looking foolish and inept, incapable of making decisions. She had little control, especially now with his mother already involved, but her heart sank as she felt her life disappear even further from what she had expected and hoped.

Twenty minutes later, Mae reentered the living room to find Tiffany, a wedding planner dressed in a short pink dress, matching heels, and heavy perfume, assembled with Jacob and Jane at the table. They were discussing flowers and music with Jane.

"Oh, there she is," Jane said, her voice tense with judgment. "Little Miss has finally managed to get dressed and is ready to join us."

Jacob glared at his mother, giving her a warning to settle down.

"Come dear. I thought you would like to see what we have been doing while you were primping and preening."

Mae approached the trio, feeling like a stranger in her own life.

Looking over the plans, she nodded; why bother questioning anything?

Her opinion was of no value. No one noticed when Mae walked away into the kitchen to make herself dry toast. She could hear the chatter of wedding plans in the distance as she leaned against the counter, trying not to scream or even worse, to turn and flee; she thought of getting into her car and abandoning the whole scene, leaving them to it.

The wedding was set for the end of the following month. By then, the weather would be warmer, and Jane had arranged for a gardener to plant bright yellow flowers along the path leading to the end of the property, where she had asked her friend, a fellow minister, to perform the service. Mae, a Catholic, had always assumed that if she were ever to get married, it would be in a church, but Jacob's family had strong ties to the Methodist church and insisted they use her clergyman. It was grossly unfair and uncomfortable.

When would Mae's voice ever be heard?

Later that night, in bed, Mae was quiet.

"Isn't this exciting? My mom has stepped in for us. We should get her something special as a thank you. I was thinking of a necklace or something to show our appreciation."

Mae groaned, rolled over, and pretended to have fallen asleep.

But she could not fall asleep and lay quietly awake, thinking about what had transpired.

She had never been asked for input about purportedly the biggest event in any woman's life, and her heart was in a mess. She felt increasingly low and defeated, all her wishes eroded. The truth was her opinion didn't matter, and Jacob and his mom weren't even hiding the fact. They went ahead making all the arrangements without considering Mae's thoughts.

Even when deciding on the menu, Mae suggested they offer a pasta dish for some folks who preferred not to eat meat.

"I have an old family recipe; I could send it to the chef. It would make my family happy."

"Pasta is for poor people," Jane scoffed, unwilling to even consider it. Jacob threw his hands up, shaking his head, knowing there was no arguing with his mother over these arrangements.

"Let's not advertise that you are pregnant, Mae, either," Jane said sternly. When she realized how brash it sounded, she followed it with, "I want everyone to celebrate the two of you. There will be plenty of time to acknowledge the baby after the wedding. This is about you."

You could have fooled me, Mae thought. *It seems to be more about you!*

As Mae replayed the day, her chest grew tight; after two hours of restless tossing and turning, she finally grew exhausted enough to sleep to avoid more stressful thoughts.

Chapter 7

On the day of the wedding, Mae woke up with a headache.

Is it nerves, hormones, or the impending feeling of doom? She wondered, now certain she was getting married for all the wrong reasons, at the wrong time, and in the wrong way. Nothing about these arrangements was anything like she or her own mother had ever imagined for her.

She tried to brush off these feelings as she slipped into the plain satin dress that Jane had gifted her weeks earlier. Sure, it was opulent and pretty, being long and sleek and in the most amazing, layered silks, and it also cleverly gave way to Mae's growing belly.

She had to concede that Jane had made a good choice, even if it wasn't what she would have selected for herself. It fit perfectly, and felt wonderful, cool against her irritated skin.

Thankfully, the weather cooperated, the warm breeze from the open window energizing. In the distance, she heard birds singing, a delightful song of hope.

She listened, taking in the melody, hoping this meant better days would come.

Mae heard the creak of the door as her mother entered. Although she had arrived earlier that morning, Jacob insisted she go directly to the hotel to rest.

"Don't you look beautiful?" Judy admired. "Is that really the dress Jane selected?"

"It is, Mom. I can't quite believe it either. Do I look pregnant in it, though?"

Mae's spirits brightened at the sight of her mother.

"And by the way, Mom, I'm so glad you're here. I've missed you so much."

Hesitating momentarily, Judy took Mae's hands, looking into her daughter's eyes.

"You do not look pregnant in the dress, no. The way it drapes at the front, it's perfect. I couldn't have chosen a better one for you."

"She had it tailored for me," said Mae, finally able to appreciate something Jane had done.

"Are you doing okay, feeling okay?" asked Judy. "You look a little drained. Is it the pregnancy? Are you getting morning sickness?"

Not wanting to ruin the mood, Mae dismissed her worries, saying, "Mom, I'm fine. Just a little tired. And well, maybe, a little overwhelmed," she admitted. "I haven't been sleeping well, so that's probably why I look washed out."

"Now that is all to be expected, dear."

But there was a heaviness in the air—unspoken words wanting to be said.

Judy waited anxiously for her daughter to speak more, but Mae quickly changed the subject.

"Glad the weather is good for us."

"Yes, me too," Judy said quietly.

"I should finish getting ready."

"Of course," Judy responded. She glanced at her daughter, noticing the dimness in her eyes. "Are you sure you're okay? You can tell me anything," Judy prodded. "You're not yourself. You're so subdued these days. Where has my vibrant, bubbly girl disappeared to?"

Mae thought sadly, *I wish I knew.* The truth was she'd become a shadow of herself.

She blushed. "No, really, I'm fine."

When Judy left, Mae let out a long exhale. She wanted desperately to tell her mother the truth. She didn't that day—a regret she would hold for many years to come.

Before long, it was time to start the ceremony.

Mae had to hand it to Jane for something else, not only for the dress. She had done a spectacular job of transforming their backyard into a wonderful oasis of beauty. The overflow of flowers took her breath away. For a moment, she looked around and felt gratitude.

Perhaps the woman had some redeeming graces after all, though admittedly, hard to find.

Jane and Jacob meticulously planned the wedding celebration, which was a spectacle far removed from the simple, pressure-free day Mae had always wanted for herself. As guests filed into the venue, commenting on the massive flower arrangements, abundant food choices, and incredibly extravagant dishware, Mae watched in awe.

Mae observed the strangers' impressed reactions to the wedding.

Mae had little family, and there was but a handful of guests she had invited. They all looked overwhelmed and ever so slightly under-dressed for this occasion, whereas on Jacob's side, it looked like a royal wedding.

She watched as her mother uncomfortably attempted conversations with Jacob's family. She, too, felt uneasy amongst the sea of strangers, now supposed family. She tried, at least at first, to mingle with the crowd, though it was inconsequential.

Mae was invisible at her own wedding, as the attention was on Jane and Jacob, and the incredible party they had thrown. Jacob's mother told everyone who listened that she had arranged it all.

A young woman approached Mae as she stood near the table. "You look beautiful," she noticed. Mae couldn't place the stranger, though she recognized her from pictures.

"I'm Amanda. I dated Jacob years ago, and we've always been close," she admitted. "I hope you don't mind that I'm here today. I wouldn't miss Jacob's wedding for the world though."

Mae searched her memory, recalling Jacob telling her that Amanda had been his first love, and she'd broken his heart when she went overseas to study art.

He once admitted that he had never forgotten Amanda and had planned to marry her, but she'd been determined to live in France, and Jacob couldn't handle the distance or her tenacity.

As she walked away, her words, "We've always been close," rang in Mae's ears.

He hadn't mentioned her since that day long ago. It would have been nice of him to ask Mae whether she minded his ex-girlfriend attending. But never mind; the girl had been nice after all, sweet and polite. But what else had Jacob not told her about their continued relationship?

She was quickly diverted from her thoughts as the photographer called for her attention.

"Could I please have the bride? We need some photos by the water fountain."

The fountain was a stunning central piece, an elaborate statue Jane had brought for ambiance. It seemed she had thought of everything.

Mae smiled at the camera, though inside, she shook. An insecurity consumed Mae at the female stranger's revelation, though this wasn't the time to bring it up.

The day's formalities were rushed, with little mention of love and commitment. There was more discussion about the salmon Jane had flown in from Alaska than the vows Jacob and Mae had just promised to one another. Mae watched from the corner as Jane walked around the guests, soaking up the compliments of the event and making small talk. Jacob was by his mother's side, embracing the attention, never even noticing Mae was absent.

It always seemed that when Jane was around, Jacob glued himself to his mother's side.

"You doing okay?" Jill said as she appeared from behind. She was drinking a rum and coke, which clearly was not her first. Mae was relieved to see her.

"Some party," Mae replied.

"It sure is. Are these people always like this?" Jill asked.

"I don't even know them that well. Jacob and I rarely visit his parents' home together. He usually goes to his folks' house without me. I never really thought much about it, but now I'm starting to wonder if he wanted to limit my interaction with them to protect me from all this," Mae said.

"It's something," Jill said.

"I feel like I don't belong here. I'm not sure anyone would notice if I left. Not even Jacob," Mae said, half joking.

"So, let's leave," Jill offered.

"Jill, I can't. What would I say?"

By now, most guests were inside the house sipping on cocktails, which felt intrusive.

She watched as strangers stood in her home, conversing about politics and the economy while she willed them to leave.

"Let's just go out and get some air at least," said Jill.

The two left through the back doors without anyone noticing. They then spent almost an hour laughing in the garden.

"You are a runaway bride," Jill said.

"Yeah, except I can't run away," Mae said as she laughed at the notion. "I live here."

Jill and Mae howled at the situation, looking at the night sky.

"Do you think they noticed you aren't even at your own wedding?" laughed Jill.

"Probably not, and if they do, Jane is happier without me there so she can enjoy time with her precious son," Mae said sarcastically. "I should get back in, though."

"One more minute," said Jill.

Jill took Mae's hand, and they watched a plane fly overhead.

"I really love you. I know this situation sucks for you, but I'm here," said Jill.

"It's not so bad. A man who dotes on me, a home, a baby on the way." Mae's voice trailed off, considering all this.

"We both know that means nothing if you're unhappy," Jill said.

"I'll learn to be happy. Maybe it's just hormones," said Mae.

"Or maybe you found yourself in a situation that you never wanted and can't find a way out of," said Jill. "I'm here to tell you there's always a way out."

Mae took a deep breath. Everything Jill was saying was right. She just didn't know what she could do about it at this point.

She was pregnant, with hardly any money, and Jacob provided comfort and security.

"I'll manage," said Mae.

As they walked back into the living room, Jacob and his mother were dancing, never realizing she'd been gone. Mae was amazed by the transformation of the house since Jane had hauled off their furniture the day before the wedding to accommodate the guests.

It was beginning to feel more like Jane's house than Mae's own.

Mae watched in amusement as Jacob twirled his mother around the makeshift dance floor. The guests watched with delight as they cheered from the side, clapping and singing along. Mae overheard one guest say, "Those two always had the best relationship. I wonder how she feels about Jacob's bride. What's her name again?"

The woman with cropped red hair who wore a skirt equally short replied, "I can't remember, but Jane calls her a gypsy. I don't think she likes her much, but when she told Jacob, he just brushed her off."

The women continued to converse, but Mae and Jill had heard enough.

They retreated down the hall to the kitchen. Jill waved as the women, embarrassed, began to whisper to each other nervously.

Mae smiled at Jill as they both laughed and grabbed a pile of crabcakes.

Jill held Mae's hand and shifted back toward the dance floor, finally giving Mae the power to enjoy the day as much as the rest of the guests.

On the floor, they moved their bodies freely. A smile emerged on Mae's face—an authentic one, maybe the first real one she'd had for years.

The best part of the wedding for Mae was being with Jill, enjoying the bond that she'd never experienced with anyone else.

Their friendship had been a constant for Mae, and she hoped it always would be; Jill was a soft place to land, a place where Mae could be her most authentic self.

Jill could see when Mae was lying to herself and had no qualms about calling her out.

Mae appreciated her honesty; no one was closer to her than Jill.

As Jill spun on the dance floor, her emerald-green dress flowing, her golden hair shining, and her blue eyes sparkling, Mae thought, *I love this woman.*

Mae hugged her, thanking her for making her wedding at least tolerable.

"Oh, for fuck's sake, Mae, we must find a way to get you out of this. But for now, let's dance!" Jill slurred, raising her glass as she put her arm around her dear friend's waist.

They danced until Mae's feet throbbed and her belly hurt from laughing. "Who knew my living room could be so much fun?" Mae said breathlessly.

Jacob approached Mae, nodding to Jill, signaling their fun was over.

"It's time to cut the cake."

It was half past midnight when the last guest had left, and Mae was exhausted. Jacob took her hand and said, "Tonight was the best night of my life."

Mae wondered, *is that because of me or your mother? You've barely spoken a word to me.*

She refrained from the question, too afraid of the answer.

Instead, she nodded and said, "I'm so tired; I need some rest."

Mae went off to sleep, the thought of her wedding night lingering in her head. She thought about her conversation with Jill, overhearing the two strangers discussing their conversation with Jane and her nuptials with Jacob. For her, she had fallen into marriage rather than choosing it.

Did she love Jacob or had he only become convenient, safe, and comfortable?

She considered these thoughts as her eyes grew tired.

Mae owed it to her baby to provide a stable home, intending to put forth her best effort.

The child was coming soon into the world, and regrets or second-guessing would not change that. Mae, too, was here, stuck at a place she would rather not be. But she did as she was expected to, finding a way to make the best of it because there really was no alternative.

Falling into a deep sleep, she didn't hear Jacob come to bed, nor did she hear the noise of the seven-strong cleaning crew Jane had hired to take care of the mess left by the guests so that when the couple awoke, the house would at least be intact again.

The following morning, Jacob lay sprawled out beside her, snoring lightly. She stared at this man, now her husband, noticing his thick hair and the defined jawline.

In her realizations from the night before, she made a conscious effort to build a life with him, but with this decision, she would lose a piece of herself in the meantime, sacrificing herself.

Mae wasn't even sure who she was anymore, but since she was so unclear about what she wanted, she at least appreciated what she had with Jacob. She looked down at her full breasts and growing stomach, deciding to finally surrender to being his wife.

An internal dialogue raged within her anyway, one that said she should try to find happiness by accepting contentment, calming her inner voice of restlessness. There was no sense in constantly telling herself she was miserable; life was as it was, and brooding would not help.

On the surface, she had little to complain about in any case, except she wasn't living authentically. She knew this; she suspected Jacob did too. Still, she was here, and their baby was on the way, so she needed to find a way to manage her defiant emotions.

It was a task like any other, something to practice and work hard at.

Could she make it work by trying harder to love him more?

The responsibility of it weighed heavily upon her conscience.

One thing was certain; she didn't want to be one of the women she had heard Jane complain about, one who was selfish and self-absorbed and was causing family breakdowns across America. The younger generation was being blamed for doing just that.

Knowing that this rhetoric was untrue despite a woman's marital status, she drowned out the negative thoughts her new mother-in-law had put in her head.

She felt Jacob stir, rolled over closer to him, and softly kissed his neck.

Her fingers caressed his body as she laid her head on his chest. Jacobs' eyes opened to find Mae on top of him, grinding her hips with a wild look of desire. She felt him become aroused by her advances as she took charge, surrendering to her desires. Their breaths became heavy, and then she collapsed on top of him, moist with sweat, satisfied and relaxed.

"Well, good morning to you," Jacob said.

It wasn't like Mae to be aggressive and make sexual advances.

Mae smiled and said sweetly, "Hello, husband,"

Jacob's smile became broad with satisfaction.

"We are going to have a great life together," he said.

"I believe that too," Mae lied.

* * *

The months flew by, and preparing for the new baby while settling into marriage had the couple constantly managing every moment. There was much to do, and the distraction was welcomed. Mae was surprised at how quickly she was content once she settled into her new role. Though she wasn't sure if it was complacency or defeat, the boredom of complicity plagued her, but the impending birth of her child shed some excitement. Jacob would provide the financial stability she now desired because of the impending birth. She could feel secure at last.

Gone were the days when she didn't have enough food.

She hadn't known better during childhood but accepted that money was scarce and always would be, even through college. It had never bothered her that much, but the thought of sparsity now made her anxious. She needed to make her marriage work, even if only for the sake of her child. Without Jacob, how would she care for this baby? She owed it to the infant to provide the comforts she had never enjoyed. After all, Jacob was a good person with a big heart and more than anything, he wanted a life with Mae and their baby. She had heard so many times of men who ran from responsibility, whereas Jacob ran toward it. Considering herself lucky for his devotion, she didn't want to squander the opportunity for normalcy.

Mae's lack of financial security left her dependent on Jacob, leaving him in charge of many of the decisions, from the decorations of the nursery to the finances and even the food they ate. It still bugged Mae at times, but she never said so. Instead, she appreciated his interest in the decisions, at least. As time passed, the fact that he was in control seemed to normalize, and Mae barely noticed. It had become second nature that Jacob steered both their lives, and Mae became accustomed to it. Whenever she showed irritation at this, he would bring home chocolates and shower her with materialistic attention, never asking her if she minded his decisions.

Even though he had a clue it bothered her, he avoided the conversation, instead offering her a cup of coffee and a loving glance.

Mae was in her third trimester when Jacob insisted she stop working.

"I like my job. I don't love it, but it's something."

Mae's protruding belly caused her to wobble as she spoke. She opened the refrigerator, grabbing a handful of grapes. "I don't want to quit work, Jacob, not yet. I want to return to it eventually and, at some point, get my law degree. This was never a long-term stop for me anyway. My plan had always been to attend law school and eventually practice law."

"Mae, why would you work when I make enough to support the both of us? You should be resting and preparing for the baby. Anyway, you will be exhausted once the baby is born, so you should get proper rest now. Please, if you can't do it for yourself, do it for me and our child."

That statement was one she loathed; it put pressure on her, inciting a guilt trip as if she would be neglecting her child if she decided to work longer—even though the baby wasn't even here!

Plus, Jacob expected Mae to stay home with their kids.

He didn't want to spend the money on daycare or risk the germs they would acquire if the baby had to be placed with lots of others while the two of them worked.

Mae argued, telling him, "Jacob, I know you mean well but sometimes, you sound like a caveman with these old-fashioned views. Women don't get dragged home by their hair anymore. Some even go out to work, you know!"

She tried to make light of it to avoid an argument.

He joined in, making Neanderthal grunts as he playfully chased her around the kitchen.

She had promised to consider what Jacob was proposing that she might become a stay-at-home mom, spending her days with their baby and looking after their home.

Sure, there were some good points, but even though Jacob made more money than Mae, she still liked earning to help out with the bills and not be entirely reliant on Jacob.

"Jacob, you have to know that I still intend on working after the baby's born. It's just not me to stay home. I've been researching childcare, and there are options. I mean quality options."

Jacobs' eyes grew wide as he slammed the pantry door. He poured himself a beer and grabbed the chips off the counter, not saying another word.

Mae sat silently stunned; what had brought this on?

She wasn't prepared for the tension or the silent treatment.

They had rarely discussed their expectations after the baby was born; she assumed she would return to work after maternity leave.

Two hours had passed, and Jacob was stewing in silence. Mae tiptoed around the house, trying to stay out of his way as she folded the laundry and tidied up.

Finally, as she was starting dinner, Jacob entered the kitchen and slammed his hands on the counter. "Dammit, Mae, why isn't anything enough for you?"

His voice was loud, though not shouting.

"I don't understand why you're upset. We never even discussed this. What made you assume I'd stop working after I gave birth? I've always liked working more than having a family; it's what I planned to do ever since I was small, Jacob. Some women dream of being moms. I dreamed of having a good education and a career. I can be a mother too, you know."

This time, Jacob looked more hurt than angry.

He was genuinely insulted by Mae's desire to go back to work. His face had paled when she said she'd always dreamed of having a career, not a family.

It was as if he considered her abnormal.

"I've worked my ass off, Mae, to provide for you and this baby. Late nights, shitty clients, demanding boss, thinking I was doing right by you. To hear that it means nothing to you is infuriating. You sound so ungrateful, you know. I would love a job like yours, where you have so little responsibility. Your day consists of answering phones and making photocopies. My day is riddled with anxiety and stress."

Mae was stunned. *Is that all my job is to him, an easy thing to pass the time?*

Jacob didn't know that she had just been promoted to head paralegal, and her boss had offered to help pay for some of her law school if she promised to stay.

Already, she was being recognized as a great employee, a strong would-be lawyer.

But why would she share any of this with her husband? He would be happier if she just admitted that women were supposed to stay home and care for kids, and that was that.

"Jacob, if you remember, I was supposed to go to law school right before I got pregnant. We discussed it. And you expect I'll give up everything to stay home with a baby I didn't want!"

The vile words had slipped out of her mouth before she could stop them.

She wished she could rewind the clock and take them back, but it was too late.

Jacob stormed out of the house, slamming the door behind him, as their hanging picture of the fine big oak tree fell to the ground, the glass smashing into tiny pieces scattered across the floor.

Mae sighed a deep breath of regret. She grabbed the dustpan and cleaned up the pieces of sharp glass that had reached the den, repeatedly replaying the argument in her head, trying to figure out what she could have done differently. An overwhelming feeling of regret turned her stomach, while her heart was racing with adrenaline.

She'd never wanted any of this and was trying to make the best of this life that had been rolled out for her. She wanted to volunteer overseas, spend time exploring the world, go to law school, have a career, have a life. *This* life was too small, Jacob ensuring it would stay that way.

Still, her gut churned at how badly she'd spoken to Jacob and about the heinous words she had said. They were toxic, and she hated herself for them.

After two in the morning, Jacob came stumbling in the front door. Immediately, Mae pushed herself off the couch as she watched him fumble his way into the kitchen.

"Jacob, you, okay?" Mae said with a soft voice.

He didn't respond immediately as she waited, feeling foolish in the doorway.

"Mae," he said, his voice slurring. "I'm not the type of man who wants to come home and deal with domestic things."

He hesitated before he continued, choosing his words carefully. "It's just that I know I won't be home to care for children with my career. I rely on you to take care of that stuff, and I'll handle the finances. I want my kids to grow up with a mother who is home and available, not off at work all day. Mae, we owe it to our child to have a present mother. You never had this kind of stability growing up. Don't you want a better life for our child?"

Jacob sounded heartfelt, clearly believing what he was saying.

Mae, however, could not believe what she was hearing. *Mothers can work and be present. Why do men hold to such unreasonable standards?* She wondered, did Jacob want a life with her because he loved her or because she was easily manipulated into the role he needed her to play?

Before she could react, he moved closer, gently touching her skin. His breath reeked of whisky and cigars. Mae felt her stomach turn as the rancid odor consumed the small space.

Plus, he'd judged her childhood, casting aspersions on her parents for bringing up their kids in near poverty like that. He was playing on it, pushing the topic to try and coerce her. It was cruel and manipulative, and she tried not to see it in him, the man she had chosen to marry.

The only thing such thoughts could do was to make her sad.

She'd never spoken ill of her living conditions growing up and remained remarkably close to her mother. Judy had done her absolute best for the family, and no one could ask for more.

Jacob didn't even like their closeness. "You talk to your mother on the phone far too much," he started saying. "Could we please cut it down to three days a week instead of every day?"

"I like the fact we talk every day," she said simply.

"Mae, I'm going to make this clear. You can't talk to your mother daily anymore. You will have your own child and a family. It's time your mother lets you live more independently."

As if he could talk! He, the man who clung to his mother's side and always gave in to her!

Before he could continue, she interrupted. "Jacob, it's none of your concern how much I check in with my mother, and I won't let you dictate to me on this matter."

Not wanting to upset his pregnant wife, he retreated.

"I didn't mean for it to come out that way. I know how much your mother means to you, but we have our own little family unit now, and I want us to build our own lives."

There was sincerity in his voice, his eyes pleading for her to believe his words.

She didn't argue further but was sure only to speak to her mother when Jacob wasn't around.

But, of course, he continued speaking to his own mother several times a day.

She didn't say a word about it.

Thoughts flooded through her head, but Jacob continued, "Mae, I need to pursue my career without worrying about also caring for a baby. I've given you so much, and I'm asking you to allow me to provide for you both. At least for now."

Mae didn't think it was an ask but instead a stern suggestion.

She shrugged as she waddled to bed, knowing her future had been decided.

That night, Mae was awoken by terrible pain in her abdomen.

Her due date wasn't for another three weeks, so she assumed it was heartburn, the thing that had plagued her throughout the pregnancy. But this time, it was different. After over an hour, when the pain didn't subside, she got out of bed to go to the bathroom. As she unsteadily wobbled her way across the room, she felt a gushing between her legs and let out a loud yelp. Groggy but immediately awake, Jacob found her leaning against the wall, breathing heavily.

"It's time," she groaned.

"Oh my gosh, Mae, now? You haven't even packed a bag yet. I thought the doctor said the due date—"

"Jacob, NOW," she hollered, cutting him off.

Jacob grabbed his keys as he hurried out the door, holding Mae up as her contractions became closer and her screams ever louder. They drove in silence to the hospital, the still air of their vehicle only punctuated by Mae's intermittent moans and yells.

Six hours later, a tiny, wailing baby boy was born on a rainy early morning.

His small limbs hung off his body. The first thing Mae noticed was his screaming mouth; he was no more excited to be in this world than she was.

A young nurse with a bright smile asked Mae, "What will you name the baby?"

Mae said nothing and stared at the ceiling, trying to process what her body had just experienced, and what it had managed to push out into the world. The pain had been horrific, and her body and mind were battling to reconcile the last six hours.

The thought of a name was too much to bear after everything she'd just endured.

After awkward moments, Jacob spoke up and offered his grandfather's name on his mother's side. "James Edward," he said, smiling down on his new son. Of all their conversations about the baby, they had never discussed names. How dare he make this decision alone?

But yet again, for a quiet life, she resigned herself to the chosen name; it would be futile to consider any other, only bringing days of raised voices and bitter words if she tried.

As the doctor put the baby's small body into Mae's shaky arms, panic took over.

She felt faint and considered refusing to take the sweet creature.

Thoughts of escaping ravaged through her mind. She looked at the door of her hospital room, wondering, *could I put the baby down on the bed and run out of this place?*

How soon would anyone notice?

Jane and Jacob could raise the child. After all, Jane thought she was more superior than everyone and better than anyone at everything! It was Jane's chance to take control.

And Jacob would be able to glue himself to his mother's skirt for a real reason.

To her shame. Mae actually imagined herself doing this, thinking how she would be free to start the life she intended. This fleeting thought brought both relief and dread.

The fantasy relieved her, but the reality was that this couldn't be possible. It brought only a sense of utter dread and of being confined and trapped forever.

Mae shook off the ugly feelings as she looked around the room, catching the watchful eye of the staff and Jacob. She was being watched. All eyes were waiting for her joyful tears to come, but none did, her face only contorting from disbelief to disinterest.

Jacob also waited for the transition of maternal love to cross Mae's face, his eyes pleading for his wife to show some emotion.

Mae stared out the window, never once looking at the baby, even when he kicked and cried.

She chose to watch the clouds float by as her child lay on her naked chest, placed there by a nurse. The crying from the newborn grew louder, no doubt sensing her tension. The crying was almost unbearable now, Mae covering her ears, wanting to yell, "Please stop!"

Eventually, a nurse, recognizing that Mae had no intention of putting the baby to her breast to feed, took him away. "We will try this again later," she said kindly. "You must be exhausted."

Mae nodded at her as she whisked the baby off to get weighed and cleaned. She heard the wails subside as the nurse gently soothed him, holding him close.

"You did great," Jacob said, sounding hopeful.

He grabbed her hand and kissed it gently. "Isn't it a miracle?" he asked with overwhelming pride. Of course, he was referring to the miracle of the birth, but she could only think of the miracle that came when the wailing finally ceased.

She had no words, staring at Jacob, silent. She rolled on her side as some tubes tugged at her skin. All she wanted to do was sleep, hoping this was just a bad dream.

"Good idea, love. Get some rest. My parents are waiting in the lobby, and I want to tell them the happy news. I'll make some calls, and then I'll be back to check on you in a little while."

By the time Jacob had gathered his keys and coat to leave, Mae had fallen fast asleep.

A nurse nudged her awake, saying softly, "Mae. Mae! The baby needs feeding."

Then she eyed Mae askance. "You haven't eaten anything while you've been with us either; you do know the importance of keeping your strength up for the baby, don't you?"

Mae was exhausted and already tired of hearing the word *baby* over and over.

Was this how life would be now?

Everything about the baby and the family, leaving no space for her to ever be herself again?

Exhaustion burned, a feeling never experienced prior to the birth of her son. Even while she was pregnant, she had never been this tired. Her skin, head, and body hurt from head to toe.

The bustling hospital's noise put her on sensory overload, driving her to pull the stiff sheets up past her chin, hoping to drown out the chaos. She wanted to rest, and the thought of having the baby latch onto her already tired body was too much to comprehend.

By now, she couldn't even keep her eyes open and her head upright.

"Mae, give it a try. It is very important you bond with the baby in the first hours of his birth."

Mae's eyes grew wide. Tears formed as she looked desperately at the nurse.

"It's okay, Mae. I'm here to help. Just take the baby and place him close to your breast. I know you're exhausted, but once he's latched on, I can stay and take him off you when he's done; that way, if you drift off to sleep while he's suckling, it will be fine. Then, you will both get what you need! How does that sound?"

It sounds unrealistic, unlikely, and impossible, thought Mae. *I will never get what I need.*

The nurse placed the baby against Mae's chest, then forced Mae's enlarged breast into the tiny mouth. His tongue licked around the area until he finally found the nipple.

He began sucking so intensely that Mae winced in pain. Now, tears were flooding as the baby continued to ravish the milk from inside her body. The nurse didn't notice Mae's immense discomfort as she walked around the room, writing notes, and replacing supplies.

"When will he stop this? It hurts," Mae complained.

"Babies feed on demand every couple of hours. Sometimes less, sometimes more. As far as the pain goes, you will get used to it, and eventually, it won't hurt anymore."

Every two hours ... sometimes more? How will I ever sleep?

Mae stared at the nurse blankly. "Why is it that after having a human live inside my body, invade my world, and violate me, I'm now expected to get used to it?"

She spoke the words aloud, but the nurse only chuckled, obviously taking it as a quip.

It wasn't one; it was a genuine complaint, a cry for help.

Mae was hating this. All those things that mothers said made it special to be a new mom, she detested already. Most mothers said that having an infant suckling was deeply relaxing.

To Mae, it was hell on earth.

She already resented this tiny, dependent human, the one who would never give her any peace. She resented the father, who seemed mostly oblivious to the demands this placed on her.

And she resented herself for getting pregnant when Jacob had given her too much champagne one night, hating them both for forgetting to use protection. Now, Jacob was off making calls and celebrating while this small human was literally sucking the life out of her already depleted body. She heard the machines beside her start beeping faster, her blood pressure soaring.

This got the attention of the nurse, who scurried toward Mae.

She took hold of the baby with urgency, noting the numbers on the machine.

"Okay, that's good for now, dear. We can supplement with formula in the nursery if you would like," she said softly. "Get some rest because he'll be wanting to feed again in a couple of hours. You'll have to grow more resilient, though; you have eighteen years or more of being wanted at every turn!"

It was supposed to be funny, but made Mae just want to cry with a visceral hurt. Gone were all her dreams and her freedom. Gone was her travel and her learning, and her work.

Mae slowed her breathing as the nurse removed the baby from her arms.

"That was good, Mae. Oh, just before you try and sleep, I'll bring him back in a little while and show you how to change his diaper."

Change his diaper, thought Mae. *Is this what life has become for me now? Changing the diapers of a leech-like human who continually wails in my presence?*

These thoughts kept circling, anxiety rising from the pit of her stomach. When her ruminations took her down a dark path, she tried to shut them out with slumber.

Sleep was the only time she felt peace; she tried to welcome it with a deliberate aim of avoiding any more thoughts of the baby. She would not wait to see the nurse change the diaper. She didn't much care if the truth be told. Instead, she drifted away, staying in a deep sleep for hours until she heard the whispers of doctors outside of her room.

"Has she been at all interested in the pregnancy, or do you think she's depressed?" a female doctor was asking Jacob. Of course, he would be clueless, so asking him was pointless.

Mae kept her eyes shut, but her ears were open as she listened to the words *postpartum depression.* Jacob was asking questions, but his voice was muffled and tense, concealing the meanings. As she allowed herself to drift off, more words came. Psychologist.

Anti-depressant. Nanny. Psychotherapy. Counseling ... On and on it went.

She began humming lightly, choosing a tune that would usually make her sleepy.

It was Brahms' Lullaby, a beautiful melody her mother's music box used to play to her when she'd been a child, unable to sleep, or if she'd been sick and confined to bed.

Jacob walked in and looked at her sheepishly when he realized she was awake.

"There is my beautiful wife," he said brightly.

She did not reciprocate, only noticing how tired he looked. But he was handsome still.

His thick brown hair showed speckles of gray, which only made him more attractive. "I hope you got lots of rest, darling. I was just with baby James; God, I can't describe, he's so beautiful. I can't believe we made that perfect human together." He kissed her forehead and looked deep into her eyes. "I love you, Mae. I know you're tired, and your body's been through so much, but our baby is here now, and you'll be a wonderful mother. I owe you so much for our baby."

There it was again: *baby, baby, baby.*

Would this be all there was to talk about? This was to be her mental prison from now on?

Mae squeezed his hand tightly, wanting to believe she would feel something toward the tiny child they had made together. *The doctor must be right. I'm depressed, that's all, and soon, when my hormones settle, I'll get better and then everything will be all right.*

If anyone had taken the trouble to ask, she'd have said all she felt was a sinking feeling of doom. She hadn't considered that motherhood could be emotionally draining or that she would lose a part of herself for someone else from the very moment of birth.

She wanted to bond with the baby, but whenever her son was brought to her, she instinctively wanted to turn away, allowing her gaze to settle on something without him in the frame.

———

Two days later, Mae was at home with James, settling into the notion of being a new family.

Jacob begrudgingly took several days off work on the doctors' advice, aiming to help with the transition. It only showed that he was resentful toward Mae, not wanting to miss work for something he believed she should have been managing by herself.

But the advice of the doctor had been stern, leaving him no choice but to oblige.

He called his mother while Mae was asleep.

"Mom, she does nothing for the baby. I'm up all night with him, feeding him and changing his diapers. She just sleeps all the time," Jacob complained.

"Well, Jacob, not all mothers can be as attentive as yours was—and still is!" Jane laughed.

"I don't have time to take care of James though, Mom. I have a career to tend to, one that pays all the bills. And all she wants to do is laze around in bed and read magazines. I wouldn't care, but they're not even useful things she's reading. It's either about law or travel, the two things we have no time for her to indulge in anymore. The time for these hobbies has passed."

"I know, Jacob. The thing is, you put up with it all and you also do too much for her. She better start pulling her weight. Maybe tell her she needs to get out of bed and be productive. My feeling is you need to start being direct with her. Not exactly an ultimatum but be forceful."

"You think so? The doctors insisted I stay home for a few days and get her a nanny because they think she's clinically depressed. What could she possibly be depressed about though? She has a baby and a husband who provides financially for her every wish."

Jacob was getting more agitated as the conversation continued.

He suddenly heard the baby fuss and rushed his mother off the phone.

"I got to go, Mom. James has woken up."

"Okay, dear, but remember I told you that girl was inept. You need to place the baby on her stomach right now and tell her to see to him. There's a saying, 'Start as you mean to go on.'"

Jacob hung up the phone, more frustrated than before.

He composed himself as he greeted Mae.

"Mae, you haven't eaten all day. I made you toast," Jacob said as he pulled open their bedroom curtains. It was mid-afternoon, and she still hadn't gotten out of bed, still wearing the same clothes from two days before. She had yet to shower since giving birth too.

He liked to think of his wife as sexy and alluring, but now she was grimy and weary.

"Look, Mae," he said in an exasperated tone. "I need to be at work tomorrow, so you'll need to get up and start helping with the baby. Plus, it will be good for you to move a bit."

Mae looked at him helplessly.

She mustered up the courage to rise stiffly and walk toward the bathroom in a slow trance.

"Then can you help me to the toilet?" she asked.

He huffed. "Mae, you're going to be all alone tomorrow. You need to start doing things for yourself."

She could only hear him say, *you're going to be all alone.* She thought, *I already am.*

In the shower, Mae let the warmth of the water consume her body, looking down at her expanded belly and filled breasts, trying to recognize her figure. She held in her sobs until she couldn't any longer. Then she cried for herself, her baby, and for the shame of feeling selfish.

She felt unworthy of her life and couldn't understand why she was so miserable.

When Jacob left for work the following morning, he kissed her on the forehead, saying, "I'll check in later." But he often forgot, so Mae expected nothing. She went to the nursery, watching James in his bassinet, sucking on his fingers. He was beautiful, exactly like his father had said.

She stared at him, trying to recognize his features. James had piercing blue eyes like Mae's and black hair like Jacob's. His chin had a cleft, resembling Jacob's, while his cheeks were full, more like Mae's. She touched James' arm and felt the warmth of his soft skin. He looked up at her and began to fuss. Mae instinctively picked him up and rocked him, humming in his ear.

This was the first time she had cared for James alone for any extended period.

She continued rocking him and smelling his head. "I'm here, baby boy. I need to get help, but I'm here," she said tearfully. She spent the day holding James, feeding him when he cried, and changing his diapers. She felt productive for the first time since his birth, but she spent much of the day in a fog, often wiping away tears between feeds and diaper changes.

Jacob never did call to check up on her, just as she knew he wouldn't.

When he was enthralled at work, he'd forgot about anything else.

He'd also had made it clear that his career was the most important thing to him, and she needed to accept it. Mae knew she needed to care for James despite her overwhelming darkness. She desperately longed to care for her baby but barely had the energy to care for herself, finding herself in bed as James cried in the other room. She kept a pillow over her head to drown out the sounds of his insistent wails, dreading the moments when she had to cater to his needs.

Was this normal? She didn't care either way because all she wanted to do was sleep.

She had never thought of herself as selfish or depressed, but suddenly, she had feelings she had never experienced before. Mae had always been easygoing, but now, the noise of the crying baby agitated her beyond belief.

She was ordinarily patient and kind but couldn't help but feel that her body was being used by this child who consumed her breast milk constantly, leaving her drained.

She hated herself for feeling this way, aware she needed to be a better parent to James.

Another three weeks went by, and Mae still felt tremendous sadness. She continued trying to feel the joy other people shared about having babies. Instead, she felt tired, used, and overwhelmed, longing to return to her job, to see Jill, or, at least, not have someone so demanding pervading her every move, infiltrating every aspect of her life.

She wanted her mother to come and visit, but Jacob insisted she wait until she was in better spirits and was coping around the house. But when would she ever cope?

Once, at her doctor's office, she'd read a leaflet about postpartum depression.

At the time, she scoffed at it, unable to imagine feeling sadness after the birth of a child.

She had even heard other women talk about going through bouts of depression after childbirth but didn't realize the magnitude of their emotions. The topic was often on news or talk shows, but Mae hadn't ever imagined becoming one of the awful statistics.

Calls from her mother inundated her, as did many of Jacob's family. She declined to speak to most of them, telling Jacob she was busy managing James or needed to rest. Out of desperation, Jacob invited her friend Jill to come and surprise her, hoping to lift her spirits.

Two days later, Jill cheerfully rang the doorbell carrying a bottle of Champagne, a tray of cheese and crackers, and three large blue balloons. The sight of her made Mae smile.

"Oh my gosh, what are you doing here?" Mae asked.

"Well, since you're either too busy or too tired to answer my calls, I decided to come see and meet this little guy," Jill said, wiggling James' tiny toes.

"You have no idea how happy I am to see you. It gets lonely being here with a baby all day. I haven't spoken to another adult for days."

"Well, you would if you'd answer the phone!" Jill quipped, smiling.

"Good point," Mae admitted.

"Tell me, how's motherhood? I give you a lot of credit. I couldn't imagine caring for anyone but myself," Jill admitted. Little did she know, this was exactly how Mae felt too.

Mae looked down at her outfit.

She was wearing unwashed sweatpants, her hair was piled in a messy bun, and her eyes were puffy. She was grateful for the company but couldn't muster the energy to shower. She suddenly felt foolish sitting in her living room with another adult who appeared so well-groomed.

Jill was carrying a handbag that matched her shoes and wearing earrings that matched her blouse; Mae was longing to one day be able to dress in something other than dirty clothes.

"Tell me, Mae, how are you?"

Mae had never kept secrets from Jill but didn't want to alarm her about her state of utter misery. "It's an adjustment for sure," offered Mae. "I'm sure I'll get the hang of it."

"No one could imagine it wouldn't be tough," Jill said thoughtfully. "He's beautiful, though, Mae. You must snuggle him all the time." Jill was watching her closely as if assessing her.

"He is perfect," Mae said softly, her eyes never meeting Jill's. "We snuggle all the time."

Jill's voice changed. "I call bullshit, Mae. How are you really feeling? You look like you haven't slept in ages, the house is a mess, and where on earth is Jacob?"

Jill always had a way of keeping it real. Their friendship had always been honest, and Jill was the one person Mae could count on to call her out.

Mae put her face in her hands and began to sob.

Jill went over to comfort her. "Let it out. Tell me how you're really feeling."

"I feel like a stranger in my own body, Jill. I feel sad all of the time. I feel overwhelmed," Mae sniffled. "I feel like I never wanted this life. I feel, I feel … I feel fucking stuck, and all I want to do is run far away and never come back. Worst of all, I feel like a fraud as a mother."

"Well, finally," Jill said as she grabbed two Champagne flutes from the cabinet. "For fuck's sake, that's the most honest thing you have said to me in years."

Mae let out a relieved laugh, grateful that her friend wasn't judging her but giving her an outlet to reveal her thoughts.

Jill filled two glasses with Champagne. She handed one to her friend, clinking glasses and saying, "To being fucking honest."

Mae took a large gulp and smiled broadly for the first time in months. "Fuck, yeah," she said.

***

The two stayed up past midnight as Mae revealed how she'd been feeling since the birth of James. She felt the weight of shame lifting off her shoulders, knowing she could honestly communicate how she felt.

Her breaths became more even, the weight on her chest easing a bit.

Jill's voice became serious again. "We need to get you help. Call your doctor in the morning and be honest about your feelings. We need to normalize depression, especially postpartum. Don't suffer in silence."

Mae didn't resist this advice, relieved to have a solution. Her excessive drinking that night made Mae realize how much trouble she was in. Thankfully, Jill had a stronger tolerance and could care for baby James until Jacob arrived home. Though Jill could sense his annoyance, he thanked her for being a wonderful and supportive friend to his wife.

"I guess she just needed to let loose for the evening," offered Jill.

"A mother should put her child first," Jacob said flatly.

The next day, Mae felt hopeful, though her head spun from too many glasses of Champagne. Of course, Jacob scolded her for her negligence, and Mae sheepishly apologized.

"This is what I mean about Jill. She has no respect for you being a mother and wife now. She wants the two of you to relive your foolish college days."

Mae hung her head in shame, even more determined to find help for how she was feeling. Once Jacob left for work—still in a terrible mood about what had occurred the night before—she saw Doctor McQuire's business card and called to make an appointment.

The doctor was a slim woman with gray hair, a soft demeanor, and wore thick glasses.

As Mae tearfully explained her feelings, the doctor listened, nodding.

"This is more typical than you may think. The statistics are staggering, and many women don't report it because of the shame and stigma attached. I'm giving my best effort to change that, so I applaud you for seeking help," she said with a smile.

Mae thanked her as she took the prescription, feeling hopeful.

The weeks went by, and slowly, Mae began to feel her ease return. The bouts of overwhelming feelings diminished, though she would sometimes feel a slight edge come.

Once the medication had regulated her mood, Mae became intoxicated with the sweet smell of her son and held him close as she rocked him to sleep. She no longer felt disconnected from him, enjoying their daily routines so much that she rarely considered returning to work. Jacob worked long hours and barely saw the child, but she didn't mind that too much since he was often ornery when he was around. Mae relaxed into motherhood, soaking in James and barely recognizing life before having a baby. Her heart was filled, but her priorities were rarely about Jacob or the harrowing responsibility of housework.

"Mae, why is there still so much unfolded laundry?" Jacob demanded.

"Because I haven't gotten to it yet, Jacob. It isn't hurting anyone, and I'm pretty certain the laundry police will not be showing up anytime soon," she joked.

Jacobs' lips curled down, showing no sign of amusement from Mae's playfulness.

Jacob had become more uptight and demanding since James's birth. He expected Mae to do things according to his schedule and in his way.

He wanted to run his home more like a military camp.

Mae missed how Jacob had once appreciated her relaxed ways, even saying this was a major part of his attraction to her. She recalled when he'd loved her free spirit; now, her very essence seemed to irk him. Since the baby had been born, there'd been a sudden shift in Jacob's mood.

Anyone would think he was the one with post-partum depression, Mae thought one day.

She chuckled, but this was serious!

Jacob was even darker and more demanding than before, leaving little room for relaxation.

She thought she sensed something hideous in him, that he might be jealous of the baby.

"How long are you going to carry him around, Mae?" Jacob snarled.

"Until he can walk," Mae said and giggled, trying to ease the tension.

Jacob exasperated, stomped toward the bedroom, slamming the door as he growled, "Fuck you. You're looking after that kid like he can't be away from you for half an hour!"

That's because he can't, you idiot, Mae said to herself. "Don't be ridiculous! He's a little baby and you're supposed to be a full-grown man."

She carried on cuddling the baby, swaddling him by her chest.

Mae was confused by Jacob's lack of humor too, something she'd once appreciated in him. Where had the old Jacob gone? What was wrong with him nowadays?

She rolled her eyes at his dramatics and continued doting on James, knowing her overly sensitive husband would soon be over his tantrum. Mae had grown accustomed to his pouting, which didn't bother her as much as it once did. She was far too busy caring for James, something that Jacob had encouraged. Now that she was full throttle mothering her son, he now held resentment. It seemed whatever she did was wrong, so she stopped caring.

Jacob tried again to make things right with Mae. He realized he was being a bit harsh, and the baby's demands were a lot for any new parent. The child's constant crying irritated him, and he only had to hear it for a few hours a day; Mae had the baby all the time. How did she cope?

"Let's get a babysitter and go to the movies," Jacob suggested.

Sitting in a darkened room enticed Mae a little, but she preferred being home.

"I'm exhausted. Let's see what's on NETFLIX," Mae offered.

Jacob was both disappointed and relieved by the suggestion. They ordered a pizza and drank bottled beers, but both parents were fast asleep within the movie's first half hour. It wasn't until the movie ended and James awoke that he realized they'd both fallen asleep.

"Wow, we are real party animals," Jacob exclaimed, laughing. It was a little sign of the old, sweeter Jacob. At least he was relaxing a bit again. That was something.

Mae was almost deliriously happy to hear the lightness in his voice.

She gently kissed his cheek and tended to James.

―――――

The good times didn't last though. While feeding James, Mae reflected on how tired she had become. She was exhausted and could barely keep up with the demands of motherhood. To add to the stress, being Jacob's wife was no easy feat because he required constant accolades and never-ending attention.

It was like looking after two kids sometimes, not one.

He would always need her to admire and fawn over whatever he had done, whether at work or at home, waiting for a rush of approval and adoration from his wife—neither of which Mae had the energy to give. However, she did her best to comment, "You look handsome," as he left for work. Jacob would perk up from the compliment. He'd once said, "Thank you, love. It's nice to know you notice me." He'd glanced in the mirror, smiling back at his own reflection like a nervous teen who'd just dressed up for a prom date. Where had these weaknesses come from?

And while he was so busy worrying about himself, he wasn't even noticing her.

I swear I could walk about the house in garbage bags, and he wouldn't notice!

She tried to take it lightly, letting it pass uncommented. God knew she had plenty of other things to get on with and to worry about. A paranoid and needy husband wasn't at the top of her list.

Despite their efforts, tension grew. Jacob seemed to become more frustrated with the way the house was run, and Mae was worn out by his demands.

She tried to balance being a good wife, caring for James, and maintaining her sanity.

However, Jacob's constant demands weighed on her morale. The same argument continued more frequently now: "My mother never kept our house a mess. What do you do all day?"

"Jacob, I'm doing the best I can. I'll get it cleaned up. Maybe if you helped with James, I'd have more time," she quipped.

For the most part, she ignored his criticism. He'd be at work most of the day, and she wouldn't have to deal with his acerbic comments. If she was lucky, he'd return late, too, and she could be in bed and pretending to sleep by the time he showed up.

Jacob glared at Mae, barely holding back his rage. Then he let loose.

"I don't need to help with James. I financially provide for this family. And for what?" he said as he threw his plate into the sink. "What about me, Mae? What about my needs?"

"As for you being the provider," she said quite calmly. "If you remember, I was desperate to continue with law school and you adamantly said no. I wanted to be a working mom."

"That's not the point," he spat. "You are not a working mom. You have a life of leisure and affluence provided by me. I expect a better show of effort from you."

Oh, I can put on a show if that's what you want! She thought to herself, snidely mocking his undeserved rant. *This is all our life is, after all. A show …*

Just as he would expect her to, Mae rushed to the sink, hoping he hadn't broken the plate.

She had received the fine crockery as a gift from her mother and would be heartbroken if Jacob's immature response had broken one of the plates. She decided at that moment to buy some cheap stoneware; he could throw that around to his heart's content. However, she first had the problem of asking him for money to buy it. She'd cross that bridge later.

"Jacob, Mae said gently, "I think you're overreacting and frankly, being an asshole."

She needed to put her husband in his place every once in a while. He would suck her up and spit her out if she allowed it. After reprimanding him, he sometimes would apologize, although it was a risk each time she did it because, at other times, he got mad.

She soon regretted her words as Jacob, filled with fury, jumped out of his seat and charged toward her. Before she could react, she felt a sharp slap across her face.

Then he opened the kitchen cabinet without warning and hurled the whole set of flowered dishes she adored. Within moments, Mae watched as china smashed across the kitchen floor.

She gasped in horror. Jacob knew how much the gift from Judy meant to her. She often spoke about it, explaining that she'd admired the dinner set for years. Judy had spent most of the year saving up for the crockery to present to them as a gift for Mae's birthday.

"Now clean this shit up," growled Jacob. As he walked out the front door, he said, "If you ever talk to me like that again, I will break you like those dishes."

Inside of her, her spirit was broken like the crockery. She couldn't believe what he'd said.

She sat on the kitchen floor, unable to reconcile what had transpired.

As she gathered what was left of the shards of china, she heard the baby crying.

"For fuck's sake," she said as her trembling hands gathered up the jagged pieces. Blood was dripping from her leg from a fragment that must have cut her. It was a surface cut but needed attention. She let the baby cry for a while as she finished cleaning up the chaos.

Once she'd washed up, she checked on her now calm son, staring at the mobile and the dangling animals. She lifted James, holding him tight, feeling his warmth calming her wobbly knees. Mae was appalled and disturbed by what Jacob had done, and she didn't know what else he could do to hurt her. She hummed in James' ear as she rocked him in her wooden rocking chair, calming them both. As James lay on her chest, Mae considered packing up and leaving.

Where would she go?

Could she manage to take James and sneak out?

The fleeting thoughts raced. Before she could react, she looked down at her sleeping child and knew she could never leave her son here. So, she sat and considered her part in Jacob's outburst and began feeling bad for dismissing his feelings. It wasn't long before she was blaming herself; when Jacob returned home, she vowed to apologize.

As she heard the keys to the door jingle, she straightened her hair, glanced at the mirror, and went to greet Jacob. He returned with whisky on his breath and a swagger in his walk.

"Jacob, you're home."

Jacob's expression no longer showed signs of anger but of regret.

"I'm sorry about before," he mumbled. "I'll replace the dishes. You are right, I was acting like an asshole."

Mae felt a relief wash over her. Jacob surely couldn't be that cruel ever again.

She reasoned he was under a lot of pressure at work, and she was being insensitive.

"No, please," Mae interrupted. "I'm sorry, too. I should be more organized and considerate about how hard you work and for everything you do for me."

Jacob brushed the hair away from her face, softly touching her cheek and kissing her passionately. He led her into the bedroom as he swiftly undressed her, pulling her body into his.

The feeling of Jacob's body aroused Mae, making her surrender to his aggressive passion. He bit her lip as he threw her onto the bed, holding her hands above her head and thrusting himself inside. Her groans were erotic, enticing Jacob's sexual desire. Their moans were in unison until both achieved orgasm, and satisfaction filled the dark room.

They lay on their backs, catching their breath as the euphoria subsided.

"Wow," said Jacob.

"That was something," Mae said as she nestled beside her husband.

"It's been a while, hasn't it?" admitted Jacob.

As the two embraced again, the sound of James came from the monitor.

Jacob laughed. "Perfect timing, son," he said playfully.

Mae kissed Jacob on the nose and grabbed her robe. "I'll be back," she said with a wink.

The tension eased. They were content, learning how to manage through parenthood. Mae simply knew not to cross Jacob's boundaries, working hard to keep the tension in the house low and to honor the requests of her demanding husband.

Though emotionally drained, she needed to compromise to make her marriage work.

Before Mae knew it, the couple were celebrating James' first birthday, and Mae couldn't be prouder to be his mother, surprisingly genuinely happy for the first time since college.

She embraced motherhood in a way she had not expected, especially after suffering from depression after James' birth. Two weeks after the celebrations, Mae learned she was pregnant again. This time, the thought of another baby excited her.

For one thing, little James would have a constant playmate.

She wanted to grow her family and couldn't wait to tell Jacob.

When he arrived home at half past ten, Mae was waiting at the candlelit kitchen table, bursting with excitement.

"Did I miss our anniversary or something?" Jacob said wearily. "What's all this?"

"Exciting news," Mae said, barely able to contain her joy.

"Mae, if this is about you returning to work, I already told you I work enough for both of us. You stay home with James and let me do my thing."

Mae was quiet for a minute, ignoring his comment but still internalizing it. She shrugged it off, not allowing him to ruin the moment.

"I'm pregnant!" she said. "I hadn't realized that I'd missed my period for a couple of months. I went to the doctor this afternoon, and I'm already three months in."

A smile spread across Jacob's face, and he hugged his wife.

The two kissed by the candlelight, sharing genuine intimacy.

"That makes me incredibly happy. I promise I'll provide a life of comfort for you and our kids," Jacob said. He paused, calculating. "Wait, will the kids be in the same grade?"

"They'll be one grade apart. It's like having twins," Mae said.

"Things are going to be hectic around here for sure. Maybe we should get someone in to help out," Jacob offered.

"I thought you would help out a bit more."

"Mae, not this again," Jacob said, exasperated. "I told you; my plate's full already."

Mae sighed, suddenly feeling foolish. "I'll be fine. I can handle it," she said.

Mae wondered why he seemed to focus on providing financially but never mentioned any emotional or practical responsibility.

She was tired and didn't want to have that conversation so late into the night.

The two held each other as they nestled up in bed together. Just as they were about to fall asleep, James' cries came from the nursery.

Mae had hoped that with her pregnancy announcement, Jacob would offer to get up with the baby more often. She waited a couple more moments, willing Jacob to offer, but when she heard the sound of his heavy breathing, she grumbled, "I'll get him."

Chapter 8

THE WIND WHISTLED THROUGH the night as the downpour of rain relentlessly hit upon the window. James, startled by the racket, stayed close to Mae for comfort.

"It's okay, sweet boy." Mae rubbed his soft curls. "Mama's here and will always take care of you. It's just a little bit of rain." Mae had also been alarmed by the fierce winds and heavy rain, but having James gave her something to focus on. The weather had been bad all day, and there were many reports of power outages and the possibility of evacuation due to the dangerous flooding around town. Mae wondered if Jacob was okay and was disappointed that he had yet to call to check up on them. She was, after all, managing a toddler while pregnant, yet when he was at work, he never called to see how they were doing. Mae had grown accustomed to it, but it bothered her that Jacob was spending more time out of the house than with his family.

Wasn't he the one who wanted all of this? she would wonder.

The more Mae considered this, the more agitated she became.

She felt she was something to check off his list of things to achieve in life rather than a choice. They were such different people with clearly opposite value systems.

She would never have seen Jacob again if she'd left on that volunteer trip.

She certainly wouldn't have chosen to spend her life with him if she hadn't gotten pregnant.

Here she was, though, content with the safety of motherhood and financially secure, but still trying to find her way to happiness.

By early evening, the rain had stopped, and Mae took James outside to jump in the puddles and look for rainbows.

"Look, Mama," he said, his eyes wide with amazement. The bright colors shone on the two as they happily splashed in the puddles dotted around the sidewalk. "I love you, Mama," James said for the first time.

Mae stopped and looked at the small boy in awe.

Tears welled in her eyes, and she felt immense love. "I love you too, my sweet boy." They wandered through the streets as the sun began to set.

"Dada, home?" James asked. James was beginning to talk more now, which fascinated Mae. His verbal skills were impressive and only growing.

"I wish I knew," Mae said softly. "Let's get some ice cream and watch a movie, James." A smile grew across his face as he began skipping home, holding his mother's hand tightly.

As the months passed and Mae's protruding belly became more obvious, she found it more difficult to move gracefully around the house. The roundness of her cheeks grew as her hips expanded further than ever. So far, she had gained over thirty pounds with this pregnancy, making it impossible to fit in any of her pregnancy clothes from the time when she'd been expecting James. She didn't mind much and wore many of the same outfits over again.

She was caring for James and rarely went anywhere worth getting dressed for.

Nowadays, her visits to the grocery store or park did not warrant nicer outfits, and she was comfortable in the few things she wore. But her husband was not happy about it.

"Are you wearing that again?" Jacob complained.

He was always well-groomed, and appearance was important to him. His blue button-down shirt with beige khakis was neatly ironed, even if he had nowhere to go. He said he couldn't understand how any grown adult wore sweatpants, even on a lazy weekend afternoon.

"It's preposterous and sloppy," he would comment when he saw people around town dressed casually. "Have a little self-respect." He sounded just like his disapproving mother.

Mae looked around, embarrassed by his inquiry, knowing he was just as disgusted by her appearance too, and his comments were a sly dig at her. "Jacob, I'm tired. I don't care what I look like. I'm carrying around a human inside my body and a toddler outside of my body."

"Mae, please go buy some clothes. I'll give you the money. It's embarrassing for both of us."

Mae walked away, looking at the ground as she felt the wrinkles of excess skin on her lower back. She went to the bathroom, glaring at the mirror, noticing the weight on her chin and neck.

She had never been one to care much about her looks.

Naturally pretty, she didn't need much makeup.

Now, though, she was growing self-conscious and removed the brush from the bathroom closet. She brushed her hair and teeth and applied a light pink rouge to her cheeks.

She glided red lip gloss across her chapped lips, hoping it would conceal the roughness.

Then she found a perfume bottle on the counter and applied a small spray between her wrists. She looked in the mirror again, pleased with her reflection.

As she returned to the living room to seek Jacob's approval, he was reading the New York Times, his eyes furrowed and his demeanor with a pensive look.

"Fucking Democrats, all they want to do is give away my hard-earned money," he grumbled.

Mae offered, "Jacob, people need help. When I was going to live in Guatemala, I was doing it to make a difference in someone's life. I think that is the intention of politicians."

"Bullshit. I'm so glad I lost your passport back then. What a stupid idea that was—"

The room went silent, and Mae felt her head spinning like an amusement ride at a carnival.

Confused, she said, "What does that mean, Jacob? You 'lost' my passport?"

Jacob was quiet as his eyes darted around the room. He hadn't realized what he'd said until it was too late to stop it. He hadn't intended ever to tell Mae what he had done.

Embarrassed, he said, "Mae, I was just trying to help. It was too dangerous for you to go."

"You had no right, Jacob." Mae was horrified by this revelation and felt a flush of heat in her cheeks. A rage began to rise in her body. "No fucking right at all, Jacob. You selfish piece of shit. You knew I had firm plans, and you manipulated me to fit into yours."

"No, Mae, I was protecting you from yourself. You were a naïve, reckless young girl who lived on idealism. I could provide a better life for you. You should be thanking me for saving you from your immaturity!"

His voice was condescending and even-toned as he looked at her defiantly.

"Fuck you, Jacob. I'd have been better off without you," she screamed.

"Well, you aren't without me, and now you are responsible for raising two kids—*my* kids—so I suggest you get over your silly childhood fantasies and grow up."

She stormed out of the house into the yard.

Mae couldn't breathe and was shaking from head to toe.

She could barely dial the number on the phone to call Jill. She wouldn't even know what she would say to her. How could he do this? The phone rang three times before Jill's voicemail came on. Mae hung up, infuriated, confused, and defeated.

That night, she avoided Jacob.

"The silent treatment is a bit futile, don't you think, Mae?" he said from the living room. His voice was both condescending and an attempt to be playful, but it came across as snarky.

Mae wasn't ready to talk to Jacob, and she spent the little time he was at home avoiding him.

It had been years since her unintentionally canceled trip, and there was nothing she could do now, but the betrayal was incredibly hurtful. Now, she saw her husband for the man he was.

Three days passed, and Mae didn't stay in the same room with Jacob for long. She busied herself with James and prepared the nursery for the new baby, who was due any day.

She had everything she needed for the new arrival but wanted to stock up on diapers and other supplies, so she didn't have to drag two children out simultaneously.

Mae worried about postpartum depression after the birth but had already spoken to her doctor, preparing to start medication sooner than she had after James had come along.

She knew more about it now and understood the hormonal post-birth changes, which she could get help with through medicine and therapy if necessary.

Mae was optimistic about having another child and excited to welcome a new baby home.

In the meantime, Jacob didn't offer to attend any doctors' appointments with her; instead, she and James went together. Luckily, James was an easy baby and stayed in his stroller as the doctor examined her, focused on his toy dinosaurs.

Once in a while, he would look up and point to Mae's belly and sweetly say, "Baby."

Jacob barely noticed how disconnected Mae was. He went about his days, unaware this newest revelation had hurt Mae deeply, creating a destruction they could never remedy.

Mae considered leaving Jacob after the baby was born and wondered where she would go. She confided in Jill about her misery.

"Life is short, Mae. Do what makes you happy. We will figure out the rest."

"I'd agree if I didn't have almost two kids to worry about."

"Well, don't have anymore, Mae. Make sure of it. Go on the pill or do something."

It dawned on Mae how pleading Jill's voice sounded.

"You've never liked Jacob, have you?" she inquired.

Jill let out a hesitant breath. She was careful with her words, avoiding stepping over boundaries. "Look, Mae, I think he controls you. I see it firsthand. I'm not going to meddle in your marriage, but no, he isn't my favorite person."

"Mine either," Mae said quietly. "I see it now."

"Maybe you can talk to him. Ask him to lay off. Perhaps even try marriage counseling."

A man like Jacob would never let his ego settle enough for that, but Jill tried to offer support and suggestions.

"The truth is, I'm worried how financially miserable he would make my life if I did leave," said Mae. Jacob had controlled the bills and banking, and she couldn't access any of the money.

Once, when Mae complained about it, Jacob insisted she had enough to worry about with the kids and that he would handle all financial matters. He would leave cash for Mae weekly for food shopping and to take the kids places. Mae initially found it a thoughtful gesture.

But now, she worried that she had no access to any money at all.

Every week, Mae would manage the money Jacob gave, saving a meager amount and hiding it away. He never asked what she spent her weekly allowance on, so she began cutting corners to stock away cash each week. Sometimes, it was ten dollars, other times five, but each week, she made sure she could hide a little something in her black snow boot at the back of her closet.

She contemplated asking Jill if she could move in with her, but when the baby arrived, Jill's studio apartment could not accommodate more people.

There was barely enough room for Jill and her cat Mittens.

Mae felt helpless, also embarrassed to be in this predicament.

How could this have happened? It was a question that rolled around in her mind constantly. Mae had once had potential. How could she have allowed him to erode it like this?

She'd planned on traveling overseas, studying law, and had an entire career planned out before she was manipulated into her current situation.

That life was a distant memory now, and Mae was resenting every moment.

While Mae cared for the family, Jacob's career continued to skyrocket.

He finally made partner at his company, which increased his income tremendously.

He had the freedom to attend nightly cocktail parties with colleagues and friends, also spending many nights with clients, becoming less available for Mae.

Loneliness submerged her, though she tried to make friends in the neighborhood. Mae's circle had become so small that it consisted of her son, weekly calls with her mother, arrangements of coffee dates with Jill that never happened, and promises she would come to visit soon.

Mae was busy managing motherhood, but she longed for adult conversation.

Noticing a flier at the local market, she jotted down the number for a mothers' group. At first, she was wary, unsure if she would fit in with many of the younger moms in the neighborhood. Despite hesitation, Mae committed to joining the group to meet her neighbors.

Besides Jill, whom she rarely saw, she had no other person to confide in or ever spend time with. She planned to attend a Mommy & Me class at the library the following day.

It was accessible to residents, and it was exciting to expose James to other kids. Knowing her baby was due soon, she hoped introducing him to other children would also help him transition to having a new baby in the house.

Mae tucked James into bed, telling him their plans for the morning.

"That's fun, Mommy," he said excitedly.

"Yes, and you can meet other kids your age. Since you will be a big brother soon, I thought we could do something with children. Would you like that?"

James smiled. "Thank you, Mommy!"

As she finished cleaning the kitchen, Mae felt an intense pain and, without hesitation, knew she was in labor. She called Jacob to tell him, but he didn't answer. She reached his secretary, who nervously told her she would go into the conference room to notify him of the news.

Forty-five minutes later, Jacob called, slightly irritated.

"Mae, I was in the middle of a meeting," he said impatiently.

The contractions were close by this time, and Mae could barely stand.

"I'm in labor. You need to come home and get James so I can get to the hospital."

"I'll call the babysitter I hired to be on call for James and then be by to pick you up." Jacob's voice softened. "Mae, I love you. I didn't mean to hurt you. See you soon."

Mae let out a yell in agony. "Hurry," she demanded.

They arrived at the hospital, and Mae was admitted immediately.

She practiced her breathing, and Jacob held her hand, encouraging her to stay calm. "You got this, beautiful," he said, rubbing her back.

Mae let out a few more screams when she heard the doctors say, "It's a boy." Before Jacob could claim their new son's name, Mae took the baby in her arms.

"Trevor," she said softly.

Jacob looked at her curiously. "Trevor?"

"Yes, Trevor," Mae said. *Welcome, baby boy.*

If Jacob was irritated by this, he didn't say. Mae held her newborn son close to her breast. This time, she felt an immediate connection to the baby.

Days later, she was sent home with her new bundle to introduce to James.

The three spent time acclimating to the new family dynamics. Jacob, in the meantime, returned to work that same day with the excuse that he had an important meeting.

"I could use some help, Jacob," Mae said one late night when he arrived home.

Her voice was soft so as not to wake the children. They both had trouble sleeping throughout the night, and Mae was already exhausted from the consistent sleep disruption.

"I can get you a nanny," Jacob offered.

I don't want a nanny. I want help from you." Mae sounded desperate. "I want a family where we spend more time together. I want us as a unit. The kids want to be settled by their dad when they can't sleep, not by some stranger."

"Well, she'll only be here in the daytime."

So what use would that be? Mae wondered. "It's the nights when they cry the most."

"You don't want a stranger in the house at night, do you?" he asked.

"No, that's the whole point."

"I don't get it," he said. "Whatever I offer, you don't want."

Jacob's eyes narrowed, seemingly surprised by Mae's emotional plea. He crossed his arms, looking disheveled at Mae in her oversized nightgown.

"Mae, I promised you I'd give you a financially secure life. One you never had, mind you, but that takes working long hours and doing things that other people won't."

Mae looked down in shame. Despite everything Jacob had done to manipulate Mae, she wanted her marriage to work for the sake of their kids, at least for now.

She wanted her children to have a secure life emotionally and financially.

"I guess I'm asking too much," she said.

"Mae, I think you're selfish. I work hard to provide, and you get to stay home. Enjoy it."

"I work hard, too, Jacob. Taking care of two children, doing all of the chores—"

Jacob interrupted. "I'm sure, Mae. But I have real work, and that pressure's a lot, so hearing you complain about sitting at home is insulting."

Mae vowed to work harder at being a better spouse, hoping to ease the tension. The following day, Jacob woke up and kissed Mae on her forehead. "Enjoy your day, love."

Mae didn't argue this time and replied, "Thank you for everything you do for me."

That day, as she was having coffee while both babies miraculously slept, she thought about the argument with Jacob prior to going into labor. They never discussed how Jacob intentionally changed her plans to go overseas, but she hadn't forgotten it. She felt bitterness inwardly but remained calm, knowing she was in a vulnerable financial predicament. Her boys needed to come first, which meant she needed to stay put and tolerate Jacob.

The more she thought about it, the more she realized how little her needs were met. She'd never gone back to work, never started law school, and hadn't done any of the things she'd intended, having been thwarted by him at every turn.

He had controlled their finances and the decision-making, and the further she got away from her old life, the more it seemed like a distant memory. Gone were the days of excitement, spontaneity, and grand plans. Mae felt trapped, and there was little she could do about it. She, of course, buried these feelings, knowing she had two children who relied on her, but deep within her soul, a nagging feeling continued to eat away at her for the way Jacob manipulated situations.

He appeared friendly, caring, and doting on the outside, but when she examined his motives, he was self-serving and manipulative. Jacob had established such a strong reputation within the community that she was often stopped by people who nonchalantly mentioned his generosity.

"You're Jacob's wife, right?" an elderly woman who lived three doors down mentioned as Mae walked the children to the park.

"Yes. I am. Do you know Jacob from the firm?" Mae asked, assuming she was a client.

"Oh no, Jacob arranged for my driveway to be plowed over the winter. He was so nice about it. He stopped by to check in on me, knowing my husband Bob had recently passed. Such a wonderful husband," she went on. "You must feel fortunate."

This was the first Mae had heard of these oh-so-benevolent acts.

She remembered another instance when she'd been at the park, and a woman stopped to tell her how much she appreciated Jacob bringing bagels to the recreation center once a month.

At first, Mae thought they had the wrong Jacob. The Jacob she knew wasn't generous with his time and rarely spent time with his family. The Jacob others knew was overextending, considerate, and caring to strangers. Why did he give so much time to strangers and so little to his family? The questions whirled in her head until she was interrupted by Trevor's cry.

She hurried to him before he could wake up his older brother, but it was too late.

James was at the nursery door. "Momma, I hungry?"

That was a quick fifteen-minute nap, she thought, but replied, "Sure thing, buddy. What would you like to eat?"

Chapter 9

As THE CHILDREN GREW older, the demands of motherhood increased. James was the easier of her two children and helped with his little brother and his tantrums. Trevor was increasingly mischievous and held little respect for authority. Mae continued to guide Trevor by setting limits and boundaries, but Jacob thwarted her efforts.

"What are you trying to do? Make them soft?" complained Jacob when Mae disciplined Trevor for hitting his older brother.

"As it is, James is sensitive and docile. I'm glad to have Trevor, who acts like a boy," Jacob said flippantly. "You allowed James to be too feminine. He was playing with dolls and baking bread with you for years. Now look at him. He's mediocre at sports at best. He spends time with the weird kids from the chess club. Trevor even told me so."

Jacob threw his hands up in disgust.

His eldest son was soft, kind, and caring, unlike Trevor, who spent his time playing contact sports, which usually ended in a brawl with the opposing players.

Trevor was no stranger to trouble either. At least once a week, Mae would receive calls home from school about fights on the playground, cheating, or being disrespectful. Jacob would answer Mae's concerns with a soft chuckle and a brash comment, "Boys will be boys."

But this was more than the unruly behavior of boys. Trevor was different from the other boys, who were energetic and boisterous but respectful.

Trevor was aggressive, even mean, satisfied by others' misery.

One day, while riding bicycles, Mae was sure that Trevor purposely put a rock in the way of James' path to watch him fall. When Mae heard James' screams, she rushed outside to see what the commotion was about. James had scraped knees and road rash on his face.

Trevor stood with a look of satisfaction and a big smile, without any concern for his brother. Another time, while swimming at the lake, knowing James wasn't a strong swimmer, Trevor urged him to swim out farther to get the ball that had floated away.

Trevor, a competitive swimmer since he was six, coaxed him until James relented.

"C'mon, James, what are you scared of?" Trevor teased.

"No, I can't," James muttered. "Why don't you get the stupid ball? You're the swimmer."

"Just get the ball, James. Why are you always such a baby? It's embarrassing being your brother sometimes. Even the kids at school ask me how I can stand to be the brother of a wimp."

James' heart raced at Trevor's words, and a surge of delusional confidence overtook his skinny limbs. He began swimming farther out into the water, unable to stand.

Mae saw this and shouted for James to leave the ball and return to shore.

With the wind and the laughter of Trevor cheering him on, James did not hear his mother's demands. As he got tired, he sank deeper into the water until his head bobbed in and out.

Mae threw down her towel and began screaming for help.

Trevor watched with amusement as his brother struggled to catch his breath, but when he saw his mother's worried eyes, he began frantically swimming toward James.

Mae could hear the gasps and coughs of poor James, desperate for breath.

Trevor reached for his brother just as his limp body went under the water; he miraculously swam him to shore. Once on land, Mae started CPR, and a gush of water and uncontrollable coughs came from the frozen boy, who had already turned a light shade of blue.

Mae cried uncontrollably, screaming at Trevor for allowing his brother to swim too far.

Trevor looked at his mother with wide eyes. "Mom, I'm sorry, I didn't mean for—"

Mae cut him off before he could continue. "Oh, of course! You never mean to, Trevor, but you somehow always do. We could have lost your brother because of you!" The slap to his face jolted both of them, and Mae began to sob. "I'm sorry. Oh, what have I done? I'm so sorry."

By then, Trevor had run away, leaving Mae stunned.

The paramedics came to take James to the hospital for observation. Jacob had already arrived as James was brought in, Mae frantically rushing behind.

"Mae, what the fuck happened? Why can't you handle anything?"

His face was red, and his voice was loud.

"Not now, Jacob,"

"Trevor called, by the way," he said slowly. "Don't expect any Mother of the Year awards."

Mae looked at Jacob in disbelief. She stared at him for another moment until she was interrupted by the doctors.

"Ma'am, he's going to be all right. Just wait in the waiting room, and I'll have a doctor come out and talk to you after we run some tests."

James spent two days in the hospital and was released. Trevor never mentioned the incident, and Jacob insisted that Mae never take the boys to the river again.

Mae replayed the incident over and over in her mind.

She just couldn't shake Trevor's part in it. *Could he really be so cruel?*

Anytime she closed her eyes, she saw James' head bobbing under the water, desperate to catch his breath as Trevor watched in callous amusement. When she brought it up to Jacob late one night, he responded, "You really are paranoid, Mae. He's just a kid."

Eventually, Mae let the incident lie and kept a watchful eye on both the boys. She busied herself with swim meets, soccer practice, football games, and various clubs they participated in, which seemed never-ending. Jacob encouraged his boys to stay active, never giving thought to the fact that Mae was the one who had to arrange all the driving and pickups, and who had to attend the plethora of games for each sport. Mae was often exhausted from their demanding schedules, while Jacob rarely went to the games, still working past ten most nights.

He always faintly smelt of bourbon and women's perfume, but Mae never mentioned either.

It was of little interest to her as long as he still came home to her and the children. She had grown into the role of mother and provider, spending most of her time doting on her sons.

"Jacob, I can't be in two places at once. Don't you want to see the boys' semi-final games? I'm sure they'd love it if you were there to see their matches."

"Yes, of course I do," Jacob said. "I'll try and move my schedule around," he said pensively.

It had felt to Mae that her requests to be involved in family life were such an imposition on Jacob. Without using words to say it, his actions and exasperation made it all too clear that he would rather be anywhere but sitting on a field. On the rare occasions he attended their games, he was distracted by texts and calls from work.

He whispered when he took the calls, too, often walking into the distance where Mae could not hear. She had suspected for some time that this was not work; he was probably carrying on illicit affairs. But, for the sake of her children, she continued to stay quiet until the disrespect became blatant and embarrassing.

She cared only that he did not ask to separate since this would destroy their kids and their family unit. But sometimes, when he was on calls more often while at home, she felt things were getting to a point where their family could collapse. She would have to confront him.

"Who the fuck are you always on the phone with?" she wanted to know, her rage more aggressive than intended.

"What? Mae, how fucking dare you?" Jacob said as he slammed their bedroom door. "I work like a fucking dog for you, Mae, and you dare to grill me about my calls?"

She stared, but he carried on. "First of all, lower your goddamn voice, you paranoid twat. Second, how fucking dare you question anything I do? I support you and the kids, and I work all the hours God sends to support your lazy ass. You had better start showing me some respect."

"Or else what?" Mae said defiantly. "I'll take half of everything if we divorce."

Something inside Mae had snapped. The feelings she had suppressed for years flooded her like a garden hose, making her no longer able to hold her emotions or her tongue.

"You took away my opportunity to travel, got me pregnant, and now I'm treated like a servant rather than a wife." Mae's voice became louder. "You are an awful father and even worse husband. You're a shell of a man with an ego bigger than the state of Montana."

She was now pointing, getting closer to him.

"All you are is a man who impresses strangers by bringing them bagels—using our family's money, I might add—and helping out neighbors when you don't even care for your own kids."

Under her breath, she gave Jacob one last verbal blow. "You are a fucking loser."

The worst insult for Jacob was pointing out his flaws. He was easily defensive and could not handle if anyone said anything negative about him. No doubt his mother Jane's constant judgment when he was a kid had made him have low self-esteem. He craved people's adulation.

He ensured he held himself to a high standing in public, so people only ever imagined he was a wonderful and loving family man. The whispers from other women about how lucky Mae was to have such a great catch fueled his desire to be liked. He listened as other men's wives gushed over him, nudging their husbands to "Be more like Jacob."

Jacob gathered more fuel for every compliment he was given and more fuel to perform the act of the neighborhood good doer. People would never realize that Jacob wore a mask.

For the first time, Jacob was risking being exposed by Mae.

"Your mask is slipping, Jacob. And I see you now," she said.

Jacob stared at Mae, stunned that she had the nerve to abuse him the way she did verbally.

She'd never spoken to him in this tone before, and he was shocked—worse, he was insulted—that someone of his caliber would be treated with anything other than the utmost respect.

Jacob was accustomed to fancy living, people revering his existence.

Part of his problem with Mae, on the other hand, was that she still saw him as average. The outside world believed otherwise. They saw him for his sophistication, power, and influence.

"You wonder why I hate being trapped here with you," snarled Jacob. "You're dull at best and have no respect for the career I've attained to keep you home, doting on your sons."

Jacob had convinced himself of his own narrative of self-importance and lived accordingly.

In a moment of bravery, Mae retorted, "I wanted to return to work. Let's not forget that, Jacob. You convinced me, no, you demanded I stay home with the kids. I was on a path, and you diverted me, intentionally ruining my life. I daren't think what really happened to my passport."

Jacob had married Mae because she was vulnerable and easily impressed.

He knew he could provide for her, still have a career, and keep the image of a family man.

He knew how to get to where he wanted to go with his ambitions, but he had to have a certain persona to gain the respect of a loyal family man.

At work, people would trust him, and then he'd acquire more business for the firm and be promoted sooner. He was smart and calculated enough to have planned for this early on, and Mae had fit the bill of who he needed by his side to accomplish his goals.

She was attractive but not showy, friendly but lacking social charisma.

More than anything else, Mae was simple to please and lacked money.

There was an added bonus; she had little family. She would be easily content with an easier lifestyle controlled by Jacob, which made her the perfect partner for him to control. Because she had few relatives and siblings, he could do all this mostly without interference.

Jacob heard the footsteps of James entering the room, and he retreated, inhaling as he composed himself. Calmly, he said, "Mae, honey, it seems you're having a bad day. I think you need to lie down and get some rest. You seem so out of sorts. Even the boys have noticed it."

Mae looked at Jacob, not thinking she'd heard him correctly.

She had just confronted him with accusations of cheating, and he'd offered her rest.

He was insisting that her suffering or her astute observations were all products of her own crazy mind, her overworked psyche and body, and her failing mental health.

Now, Jacob's voice was soft. "Listen, I know I'm not perfect, but I can see now how much trouble you are having handling motherhood. It's okay to get help. Remember how depressed you were after having the boys? Maybe it's coming back."

He grabbed James' shoulder. James, well into his teen years, was just as tall as his father and looked alarmed. "It's okay, buddy. Your mother is having a moment."

James looked at his mother, then his father, feeling the tension in the room.

"We wonder where Trevor gets it," Jacob said to James with a smirk.

James shrugged, not wanting to be a part of whatever he'd walked in on, and said, "Okay, as long as you guys are cool."

"Yes, we're cool," he said, staring at Mae as her shoulders slumped.

Jacob's voice was sincere in front of James, which made Mae start to doubt her feelings of rage. Maybe she really was stressed, imagining all this deviousness in Jacob.

James left the room, giving his father a high-five before departing.

"Jacob, I had mild postpartum depression with James and got help. If you look back, you'll see it wasn't with both boys." Mae found herself justifying the facts.

"Sweetie, I know you don't remember much, but it was a lot more than that. I tried to help you as much as possible, but you were in such a bad state," Jacob said, trailing off.

Mae was quiet momentarily, trying to recall all those years back.

She hadn't remembered the severity of her depression, not even remembering Jacob noticing or helping, despite his claims that he'd had to step in so often.

She thought for another moment before she heard Jacob say, "It's okay, Mae, I forgive you."

He walked out of the room, leaving Mae confused. Her cheeks felt hot with shame as she desperately tried to reconcile what Jacob proclaimed. Had she been delusional all this time?

Was she imagining that he persecuted her?

It was possible.

She felt ungrateful and foolish for even thinking Jacob could do such awful acts.

"I have to be a better wife," she mumbled, unsure of the reality.

Mae made an earnest effort to improve for the sake of her marriage, her children, and her sanity. From then on, she focused more on Jacob, complimenting him and showing her gratitude inside and outside the bedroom.

She invested in her clothing and figure and worked hard to be everything Jacob demanded.

He was now a renowned businessman, often on television and at public speaking events, sharing his knowledge about finance. Mae continued to play the part of the doting housewife and no longer saved money in a secret stash. She had felt foolish for having done so in the past, spending the money she had saved on cologne and other gifts for Jacob.

He had convinced her she'd been hurtful, and she strived to be better.

As he had mentioned, she didn't want to turn out like her mother, alone and broke.

Jill called again for the fifth time. When Mae answered, Jill was agitated. "Mae, jeez, where have you been? I keep calling, and you never return my calls. I've been so worried."

"Jill, life gets busy when you have kids, a marriage, and a home. What's so urgent?"

There was a condescending tone in Mae's voice that Jill ignored but no doubt noted. The two made plans to see one another the following Friday. They met for coffee at a cafe not far from Mae's house since Jacob didn't like Mae being out for too long, insisting she stay close to home.

Mae didn't want to alarm Jill and give her friend yet another reason to criticize Jacob, so she made an excuse that her schedule was busy with the kids. She'd asked if Jill could travel toward her this time. Usually, they met halfway and went for dinner and drinks, but now, every time Jill suggested it, Mae found an excuse for why she couldn't possibly make it, not right now.

Two weeks prior, Mae had canceled at the last minute, saying she had a headache. The time before, she'd told Jill she had car trouble. The time before that, she claimed that James had a fever and she didn't want to leave him alone. When Mae agreed to a coffee date, Jill took her up on the offer without hesitation; she needed to see for herself if Mae was okay.

Jill, who always kept Mae accountable, questioned her line of thinking.

"Mae," she said gently. "It sounds like Jacob is changing the narrative a bit. What's with this sudden husband worshiping?" Jill's voice was playful.

Mae's eyes narrowed. "No, Jill, I get it now. It's me. I'm so unsettled with my thoughts, as I always have been. It's time I grew up."

Jill crossed her arms, annoyed by this new proclamation. "This sounds awfully like Jacob and not my independent, free-spirited friend. Those sound suspiciously like his words."

"Jill, please, let's enjoy the day. I don't have much time, and I have to get my hair and makeup done for an event tonight to honor Jacob for his work at the Children's Foundation."

"Hair, makeup ... Mae, c'mon, since when? Who are you, becoming a puppet of your husband's?"

Mae turned in fury.

"How dare you, Jill? My husband does many wonderful things for our community, and I've spent years taking it for granted. If you can't accept my marriage, then you don't accept me."

Jill was flabbergasted.

The conversation escalated to an argument quickly, as if Mae's intention.

Jill watched Mae's expression change. She seemed nervous the entire day, quieter than usual, and unwilling to share her feelings.

Mae thought of the conversation she'd had with Jacob before she left.

"You know she is jealous of you?" he'd said.

"Jealous? Jill? I don't think so," Mae said, a little more defensively than intended.

"Notice how she's always tried to cause a rift between us. She wants you alone like she is. Just be careful," Jacob warned.

His words rang in her ears on the drive to meet Jill.

"Mae, I have nothing but good intentions for you. But when I ask how you are and about your busy schedule, it's because I care about you and want to ensure you care for yourself, too. Motherhood should not define you, Mae. Being a wife also shouldn't be who you are."

Mae managed to skirt the conversation, twisting it to something more general about the weather and the kids' report cards. Jill said she felt a distance between the friends and suspected it was Jacob's doing, though she had no proof.

"How's Jacob doing, anyway?" Jill asked, trying to change the subject and de-escalate the rising animosity in Mae's voice.

"He is doing wonderfully. I don't know how he manages everything," Mae gushed.

Jill looked at Mae curiously, as if to hide her annoyance. "What is happening? I'm watching my beautiful, feisty, independent friend turn into a robot. You're like an automaton Jacob fan."

"I'm pretty tired of these accusations. I think Jacob's right. You're jealous of me."

"Jealous? Mae, no, I'm worried. Can't you see that Jacob is controlling and manipulating you? He's been doing this since the beginning of your relationship. At first, at least you were aware of it, but now you are completely oblivious to what is so clearly obvious."

"Fuck you, Jill," Mae said. "You don't know a thing about me, about relationships, or marriage. And here you come in with accusations about something you know nothing about."

Before Mae could stop herself, she added, "Jacob says you are jealous of me and my life, and I didn't want to believe it. But he's right! Go find your own life, Jill, and stay the fuck out of mine." She slammed her clenched fist on the table.

Mae got up from the chair, grabbed her coat, and left her half-eaten croissant and coffee behind. As she stormed out of the cafe, she turned one last time to see her friend.

She cried out at Jill, "Don't ever fucking call me again. You hear me? You're dead to me."

As Mae stormed out, she could feel her knees get weak. She leaned against the new red Mercedes Jacob had bought for her as a reward for losing weight.

Her manicured fingers caressed her wet cheeks as she sobbed into her hands.

She quickly dismissed the feelings of sadness as the phone rang, and Jacob was on the line.

"Almost home, hon. I have golf lessons in an hour."

"Yes, of course, I'm so forgetful sometimes. I'm on my way," Mae said, quivering.

"I know, sweetie. I tell you that all the time. Good thing you have me to keep you in check!"

That night, as Mae was getting to bed, she replayed the conversation with Jill. They had been friends for decades, and she couldn't believe how disrespectful she'd been toward her marriage.

She hesitated for a moment as she considered Jill's concern. Thinking about it, her mother had said something similar last week. When Judy had called, her voice had been strained.

"Hi, honey. How are you?" she'd said, trying to sound casual.

"I'm good, Mom. Busy with the kids."

"I've called you many times, and you haven't returned my calls. Are you okay?"

Mae had tried to remember missed calls from her mother but couldn't recall any. "I didn't get any," Mae replied.

"Well, I left you messages and didn't hear back. I was getting worried," Judy said.

Jacob, who was lurking in the background, chimed in, "Mae, don't you remember I told you your mother called last week?"

Mae hadn't remembered that at all.

Embarrassed, she said, "Gosh, no, I don't remember that! I'm losing my faculties!"

Jacob cut her off before she could finish her thought. "Oh, sweetie," he said loud enough for Judy to hear. "You need to rest more."

Mae replayed that conversation, wondering if she had forgotten or if Jill had called her mother, concerned. She was feeling violated and watched, which made her more paranoid.

She ignored these feelings, knowing her attention needed to remain on Jacob and the kids. James was graduating from high school soon, and Mae had a lot on her mind. She didn't want to cause problems, so she rescinded her thoughts, knowing she often forgot things. Things were going well for them, and she didn't want intrusive thoughts to ruin her stable family life.

Chapter 10

Mae snuggled into her empty bed, wondering how long it would be until Jacob arrived home. Over the past few months, he'd been arriving even later than usual, blaming business meetings and deadlines. She felt sorry for him, imagining him at his desk late into the night.

One night, Mae overheard Jacob whispering on the phone. While she couldn't make out the context of the call, she was sure she heard him say the name Amanda.

Mae thought back to her wedding and meeting Amanda, the tall, slim woman with the red highlighted hair. She recalled her shock when Amanda had introduced herself as Jacob's friend, also her unease at how the two still kept in touch after the years since their relationship fizzled.

Mae's head swirled with questions, but she would risk her relationship if she broached the subject. It had been a few years by now, and she and Jacob were finally in a good place.

Mae didn't want to disrupt the peace now residing within her home.

She struggled, however, with the reality of Jacob's whereabouts. Instead of perseverating about it, she chose to ignore the alarming signs.

She wanted to tell him about the fallout with Jill and thank him for his advice about letting go of the friendship. After all, it was with his encouragement that Mae could stand up to Jill and stand by her marriage.

She longed for his approval and appreciation for choosing their marriage over the long-standing friendship. Instead, she lay awake, tired but unable to sleep, feeling insecure.

As she rolled over in search of sleep in her bed vacant of Jacob, she looked at the clock one last time. It was half past midnight, her eyes growing tired.

She glanced at her phone, hoping for a text from Jacob or even Jill, but neither had reached out. She scrolled to Jill's last text, contemplating sending her one to apologize, but recalled Jacob saying, "Sometimes, we outgrow people, Mae. Jill and you have nothing in common anymore. She never grew up. You have a beautiful life, and she has a studio apartment and a cat."

With Jacob's words still ringing in her ear, she scrolled to Jill's contact information on her cell phone and blocked the number.

She pulled the sheets up to her chin as sleep began to take over.

Without Jill's companionship and with the increasing distance between herself and her mother, Mae struggled for connection.

She had hoped Jacob would notice the change in her commitment to their marriage and reciprocate; instead, he only became more distant and curter.

"Honey, what's going on? You rarely come home, and I miss you," Mae said.

"One of us needs to make a living," Jacob said. His eyes were cold, and his voice dismissive.

She still resented when he said things like *one of us.*

God knew, she still wanted to contribute financially but he thwarted her at every turn.

"Is something going on with our finances?" inquired Mae. "I could get a job to help out."

Jacob slammed his laptop shut. "Mae, you have no fucking idea, do you?" he snarled. "I'm under pressure at work, and coming home to you is exasperating."

"I'm sorry, I don't mean it to be."

Mae found herself apologizing more frequently, not knowing what she was supposed to have done. Jacob became easily angered now, having little patience.

He stood up, slamming a nearby book on the floor.

"Do you know how annoying you can be, Mae? I have no idea how I continue to put up with you. I should have thrown you to the curb years ago. I could have raised the boys without you."

Jacob's eyes were steady on her, his voice increasing with each syllable.

Mae felt her ears turn red. Her breathing began to shallow, and she was scared of reacting while her anger rose. She had practiced breathing exercises just as she'd read in a blog about keeping control—but rage was taking over.

"What the fuck does that mean, Jacob? I've been working hard to satisfy you, and no matter what I do, it isn't enough."

"Maybe you aren't enough?" Jacob cried. "Have you ever thought about that?"

Mae froze with an unrelenting sense of insecurity.

Without thinking further, she blurted, "Is this about Amanda? I heard you on the phone a few weeks ago. You're never home and you're more distant than usual."

Jacob's cheeks reddened. He bit his inner cheek.

Mae couldn't decipher whether it was from embarrassment or rage.

"You fucking bitch," he screamed. "How dare you question me? My relationships are not your concern. How about you care for the kids and house and let me worry about my life?"

Mae knew at that moment that her suspicions had been confirmed. Jacob was having an affair and was becoming bolder about it. She dropped the subject as he stormed from the house.

It would be three days before he returned, ignoring her and their boys for two weeks.

Only at James' graduation did he take her hand as they entered the massive high school stadium. He would wave at parents, community leaders, and teachers attending the graduation ceremony. Mae knew this was for show but kept her head up, smiling weakly.

"Looking good, my man," a bald man said.

"Thank you. You are looking good yourself, Bob. How's the family?" Jacob said.

"Everyone is good. I see you and the Mrs. are as happy as ever."

"She's the best," Jacob boasted.

Mae looked appalled and downcast at his blatant lies and manipulation. She noticed the ruse he had presented in the past, but now it was far beyond her comprehension.

The two men shook hands while Jacob aggressively squeezed Mae's hand tightly.

She watched as the hopeful graduates formed a line. Students filled with potential and broad smiles chatted amongst themselves, anticipating the start of the ceremony.

What would happen to these young minds if they, too, would one day be withered by life? She wished she could go back in time and make different decisions.

As her heart lamented, she watched James scouring the crowd looking for her, giving a big wave and mouthing the words, "Thanks, Mom." She put her hand on her heart and blew him a kiss, knowing she was right where she wanted to be despite her relationship with Jacob.

Chapter 11

James decided to stay local for college. The security of home gave him peace of mind, and the short twenty-minute commute to campus made his decision easy.

Mae supported James' decision and was secretly relieved, knowing that he positively influenced Trevor, who was still far less predictable. Throughout childhood, and as the brothers grew, it was clear that James was more cautious and thoughtful, whereas Trevor's behavior could be reckless. Mae kept a watchful eye on Trevor but allowed the boys to be teenagers.

Making mistakes was a part of development, but Trevor always seemed to find trouble. He had already been on school probation for a fistfight with another boy. He later described the event as "settling beef." She'd reprimanded him for using violence, but Jacob had quickly said, "Oh, Mae, enough. Let boys be boys already."

Arguing with Jacob was a losing battle, but she continued to influence the boys positively.

"Fist fighting is unacceptable behavior and will have you revoked from sports."

"We know, Mom. We aren't stupid," they'd complain.

She had hoped the constant reminders would sink in, but her hands were tied when she had Jacob egging them on.

To relieve stress, Mae decided it was time to start taking care of herself and exercising more frequently. As the weeks passed, she noticed her muscles tone and her belly tighten. She was proud of her progress, watching her calorie intake, dedicating three days a week to cardio by walking briskly in the park and another three for light weights, leaving one day a week for rest.

Mae enjoyed her walks in the park, the scenery so peaceful and the energy of nature invigorating. The path lined with oak trees and manicured lawns surrounded lush gardens.

Young couples laughed, holding hands, and families picnicked on the abundant green grass. Friends and athletes used the path as training for marathons and midday walks. The path was always filled with people enjoying the atmosphere and natural beauty it offered. In the spring, the flowers bloomed in radiant colors with the sweet aroma of summer's arrival.

The fall was Mae's favorite time at the park as she enjoyed watching the trees turn colors and the sound of crunching leaves beneath her feet. She walked with ease through the park, ensuring she got her heart rate up but still taking time to listen to the birds chirping.

Hearing the birds reminded Mae of when she'd been young and had first met Jacob. What had happened to the young couple who would frequent the park for picnics?

As Mae became lost in her thoughts, she failed to realize that the path widened and narrowed in one section, becoming two roads in one.

Clumsily, she stumbled over a branch and came too close to a man walking his Golden Retriever. The dog yelped as the tall man tripped over the dog, causing him to lose balance.

"Oh my gosh, I'm so sorry. There was a branch, and I didn't see it until it was too late," Mae said sheepishly.

"It's okay. I think Lannie here is being a little overdramatic," the man said with a chuckle as he petted the dog's wagging tail.

He reached into his pocket and took out a small treat as Lannie sat obediently.

"I'm really sorry again," Mae said as she started to walk away.

"Really, you shouldn't apologize. It was actually my fault. I was caught off guard as you passed and could have made a better effort to avoid you, but I let myself get distracted."

Mae blushed, welcoming the attention. It had been a long time since she'd enjoyed an adult conversation, and she was intrigued by the stranger. She couldn't remember the last time she'd been given a compliment, a rush of excitement running through her veins.

"Mind if Lannie and I walk some of the way with you?"

Mae blurted out, "Not at all." Her eagerness for companionship surprised her, though she did not regret accepting the stranger's invitation.

"I'm Mae, by the way."

"Hello, Mae, I'm Patrick, and you met Lannie already," he said with a smile.

Mae felt her heart race as his blue eyes looked at her curiously.

His jawline was sharp, his thin face accenting deep dimples.

She stumbled on her words, distracted by their instant connection.

"I love walking. I come here a lot to exercise and clear my head," Mae said.

"I know," he said, laughing. "I mean, I've seen you here a lot and noticed you, but you never noticed me." He said this jokingly and made a sad face, mocking his defeat.

"Well, I certainly notice you now."

The two walked the path, chatting as time went by more quickly than Mae had anticipated.

When she heard her phone ring, she was startled by the disruption; she'd been out far longer than intended! Noticing the time, she reached into her back pocket to retrieve the phone.

"Oh dear," she said nervously. "I have to go. I've lost track of time, and my son is finished with practice. If I don't have dinner ready for them, they'll ransack the snack drawer!"

"Growing boys have big appetites."

"That's for sure. Oh, and thanks for the walk and chat," she called back as she left for her car.

"I'll be here tomorrow at the same time. Meet me," Patrick said, hopeful.

Mae waved and took a long, deep exhale as she got into her car. She had never been late for the boys and worried they would call their father when she wasn't there at her usual time.

How could she explain herself?

Her hands trembled as she approached the pickup line at the high school. Trevor's car had been in the shop, and she'd promised to pick him up to avoid taking the bus home.

Trevor was waiting alone as she pulled up close.

"Trevor, I'm so sorry. I was running errands and lost track of time."

"No worries, Mom," Trevor said casually.

"No, really, Trevor, it won't happen again. Were you waiting long? I just—" Mae was overly apologetic and worried that Jacob would call her irresponsible if he found out.

Just last week, she'd forgotten to pick up his dry cleaning, and Jacob had been so angry he'd smashed another precious plate against the wall. Jacob had never replenished those he'd broken.

"It was an innocent mistake, Jacob," she had explained. "I had a headache and fell asleep, and by the time I awoke, the store had closed."

"Irresponsible cunt," he retorted. "You really could not survive in this world without me, Mae. You're lucky the boys are around, or I would have thrown you out by now."

Mae didn't sleep that night, worried that Jacob's wrath would continue into the morning as it sometimes did. However, as the sun rose, he reached for her, caressing her body.

Groggy, Mae felt his hard penis push up against her from behind, forcing himself inside.

The quick motions as she awoke became more aggressive as he grabbed the back of her hair, pulling her in and out, moaning loudly in her ear. When he was finished, he slipped out of her, kissed her neck, and took a shower, leaving Mae to feel violated.

The flashback of that night made her quiver. She was jolted back to the present when she heard Trevor say in his teenage sarcasm, "Mom, relax, it's fine. I waited for like five minutes."

As she prepared dinner for the boys, she couldn't stop thinking about the stranger she had met. She hadn't ever felt so strongly about someone she had just encountered, and she couldn't help but wonder if he felt it, too. She felt nervous about seeing him the following day.

She would be there on the path and found herself longing for the next morning.

Mae was quieter at dinner and lost in her thoughts of the afternoon, also feeling shame for the unexpected emotions the stranger had mustered up.

She was disappointed in herself too. After all this time of admonishing and accusing her husband of having affairs, here she was, about to embark on one. But it was too late for regrets, too late to stop what she was doing. She had agreed to meet Patrick and wouldn't be a no-show.

Mae went to bed that night filled with anticipation of running into him.

She hoped to time the walk perfectly, knowing his and Lannie's daily route. Mae would be more careful about the time so that she wouldn't be late or cause suspicion to Jacob.

The last thing she needed was for Jacob to find out she'd had a conversation with another man. She could only imagine what Jacob would do if he found out. Maybe she would deserve it.

His jealousy was out of hand though, and his rage had become more violent over the passing months. Just weeks prior, while dining out, a waiter had smiled at Mae as they left the restaurant.

For the rest of the evening, Jacob had accused her of being flirty, sending mixed signals.

"You bitch," he shouted. "Anything to embarrass me, Mae. After everything I do for you, you humiliate me at a restaurant I frequent. And look at you, dressed like a whore."

Mae was dumbfounded. She'd dressed in a black lace dress, showing off her figure to impress Jacob that night. She'd only hoped he would find her attractive and even pay her a compliment. Instead, he responded, "It's nice to see you dressed in something other than leggings. But not so good to see that you use your attire to flaunt yourself to other men."

"Jacob, I didn't do anything," Mae said, trying to de-escalate the situation.

"Stop pretending you're innocent. I saw the way you looked at that waiter. What? Do you want to fuck him? Go fuck him if you want it so much."

"No. No ..." Mae pleaded.

"I knew you were a low life when I married you and tried to help improve your social status. I should have let you go to a third-world country like the trash you are!"

Mae felt tears burn her tired eyes.

Jacob was no longer apologizing for ruining her plans all those years ago. That had ended long ago. She would never win an argument with him, so she just stared helplessly out the window and was quiet for the rest of the ride home, listening to Jacob rant about her behavior.

When he finally finished berating her, all she could do was reach for his arm gently and say, "I'm sorry, Jacob. You're right. I will try to be better. Thank you for being patient with me."

Jacob looked at her with satisfaction. "You had better," he responded. "Really, Mae, a waiter? When you have the top financial advisor in the region?"

When they arrived home, Mae knew what was expected.

They entered the bedroom, and she knelt and slowly unzipped his too-tight pants. Jacob allowed himself to be fully satisfied, thrusting himself into her mouth.

She knew not to complain about the discomfort, surrendering to his sexual demands. When he was finished, he went into the bathroom to wash, leaving Mae on her knees, humiliated.

Jacob's sexual desires were becoming more frequent and less intimate.

His appetite for rough sex was growing, and the one time Mae had tried to object, he'd replied, "If I don't get it with you, I'll go elsewhere." Mae suspected he already did, but she wouldn't mention it. She knew the wrath she would endure if she dared to talk back.

Puzzled by his odd mood swings, she started snooping through his drawers for an explanation for his bizarre behavior. While putting away laundry, she noticed his messy clothes on one side of the drawer. Taking out the shirts to refold them, she found a white powder that she suspected was cocaine. *Are all his violent outbursts triggered by drug abuse?*

Conflicted about bringing it up, she broached the topic lightly.

She left the bag on the top of his dresser, indicating that she had found it. She waited to see if he would mention it and then decide how to handle it.

It wasn't long until Jacob mentioned the empty bag.

"Listen, Mae, I don't want you to think there's a problem," he said, holding the bag in the air. "It's an occasional thing and harmless."

"There is nothing harmless about cocaine."

"Okay, you're right," he conceded.

Mae thought that would be the end of it, but things only got worse as he yearned for more drugs, increasing his intake as the weeks went on.

He was violent both in and out of the bedroom, and Mae was out of ideas on how to stop it. She tried to avoid conflict and stay out of his way, hoping he would eventually get tired of the drugs. To her dismay, he was visibly changing in appearance.

His eyes were often red, and his once-chiseled chin had become emaciated.

Jacob was becoming unreachable. His once gentle touch had been replaced by irrational behavior and condescending remarks. He now viewed her as a domestic servant, expected to cave to all of his needs. She continued to try to repair her marriage, but the once loving man was now consumed by a desire for power and control.

Mae had surrendered, left empty inside.

She had no one to talk to and hadn't heard from Jill since Jacob had texted her, saying never to contact his family again. She'd watched as he scrolled through her phone.

"Is that my phone?"

"It is," Jacob admitted. "I temporarily unblocked Jill's number and took care of that situation for good. I don't think you'll have to worry about her poisoning your mind anymore."

Mae's heart raced.

"What have you done?"

"I told her never to contact you, or I'll ensure she never works again. She knows how powerful I am, and I'll follow through with my threat."

Jacob peered over his glasses, ensuring Mae understood what was at stake for her friend.

Mae had become frightened of what Jacob would do if she disobeyed his requests.

She sank into her life to make matters easier, withdrawing in fear.

The only relief Mae had was her exercise routines. She continued walking in the park, hoping to run into the handsome stranger. Intrigued by her chance to meet with Patrick and his pup Lannie, she looked forward to seeing them both again. Even in the short encounters, she felt heard and respected, something she hadn't experienced in her marriage for a long time.

She was desperate for attention and connection and couldn't recall the last time Jacob had been interested in anything she had to say.

Patrick spent over an hour asking Mae about her hobbies. She realized she didn't have any these days; regardless, he kept pressing, wanting to know more about what she enjoyed doing.

"You must like doing something other than taking care of your kids and housework."

Mae was quiet. "Jeez, I've no idea," she responded.

She couldn't stop thinking about Patrick's comment.

When had her children and husband denied her this, and how had she allowed it?

A wave of panic swept through her, considering how life somehow had gotten away.

The conversation with Patrick replayed in Mae's mind throughout the day. Later that evening, sitting on her bed, she glanced across the room to the mirror and stared at her reflection. She tried to remember the young, energetic woman with curiosity and zest for life, but the image reflected back had vacant eyes, brittle hair, dull skin, and a forced smile.

Patrick, if nothing else, sparked something inside her: curiosity about who she was other than a mother and wife. Her conversation with Patrick that day left her longing for more.

She was bored with her life. The life she'd intended for herself had taken so many wrong turns, leaving her unsatisfied and a stranger living within her own body. She tried to remember when she had forgotten who she was, just existing as a vacant shadow of herself.

With feelings of unfulfillment, Mae turned on her computer and scanned the internet for job opportunities.

She had been thinking more frequently about returning to school, now intent on obtaining a real estate license. It seemed like a random profession at first, but Mae wanted to enter the workforce, and this would fit her schedule because of its flexibility and her need for availability for the boys. She was excited and decided to think more about the prospect over the coming weeks. She hadn't forgotten her dreams of law school either, but it no longer seemed attainable. Jacob would never pay the hefty tuition, and she had no money of her own.

He kept her small in his big world, reminding her regularly of his importance, repeatedly telling her how lucky she was to be married to the smartest motherfucker around.

"You know, Mae, everyone finds me interesting. Amazing that someone like me has been married so long," he said as he slicked back his thick, dark hair. "Women keep coming to me."

"Jacob, what does that even mean?" Mae said with irritation, ignoring his snarky comments and watching from across the room as he admired himself in the mirror.

Whenever Mae thought about her conversations with her husband, she realized he spoke only of himself, his work, or how Mae had failed him.

Desperate to get some space from him, she suggested taking the boys on a small vacation.

"A vacation," he snarled. "Your entire life is a vacation, Mae. You are going to have to wait to spend more of my money."

Defeated, Mae conceded, "I thought it would be nice for our boys, that's all."

By the time she'd finished her sentence, Jacob was already watching the news and had stopped paying attention.

She would head for the park the following day, remembering Patrick's invitation to meet.

Chapter 12

For the first time in over a decade, Mae woke the next day with excitement. She put on her gray leggings that showed off her figure, hiding her tummy and accentuating her bottom. She wore a light blue t-shirt that sat a little snugly on her breasts and applied lip gloss and light makeup, which she hadn't done before. She reminded herself to change before her boys or Jacob could notice her appearance. She had to place her clothes at the bottom of the dirty laundry pile to ensure Jacob wouldn't see the change in her wardrobe.

He monitored Mae's every move, though he spent little time interested in her as his wife.

His cocaine use had not diminished, though it hadn't increased either. Mae couldn't be sure how much he was using, but for now, he'd settled into the routine of weekend highs and, by Sunday evening, dark, moody lows. He was becoming paranoid and even more controlling.

When she had her period, he'd comment on the number of tampons she used and the cost of the product. For a man who was rarely home, little got by him without him noticing.

She was taking a chance by meeting Patrick but couldn't imagine letting the opportunity slip through her fingers. She left the house and headed on the trail, waiting anxiously for him to meet her as they'd agreed. When he didn't show up, her mouth curved down. She looked at her watch, wondering if she had gotten the time wrong. Mae waited, embarrassed, hoping to hear the sound of Lannie's bark in the distance. By half past noon, she had given up and started walking back to her car, humiliated and angry. She heard a deep voice calling her name as she neared the parking lot. When she turned, there was Patrick, looking nervous and disheveled.

"Mae, wait, please," he said breathlessly.

As he approached, she was taken aback by a foul odor.

She looked at him, puzzled, unable to speak.

"Mae, please, wait." Patrick hurried toward her, face flushed. "I'm so sorry," he said, anguished. "Lannie got sprayed by a skunk, and I've spent the morning desperately trying to get the repugnant smell out of her fur."

Mae giggled as she lifted her shirt over her nose to shield the odor emanating from Patrick.

"Well, I've heard some excuses in my day, but this is a doozy," Mae said, smiling.

"You don't believe me?"

"How could I not believe you? You stink!"

The two laughed, and a lightness took over Mae.

She hadn't laughed so freely in ages. Despite the circumstances, she found herself happy.

Patrick promised to get the stench out of his hair and meet Mae the following day with Lannie at the same time. Mae waved as she opened her car door and watched as Patrick hurried away.

As she pulled into the driveway of her house, she felt the ping of her cell phone.

Jacob had sent her a text. 'Where the fuck are you?' He never texted her during the day.

She exited the car and entered the foyer to find his briefcase by the doorway.

Her keys rattled in her pocket as she called him. "Jacob?"

"I'm in the bathroom. Where the fuck have you been? I have a stomach virus, and you're off enjoying the day." Mae could have sworn she heard him say, "You will pay for this, bitch," under his breath but heard the toilet flush soon after.

Thankfully, Jacob was so preoccupied with his illness that there was no further questioning about the afternoon. Mae, nervous that Jacob would still be home in the morning, paced the living room, thinking how she could notify Patrick if that were the case.

She waited to hear stirring from the bedroom to indicate that Jacob was feeling better; instead, there was silence.

Mae slept in the guest room that evening so as not to disturb Jacob. When she awoke, she was surprised by how rested she felt. She looked around the room.

Why haven't I spent more time here? The large windows overlooking the backyard and the small seating area were peaceful and comfortable for solace and reflection.

She stretched her rested body before leaving the bed.

This would be a perfect room for when I go back to school for my real estate license, she thought. The vacancy of that space was sad. Plus, she hadn't been in school since college and knew that with the boys' schedules and her responsibilities to Jacob, it would be difficult to concentrate. She would consider going to the library for quiet time, but Jacob would protest that idea, insisting she be available at home if the boys needed something.

She considered talking to Jacob about it once he was feeling well. She made the bed and walked into the living room, hoping to find Jacob's briefcase missing from the foyer.

Her heart sank; the black leather bag was sitting in the same space it had the day before.

She would not be able to meet Patrick that afternoon.

She had no contact information for him either to let him know she wouldn't see him that day. She hoped he wouldn't think the skunk incident had scared her off. Maybe this was a sign not to meet him at all. Mae felt a surge of guilt and considered never returning to the path. She weighed her options, but leaving her house with Jacob at home would be too risky. Even if he slept all day, he would question and monitor her movements, becoming suspicious if she left.

Mae exhaled, the weight of depression surfacing.

The brevity of excitement had allowed her to imagine life as someone more than a beaten-down homemaker with an overbearing, abusive, narcissistic husband.

As much as she loved her boys, they could also be entitled, spoiled, and demanding, following in their father's footsteps. Consistent runs to fill the refrigerator, loads of laundry, and complaints about dinner only further pushed Mae to her limits. While James was more appreciative of her efforts, Trevor, like his father, was often condescending and disrespectful.

He would use a half-joking tone, but his words stung Mae, leaving her defeated.

He was tall and muscular like his father, and his good looks made him popular with the girls at school, which only fed his ego. Like father, like son.

"Mom," Trevor would say, traipsing through the front door in his dirty cleats. "There better be food ready. I'm starving."

Mae would have dinner prepared in anticipation of the famished teenager.

When he set the baked chicken, potatoes, and string beans down next to him, he would scoff, "Chicken again? Can't you think of something better to cook?"

Trevor would put his head down, clearing his plate and taking seconds.

When finished, he would leave his dirty plate behind and grunt as he left the kitchen. On numerous occasions, Mae would instruct Trevor to clear his plate, and he would reluctantly do so but complain she had nothing better to do and he had to study. After a while, Mae became so accustomed to and exhausted by Trevor's complaints that she succumbed to his disrespect.

She found herself cleaning the kitchen as he stomped away, slamming his door moments later.

On the other hand, James would enter quietly, taking off his shoes and hanging up his jacket.

"Hey, Mom," he would say cheerfully.

James often stayed after school for study groups and meetings, but he was happy to come home at the end of the day to discuss what he had learned at college.

He enjoyed reporting to his mother about his day, providing her with every detail.

Mae appreciated that, unlike Trevor, James cared about what his mother thought.

In recent months, she had noticed Trevor changing.

She couldn't quite put her finger on it, but his moods would swing from high to low. He rarely ate the way he had done weeks prior, and his face was becoming gaunt.

"Are you feeling okay?" she'd ask.

"Yeah, I'm fine. Why do you keep bugging me? You've asked me this three times this week," Trevor said defensively.

Mae eyed her son curiously.

His eyes looked vacant, but before she could question him again, he was already changing the subject. There was something familiar about his behavior, but she couldn't put her finger on it.

"My eighteenth birthday's in three days, Mom. I'll be an official adult. You better treat me like one and stay out of my personal life."

Mae looked at her son blankly. His voice had a different cadence, one that she did not recognize as his. It was more the way Jacob spoke when coming down from a high.

She ignored the signs, trying to keep the home upbeat. The boys noticed their father's dark mood and compensated for the tension by being overly optimistic.

"I can't believe I'll have two adult sons. Time goes quickly," Mae said, looking in the backyard at the old playset she had yet to remove.

She was interrupted by her thoughts as Trevor brushed past, late for football practice.

He had lost track of time a lot lately, and Mae gently reminded him, "Aren't you supposed to be at practice?"

Panicked, Trevor raced into his room to change and was soon out the door.

"Are you sure everything is okay?" Mae yelled as she watched Trevor disappear down the road.

Occasionally, Trevor would share one of his achievements with Mae and celebrate by holding her tightly in a bear hug. As long as the boy was winning and being celebrated, he was in a good mood. When he failed to block a tackle or if his team lost, he became dark, moody, and lashed out at anyone in his way. Mae knew when to leave her bad-tempered teenager alone.

Trevor and James got along well despite having different mannerisms and personalities. If Trevor was sour about something, James could cheer him up.

But when Trevor displayed his dark moods, even James retreated.

The day after Jacob's stomach virus, he returned to work, frustrated to have stayed home.

"What a fucking waste of a workday," he groaned as he left, slamming the door behind him as the rain poured relentlessly, hitting the sidewalk.

Mae watched the large drops spattering Jacob's windshield as he pulled away.

Another day passed, and she was unable to see Patrick then either.

The day after that, James had a doctor's appointment, to which Mae had to accompany him. By the time Friday rolled around, she had thought better than to go for a walk on the path, fearing the universe was intentionally giving her a sign to stay away. Though she was thinking of all the reasons not to pursue Patrick, she found herself longing to see him again.

"This is ridiculous," she huffed. "Why am I putting myself in this situation? I'm not an adulterer." These were the times she most missed Jill. She picked up the phone three times that month and dialed her number, only to lose her nerve and hang up.

Her conversations with her mother were becoming more infrequent too. Jacob made a fuss whenever he checked the caller ID and saw her number pop up.

"Jesus, Mae, why does your mother keep calling?" he asked.

"Jacob, she wants to check in with me and see how the boys are doing. What's your problem with my mother anyway?" Mae felt her face flush.

Jacob had always liked Judy, but now he saw her as a threat.

His fists clenched as he approached. "Don't question me. I pay the fucking bills, and your mother's constant calls are intrusive," Jacob said, his voice rising.

James and Trevor had gone out for burgers, and she was grateful they weren't home.

The conversation with Jacob would escalate quickly, and for the first time, she didn't care. She'd become tired of him controlling her relationships and missed having an identity.

She charged at him uncharacteristically.

"Your mother calls you every day. She visits once a week. If my mother wants to call and check in on her daughter and grandsons, she has every right."

Jacob glared at Mae, his pupils enlarged and his breath heavy.

Before Mae realized it, he threw a plate at her head, then grabbed her by the hair and pounded her face onto the counter. Mae's eyes flickered in disbelief, her head bleeding.

Jacob paused for a moment, realizing what had just transpired. He left the house, slamming the door and saying, "You push me to my limits, you bitch."

When Mae heard Jacob's engine screech down the street, she pulled herself up from the floor, noticing blood dripping down her head for the first time.

Her hands shaking, she reached for a dish rag and put it on the side of her head, putting pressure on the wound. She was too stunned to cry but had gasped in disbelief.

Her boys would be home soon, and she didn't want them to see her in this state.

The burger place wasn't far from home, and it had already been an hour since they'd left.

Mae quickly cleaned up the blood off the floor and checked her reflection to find a small laceration on the left side of her face.

The blood was worse than the injury, and for that, Mae was thankful.

When she heard the car door slam and her sons approaching, she quickly retreated to her bedroom to apply makeup to the slow-appearing bruise. She checked the mirror and put on rose-colored lipstick as she fixed her hair. When she exited her bedroom, the boys were lounging on the couch, surfing the sports channel to check the football score.

"Hey, boys," she said. The boys looked in her direction, giving a quick nod as they discussed the stats of their favorite teams.

"No way, bro," James said as Trevor speculated who would be playing in the Superbowl.

"Bro, you trippin'," Trevor replied, laughing.

Mae watched as the two teens interacted, grateful for their bond.

Her boys were growing up quickly, each handsome in their own way.

As much as she thought about leaving Jacob, she wouldn't want to disrupt the boys' lives.

Plus, there were the finances to consider.

Jacob would be vindictive if she tried to leave. Now that he'd assaulted her, she also began to worry about her safety. Jacob could be capable of doing anything to her or even to the boys as a way to get back at her, his temper increasingly unpredictable.

Mae looked out the living room window at the sunset, hoping Jacob wouldn't return until the boys had gone to bed.

He only usually showed up past midnight.

She heard the engine stop, and with hesitation, the car door slammed shut.

Her body tensed when the keys jiggled and poked into the front door keyhole.

She didn't want another altercation with Jacob, especially with the boys in the room next door. When Jacob walked through the house, she heard the stumbling footsteps, clumsily finding his way through the property. Mae assumed he'd been drinking again.

He had always been drinking lately, blaming it on networking and business meetings, but it had become excessive even on the weekends when he was home.

Mae listened as he stopped at their bedroom door. He hesitated, and to her surprise, she heard him make his way to the guest bedroom. A long-appreciated exhale left Mae's tense body.

Once she knew he wouldn't be entering their bedroom, she fell asleep.

Chapter 13

Neither of the two discussed what had transpired that day in the kitchen. Mae more or less avoided Jacob while he worked hard to be kinder. There began to be a noticeable change in him; he was becoming more appreciative, more loving.

His voice was gentle, his mannerisms softer. "Mae, I'm grabbing a coffee. Can I get you one?" The first time he offered, Mae was caught off guard. She stumbled on her words and mindlessly said yes just to appease him. It was nearly four in the afternoon, and generally, she only drank coffee in the mornings, but Jacob's offer had come out of nowhere.

She had stayed out of his way for the last few days, fearing another altercation. She had nothing to say to him, and her rage was continuing to grow inside her.

Mae had slowly disconnected from her marriage, despising Jacob despite his latest efforts.

Her heart would race when they were in the same room.

Whenever the boys were present, Mae would talk more to them, knowing she was in relative safety while the children were around. If her husband asked her a question, Mae rarely made eye contact and responded as briefly and politely as possible, not to anger him.

She desperately tried to only be alone with Jacob if her sons were present.

Finally, there was a breaking point when both boys left for school, and Jacob stayed behind. He was usually out of the house before they were out of bed, but today, he lagged around, waiting for them to leave. Mae put her cell phone and car key into her oversized coat pocket, ready to make a run for it if she needed to.

"Mae, we need to talk about the other day," he said softly. "I feel terrible. I haven't been able to sleep, knowing that across the hall, you were in our bedroom thinking of me as a monster. I'm so sorry for my behavior. I don't know what's come over me lately. I lost a couple of clients, my boss is on my back, and I'm overwhelmed with the bills."

He looked down in shame, slumping his shoulders. "I lost some money in the stock market too, by the way. Actually, it's a lot of money, and I'm really worried."

Mae looked at him with wide eyes. She tried to speak, but nothing came out.

"Mae, I know I drink too much. I'm selfish and careless with my words and actions, but I want to change. I need to change."

Mae fidgeted with her hands, uncomfortable at Jacob's acknowledgment.

"I think there's more to this, Jacob," said Mae.

Jacob's head lowered.

"The drugs?" she continued.

He nodded, throwing her into a quandary. It was easier to hate him when he was abusive or dismissive, but now he was sorry. In her mind, she had waited for this for years. So, why was it so goddamn hard to enjoy the moment?

She'd been wanting him to change, seeing his flaws, and now that he wanted to make amends, Mae felt nothing. This was too much to handle. She grabbed her purse, donned her oversized coat, and left the house, leaving Jacob tearful in the kitchen with his head in his hands.

Not knowing where she was going, she drove until she found herself by the path where she walked. She glanced at her watch, knowing it was almost the time when Patrick walked Lannie.

She exited her car and started walking, hoping the universe would put him on her path. While her mind was racing, trying to reconcile what Jacob had announced, her heart was searching for Patrick. She had walked almost a mile when her hope began to diminish.

She watched as friends chatted amongst themselves, couples argued, and children played.

It was painfully obvious how lonely she had become. Uncontrollable tears formed in her eyes, streaking down her thin face. Her nose began to run as her eyes swelled.

She found a park bench to sit on and put her hands over her face. Now sobbing, Mae looked around in embarrassment. It was unlike her to show emotion, especially in public. Moments later, when she could compose herself, she stood, unsure which direction to go.

She was drained, tired of putting on a happy face for the sake of others.

Had she grown so invisible?

She kept walking until her legs were tired, catching herself holding in more tears. When she reached her car, there he was, Patrick. Mae's face brightened as her smile widened. Her pace quickened as she approached, giggling under her breath in disbelief.

"Well, well, well, finally," Patrick said lightheartedly.

"P-Patrick. My goodness. How did you—"

Mae was stuttering, unable to form the words as her brain raced.

"I've come back to this spot every day hoping you'd show up," he said with a grin.

"Patrick, look, please, I didn't stand you up. It's just that—"

"Shhh," Patrick said, moving closer. "You can explain as we walk."

"Where's Lannie?" asked Mae, concerned.

"My little princess is getting groomed after what I call the Skunk Episode. Believe it or not, Lannie once again got sprayed. I have about an hour and a half before I need to pick her up. Getting that stench out has taken numerous baths. Silly pup."

Despite Mae being physically exhausted, she suddenly had a rush of adrenaline, explaining the nature of her family life and how unhappy she had been.

She talked for almost an hour, releasing thoughts and emotions, barely stopping to catch her breath. She looked at Patrick sheepishly when she was exhausted from talking.

She hadn't let him respond.

"I'm so sorry. I just threw up every emotion bottled up inside of me for decades."

Patrick looked at her curiously. "Why would you be sorry? I'm honored that you're sharing your challenges." He showed no sign of judgment or hesitation. "Mae, I recently left a marriage, and I know how hard it is to live with a person who breaks your soul."

Patrick stopped walking and faced Mae. "This sounds like more than a troubled marriage. It's abuse, Mae. Do you see that? He's mentally, financially, and verbally abusing you, habitually."

Abuse. The hideous word rang in Mae's ear.

She didn't want to consider it, almost defensive. "Jacob is controlling and isn't always the kindest, but an abuser? I don't know if I'd go that far."

"Abuse comes in different forms. Emotional and financial abuse is still abuse," he said.

Mae looked down at the falling leaves, noticing their radiant colors. She picked one to examine, handing it to Patrick, signaling the conversation was over.

Mae's brown hair fell from its bun as they approached the parking lot, causing it to blow in her face. She pushed back the hair from her eyes as she took in the cool fall air.

Patrick took a card out of his back pocket.

"My cell number is on there. Call if you need to talk or in case of anything."

As she took the card from his hand, Mae brushed her skin against his, excitedly causing her stomach to clench. Their eyes met, and she smiled, grateful for his gesture.

She watched as he drove away in his black Ford pickup truck.

She entered her car. It had been odd to see him without Lannie, but she watched as he lifted his hand to wave in his rearview mirror. Mae had never felt like this about anyone before. She had fallen into her relationship with Jacob, missing the falling in love part.

In any case, it probably would have been impossible to fall in love with Jacob; he was far too in love with himself to allow anyone close to his heart or to care for them.

She couldn't wait to see Patrick again as she rubbed her finger across his name on the business card. "Patrick Bates, Media Marketer," she read out loud.

She had better hide the card for fear that Jacob would find it and ask questions. She opened her wallet and put it in the back pocket of the soft leather bag. Jacob had never sifted through her belongings as far as she knew, but still, she put it into the pocket that kept her mascara.

Smiling, she drove down the road, heading back home.

The boys were home early from practice; as she pulled into the driveway, she could see through the kitchen window that James and Trevor were having a heated discussion. She rushed out of the car and up the stairs, entering the foyer of their brick home. James was trying to grab something from Trevor's hands, pulling a small plastic bag between the two boys.

"What is going on?" Mae demanded.

The boys went silent. Mae looked at James first, noticing his concern, and then she faced Trevor, whose eyes were red and pupils dilated. Trevor's eyes rolled as he steadied himself on the counter. James grabbed the boy, holding him against his body.

"Get the fuck off of me, James," Trevor said, slurring his words.

"Trevor, please, let me help."

Mae looked into her son's eyes, knowing he wasn't sober.

"What did you take, Trevor?" Mae screamed.

"Don't you dare say a fucking word," Trevor said to his brother.

James' eyes pleaded *I can't keep doing this, man.*

"What've you been doing?" Mae knew that a secret was being kept and something serious had transpired.

Trevor pushed away from James' grip, trying to break free.

Mae instinctively ran to Trevor to prevent him from leaving.

"Trevor!" she called out. "Someone better tell me what is going on!"

He pushed past his mother and stormed out of the house, slamming the front door behind him.

James looked at his mother and said, "I'll get him."

Mae paced around the kitchen, trying to figure out what to do. She replayed the conversation between the boys, trying to figure out what had happened.

Mae didn't smell alcohol on Trevor's breath. But what was he on to make him behave so out of sorts?

Forty minutes later, James returned with Trevor in worse shape than when they'd left.

"Mom, I'm sorry. I tried to help him, but he met his guy, and before I could stop him ..." James' voice trailed off.

"What did he take, James?"

When James didn't answer, Mae pounded his chest and screamed, "James, goddammit, what is he on?" Mae's voice was loud, and for the first time, he heard his mother panicking.

"Mom, I'm not sure. It started as painkillers, then oxycodone, and now Xanax."

Mae's head was spinning. "It started out ..." she muttered.

"I wanted to tell you so many times. He promised he'd stop," James cried.

"How long has this been going on?"

"I'm not sure. Maybe three months."

Mae looked at Trevor, slumped on the couch. She could barely recognize her youngest son. Recently, she had noticed that his eyes were hollow and he was often unsteady on his feet.

He'd answer, "I'm fine, just tired."

Mae had thought it was his moody teenage hormones that had him so grumpy.

How did I miss this? she thought now.

She thought back to when the boys would shoot looks back and forth at the dinner table, and she would hear the boys argue behind closed doors and assume it was sibling arguments.

Mae was at a loss; what should she do with this unexpected news?

She quickly googled a helpline and called the number. She didn't know what kind of drugs Trevor had taken, though he didn't seem to be in any imminent danger.

The helpline suggested monitoring him if he didn't appear in medical trouble and discussing this with him tomorrow. The kind lady on the phone provided information and websites as well as therapists to consider. After Mae hung up, she looked at Trevor passed out on the couch, his body smaller than she recalled and his face thinner. She wanted to cry, but she was outraged and scared. James' eyes were wide with fright.

"Mom, is he going to be all right?"

"How many times have you seen him like this?"

James' voice trembled, his eyes glassy. "I don't know, maybe, four or five."

"And it didn't occur to you to tell me!" Mae was angry.

"He told me he'd never talk to me again if I did. I thought I could help him and that it was just a phase," James rambled.

Mae could hear James' whimper as she screamed, "Well, fucking look at him, James! And you're right! You're right that maybe he wouldn't speak to you ever again because he'd be dead, James! He'd be dead! Have you ever thought of that, you stupid child?"

After the words slipped out of her mouth, she began to sob.

"I'm sorry, I'm so sorry. I'm just scared."

Tears rained out of her eyes uncontrollably, and she gasped for air.

James moved closer to his mother, whose head rested on his chest. She could feel his heart racing inside his chest as she buried her face in his warm embrace.

"It's okay, Mom. I'm sorry I didn't tell you. I hate keeping secrets. I wasn't sure what to do."

Mae looked at her much taller son. "I know, sweetie. I'm not mad at you. We just need to make sure he stops this before something terrible happens."

James released his mother's grip and walked to the couch where his brother was still sprawled. He patted him on the shoulder as he went into his own room, quietly closing the door.

This had been traumatic for both of them, and Mae knew he needed time to process it.

She picked up the phone to call Jacob but then put it down. A new panic overtook her; she would have to contend with him berating her for not keeping a closer eye on their son.

Somehow, this would be her fault, and she feared the consequences.

She imagined him screaming at her for being neglectful or foolish.

Oh, and he would be sure to mention that it was her job to keep the kids in line and how he worked much too hard to deal with this shit.

The last two arguments had led to incredible violence.

He would force himself inside of her, pounding her as she screamed in pain.

He would make sure the boys were out when he attacked, ensuring they were not present to witness it. Once the door closed, and they were gone, he would grab her by the hair, screaming profanities. "Fucking useless bitch. You'll have to take what's coming to you."

Mae would be helpless as he unzipped his pants and shoved himself in her mouth, holding her head so that she could barely breathe. Then, he would grab her, smack her across the face, and throw her down while demanding she take down her pants.

He would thrust himself relentlessly from behind, intentionally causing her pain.

When he was done, he would spit on her weak body and say, "That's what you get."

He usually showered immediately after, and when the boys returned from the gym, he would smile at them and casually make small talk.

Meanwhile, Mae would spend the rest of the evening in bed, trembling, while Jacob would complain to their boys that Mom was too tired and too darn lazy to make dinner again.

She replayed the scenario over and over, knowing what she had to do.

Mae looked down to see her hands shaking. She would not tell Jacob.

After their last interaction, it was so easy to trigger him. She would manage this on her own, making sure Trevor stopped this behavior, and Jacob would never find out.

Four hours later, Trevor began to stir, moving his fingers slowly and then his arms.

Mae watched from a distance, careful not to startle him as he awoke. She was inexperienced with drug abuse and gingerly approached her son as if terrified of him.

"Trevor, it's Mom, sweetie," she said faintly.

Trevor's eyes shot open, darting around the room, confused. He felt his face, unable to reconcile what had happened. He reached for the bottle of water that Mae had left on the table next to him, gulping down the liquid at record speed. When he placed the bottle down, he looked at his mom, attempting to explain. "Jeez, Mom, I don't feel well. I must have eaten something bad after I went to the gym." His voice was sincere, almost rehearsed.

Had Mae not been there to witness what had transpired, she might have believed it.

"Trevor, that's not what happened," she snapped. "You know it, and I know it."

Trevor flinched, not expecting his mother to be this blunt.

"What are you talking about, Mom? I'm fine. Why are you always on my case? Dad's right about you. You are constantly nagging everyone and then playing the victim."

Mae knew Jacob would talk poorly about her in front of the boys, but she was disappointed that Trevor would partake in the vile conversation initiated by their father.

Jacob made her out to be the problem within the family. She also knew how convincing he could be. Never mind. She imagined James better understood who Jacob was, but Trevor, closer to his father, seemed to believe every word of his father's rehearsed vitriol.

It was confusing to Mae that Jacob would speak to her one way and then turn on his charisma to become a loving husband in front of the boys.

If he ever paid her compliments in front of the boys, it meant he was stewing about something she was supposed to have done. The constant emotional damage was exhausting.

"Trevor, do you even remember what happened? Mae asked, concerned.

"Mom, I know, I know, I'm sorry. I tried a pill that a friend gave me, and it just got out of control. All my friends do them, and I wanted to be part of the crowd. I swear I will never do it again." Trevor was talking fast, throwing every excuse at Mae.

She sat silently, waiting for him to finish.

Mae didn't know what to make of this situation. She herself had experimented with drugs in her youth, remembering the days of getting high with her friends in the park, taking acid and mushrooms, then eventually losing interest. How could she fault Trevor for the same behavior she'd engaged in as a teenager? She felt like a hypocrite.

But hadn't she taught him the dangers of drugs, warning him of experimenting with the drugs that were available today? "Trevor, I'm worried. How do I know you were experimenting and that you don't have a real ongoing problem?"

"Mom, c'mon, I'm on the football team. I have great grades and plenty of friends. Do you really think I'd manage all of that if I were some sort of druggie?"

It was true. He had just been crowned Homecoming King, and colleges were coming out to scout him for a football scholarship.

A nagging feeling ate at her insides. She ignored the voice in her head and trusted that her son was just experiencing his teenage years, and it had gotten out of hand.

"Trevor, I'm serious. Drugs are nothing to play around with. You can get in a lot of trouble."

Trevor stood up, uneasy on his feet. He braced himself against the wall briefly and then went toward his mother. "Mom, look, I made a mistake. I'll never do it again."

His eyes grew wide as he ran his hands through his hair.

"Promise," said Mae, hopeful.

"Pinky promise, Mom."

Mae looked into her son's eyes, seeing remorse and sincerity. She hugged him once more before he broke away. "I'm going to take a shower. Thanks for everything," he said, walking toward the bathroom. Before he closed the door, he peered his head back out.

"Hey, Mom, can we just keep this between us?"

"Our secret," said Mae.

Mae walked to Trevor's bedroom, hesitating, still not reassured that this was an adolescent mistake. She touched his door before deciding to leave it alone. Jacob wasn't a pillar of an example when it came to sobriety, and Mae wondered, *how much does Trevor know?*

With an unsettling feeling in the pit of her stomach, she sat in the kitchen with a cup of coffee, pensive, looking out the back window. She envisioned her young sons playing, laughing through the toddler years, amazed at the wonderment of what they would now consider mundane.

She enjoyed being a mother these days, even in the challenging times.

But she missed the younger years when life had been simpler.

Now that the boys were both legal adults, a piece of Mae had faded into the background.

She felt free again, something which both scared and excited her.

It was odd for Mae to go from feeling needed to needing her children.

She'd watched them thrive in high school, and now James was busy at college, and Trevor was completing his senior year, she questioned her place. What was she good for now?

Chapter 14

Mae had inquired about getting her real estate license, even mentioning to Jacob her plans to change the guest room into an office but had yet to begin the project or register.

Every time she meant to take the plunge, something got in the way.

Although her top priority now was to ensure that Trevor was being truthful about his drug usage and to keep an extra eye on him, she set a date on her calendar for this Wednesday. It was the date she would register for classes and start cleaning out the guest room.

For the following days, Trevor was on his best behavior, waking early for school, making his bed, and being affectionate to Mae.

James would eye him suspiciously as they got ready for classes. He darted a sympathetic look to Mae, who thought he was too unforgiving of his brother's poor judgment.

When Trevor left for school early to get extra geometry help, James approached. "Mom, don't you think his sudden transformation is odd?"

"I think it's great," Mae said.

"But don't you think it feels a bit forced?"

"James, give your brother a break. He made a mistake. He owned up to it and is trying to be better." Mae's voice was more defensive than she intended.

"Okay, Mom, if you say so, I don't want you to be blindsided again."

"If you know something this time, please, James, come to me before it's too late."

"What about Dad?" asked James. "What does he think about this?"

Mae placed her coffee mug on the counter. "It's complicated with your father. He will only want to find blame, which isn't good for anyone."

James looked at his mother, incredulous. "So, you didn't tell Dad?"

"No, James, I didn't. And you shouldn't either. It will only make matters worse. I have this under control."

James gathered the rest of his belongings, almost forgetting his car key on the counter.

"Have a good day, Mom," he said as he rushed out of the house.

Mae glanced at the calendar hanging beside the refrigerator.

There was a big red X on it for today. *Wednesday, right? Today is the day I promised myself to register for classes.* Mae went online and started filling out the registration forms.

Next, she measured the guest room to see what furniture would fit, settling on a long, red desk with two drawers on each side. She decided to paint the room a warm ivory and accent the space with red lamps, throw rugs, and a large panoramic picture of the San Francisco Bay.

San Francisco had been one of her favorite places as a kid, the picture reminding her of a time when she'd had passion and desire for a life of her own.

She ordered a red picture frame to accent the desk and lamps, a frisson of excitement coming over her body. *Finally, something of my own,* she thought.

That evening at dinner, Mae told Jacob and the boys of her plans; the kids appeared excited about her new endeavor. Jacob looked down at his plate as she discussed her plans for the guest room. Mae hadn't intended to tell Jacob until after the project was complete, but he had gotten home early that night after a meeting was canceled.

"That's great, Mom," James said. "I'm really happy you're doing something for yourself."

Jacob's eyes darted toward his son, who quickly knew to change the subject.

Jacob finished eating dinner, leaving the table to pour Scotch over rocks.

He sipped the drink as he stared off toward the guest bedroom.

It took nearly all day to finish the painting.

She thought of hiring painters but felt guilty about spending money on furniture and the classes. She liked painting, and the room was small enough that it was manageable.

While Jacob scrolled through his phone, Mae spent the evening packing up items from the guest room. Both boys had plans that night, and Mae had time to complete the project.

By the night's end, she was exhausted from packing and cleaning the space in preparation for the furniture delivery due to arrive by the end of the week.

Mae went to bed proud of herself and her determination to finally start pursuing her dreams.

The following morning, she was still in bed when she heard Jacob's voice by the front door, talking to another man. She heard him say, "I'll show you the way," but rolled over and fell back asleep. Three hours later, when she awoke, she made her morning coffee and started her day.

She had overslept by an hour, but thankfully, it was the weekend, so she didn't need to be up to see the boys off to school. She dressed in jeans and a pink sweater, fixing her hair in a messy bun. Jacob would criticize her if she wore pajamas and looked untidy out of the bedroom.

As she was pouring her second cup of coffee, she heard a noise from the guest room.

Carrying the hot liquid, she went toward the freshly painted area to find Jacob walking on a newly purchased treadmill.

He breathlessly said, "I thought this space would be good as a gym. The boys and I can work out together, and you can join us, too. Didn't you say you wanted to get into better shape?"

Mae stood by the door, mouth agape. Tears filled her eyes; she was genuinely speechless.

Grabbing her pocketbook, she stormed out of the house, her head spinning, her body shaking, and her blood boiling. Jacob had done some terrible things to her, but this one was humiliating.

Mae's face flushed, her eyes burned, and her chest felt as though an elephant was sitting on top of it. She raced to her car, started the ignition, and heard her tires squeal.

She didn't know where to go as she sped through the streets, unable to catch her breath as she screamed into the air, "FUCKER!"

Had she ever been this angry before? It was doubtful.

Jacob's smug look burned into her psyche, the look when she'd seen her office become his gym. As it was, he and the boys had memberships at expensive gyms and didn't need this small space. She'd wanted one thing for herself, and he, that bastard, wouldn't let it happen.

He was intimidated by her and would do anything to keep her small.

He was fearful of her success, ready to diminish any goal she set. Time and again, Jacob sabotaged Mae's autonomy, wanting her life to revolve solely around him and the boys.

The problem was the boys were getting older, and Mae grew tired of being used as a domestic doormat. She had long since fallen out of love with Jacob. His vague notion of sobriety and forgiveness were passing thoughts, a sham; he had no intention of stopping his behavior.

As Mae drove, she thought back to the last abusive outburst a month prior.

It was clear that Jacob would now find other ways to torment her into submission.

This time, Mae had had enough. As he lunged toward her when she stood defiant, her chest out, she took hold of the pepper spray Patrick had given her, holding it out toward Jacob.

"You take one step further, Jacob, and I swear—"

Jacob reached for her wrists as Mae kicked him in his groin. He cowered to the floor, looking up as she stood over him with her cell phone out, recording the conversation.

"I have many recordings, Jacob. And even if you get rid of them, I have sent them to people. I will call the police if you come near me again. And I will be sure to post these recordings on every social media platform and to the people at your work. They'll all see who you are."

Mae was done and would follow through with her threats. She suspected that was why he decided to torment her in a new way, to break her down and show her his power and her weakness. The home gym was intended as his revenge for her finally fighting back.

From the pathetic look on his face, he knew she had him cornered.

Mae pulled into a parking spot on the walking path. She put her head in her hands and sobbed, releasing the built-up emotions of Trevor's recent drug usage, James' distancing from her, Jacob's constant abuse, and the overwhelming feelings of defeat. She wanted to escape and start over. As much as she loved her boys, she longed for a different life. A life that she had wanted when she was in college. A life filled with wonder, hope, thrills, and spontaneity. A life without being married to Jacob. A life without being a mother. A life where she did what was best for herself without guilt or shame. A life she knew she missed because she'd let Jacob coerce her into a different direction. She regretted the life she had now and maybe even hated it.

She sank into the driver's seat, pushing her head back against the headrest.

She tried to regain her breath, wiping her nose but letting the tears fall. When she couldn't cry another tear, she noticed the sun was beginning to set.

It set earlier these days, and it already felt late. She was emotionally drained, her eyes swollen from countless tears, and her body weak from exhaustion. Mae exited the car and felt the cool breeze hit her face. She inhaled a deep breath, taking in the fall smell. The cool breeze reminded her of her college days and the bonfires she would go to at the beach. She heard the crackling of leaves blow past as she stretched her legs, startled when a stray cat ran by. She leaned against the car, gathering her thoughts and watching the sun disappear from the sky.

She wasn't ready to go back home, but she had no other place to find solace.

Returning to her car, Mae noticed her pocketbook on the passenger seat. She unzipped the secret compartment where she had put Patrick's number.

She held the card out, staring at it, afraid to ring him.

Then she put the card back into the compartment and zipped it again.

She started the engine and sat momentarily as the heat consumed the cabin, wanting warmth and safety before returning to her house to confront Jacob. She didn't know what she would do or say, but she needed to be calm before addressing him. He would find a way to turn the story around and make her look crazy, same as ever. He had done it so many times before.

She would look ungrateful for not appreciating the home gym he'd made for the family to use and call her selfish for wanting an entire room for her personal use despite him having a study.

She'd have to stay calm and steady to have any impact on Jacob.

She didn't want to appear hysterical or let him think he had gotten to her; otherwise, he'd accuse her of masterminding a plan to humiliate him and damage others' perceptions of him.

No one could ever point out a flaw with Jacob, or he would immediately become defensive. The defensiveness would ultimately lead to anger, and then the anger would lead to abuse.

She had experienced this many times before and had learned to stay calm and quiet. She just didn't know how much longer she could handle being married to Jacob.

She was suffocating within his control, lately wanting to break free more frequently.

For years, she had lived in fear and shame, not even recognizing the abuse. Jacob slowly and intentionally took over her life before she could realize what was happening.

Even now, Mae would question if his intentions were pure or if she was being dramatic. He manipulated situations, making her appear unreasonable.

Even when she called her mother, he would linger to listen to their conversations.

She wanted to express discontent but was afraid of her response.

Unable to handle disappointing her mother with a failed marriage, she pretended to be upbeat and cheerful, though she was dying inside.

She didn't think her mother would believe her because Jacob put on a show when she visited. He was funny, charming, and a wonderful host. Judy would have no reason to think that she was unhappy. Jacob was a spectacular performer in the people's presence if nothing else.

He would be affectionate and helpful to Mae and an attentive host to Judy.

Judy would comment, "What a catch, Mae. I'm glad you didn't make the same mistakes I did. It's nice to see you happy and settled. He's a good man." Mae looked at Judy, hoping she would see the distress in her eyes. "I can rest easier knowing you're being taken care of, baby."

Judy put her hand on Mae's, finally meeting her eyes. "Sweetie, you okay?"

"Oh, yes, Mom, just tired." Then she looked back at her mother; now was her chance. "Actually, Mom, I want to talk to you about something."

Just then, Jacob walked into the living room, holding a tray of desserts and coffee. He darted Mae a look and then glanced at Judy with a soft smile.

"So, what are you ladies talking about?"

His voice was playful, but his eyes did not leave Mae.

"Actually, Jacob, I was just telling Mae how grateful I am that she found such a good man. There aren't a lot of them out there, ya know."

"Why, thank you, Judy. It is nice that *someone* recognizes that," Jacob said.

"Oh, honey, I'm sure my dear daughter appreciates everything you do. Look at this place. It's a palace," Judy said, glancing around the room at the large windows, Persian rugs, and crystal chandelier. "Who couldn't be happy in this home?"

Mae felt her shoulders slump and her stomach curl, knowing she would never escape Jacob or his manipulation. He was too good at it. He was charming, charismatic, and an expert at getting his way. Not even her mother would believe Jacob was a monster behind closed doors.

She would not tell her mother after all. There was no point in it.

Mae watched Jacob take an interest in Judy and her recent high blood pressure health scare. He reminded her, "Well, Judy, let's not do anything to make that blood pressure rise, shall we?"

Judy chuckled under her breath as Mae stared in disbelief.

She wished she could talk to Jill. She would understand. She would never have fallen for Jacob's pretend charm if she were here. No, she'd always give solid advice.

Mae stood up, clearing the crumbs from the coffee table.

Jacob interrupted before she could gather the particles.

"Mae, love, please spend time with your mother. You do too much already." Before she could respond, Jacob had returned the dishes to the tray and disappeared into the kitchen.

Chapter 15

Mae continued with the facade of happiness but planned to leave after Trevor graduated from high school. By then, the boys would be grown, and she wouldn't have to worry about supporting them. Jacob would lavish them with gifts and buy their affection, proving he was the superior parent. Of course, this wouldn't be true, and the boys would see right through it, but they'd play along because it would be in their best financial interest.

She planned to eventually admit the truth to her mother. Just not for a while.

However, for now, Jacob was manipulating Judy too, and Mae was afraid to confide her plans. She had to find another way or be stuck in this situation.

How much longer could she mentally take it, staying in this marriage, defeated and desperate?

Later that week, Mae went out for a drive to escape the tension in the house.

She drove through the dark streets, barely noticing her surroundings.

When she pulled into the first parking lot, she found it was Jake's Pub & Grill. She hadn't eaten, was hungry, tired, and needed a drink to calm her nerves. She found a seat at the bar and browsed the beer selection, settling on a Guinness that went down quickly and smoothly.

By the time the waiter returned to take her order, she had already finished another two beers, feeling tipsy but content. She ordered a burger with fries, enjoying the taste of the meal without having to service her boys and husband.

When was the last time I sat and ate a meal without someone asking me for something? she wondered. By the fourth beer, she realized she had drunk too much and shouldn't drive home.

She replayed the last couple of days in her head: the home gym, the memories of her mother's previous visit, Trevor's drug use. She was exasperated by the weight of it all.

She ordered another beer as she tried to focus her energy on the relaxed feeling of tipsiness instead of the dread that was her life. She reached for her pocketbook to apply lip gloss, and Patrick's business card slipped to the floor.

She reached for it, holding it, contemplating if she should call this late. With the courage of the alcohol consumed, she reached for her cell phone and dialed his number.

A sleepy Patrick answered.

"Hi, Patrick. It's me, Mae. I'm sorry to bother you. It's just—"

"Mae," Patrick said with a sudden excitement in his voice. "Are you okay?"

"Not really. I didn't know where else to go. I'm at Jake's Pub and don't want to return home."

"I'm on my way."

There was a click on the phone, and a sudden panic ran through her body. Feeling the effects of the alcohol, she was grateful that Patrick would soon arrive.

He walked in with baggy jeans and a blue sweatshirt. He ran his fingers through his hair and scoped the bar, looking for Mae, who was taking another large gulp from her glass.

"Whoa there, lady," he said.

"Patrick, thank you for coming. Good to see you. I'm sorry I haven't reached out but there's just a lot going on at home."

"Understood. I'm here now. So, tell me, what's a pretty lady doing at a place like this?"

He set off laughing at the awful pickup line.

Mae found herself laughing for the first time all week. "You do realize that was terrible?"

"Ya think?" he said with a wink.

Patrick ordered a Miller Lite, and the two moved to a table for privacy. Mae told him what had transpired and her troubles within her home. He listened intently, allowing Mae to express her frustrations without interruption. Patrick was a good listener, and since Mae never could express her feelings, she was grateful for the opportunity.

"Wow, Mae, that's a lot. I'm sorry."

"Me too," she said.

A release rushed through her body. Around Patrick, she was relaxed and felt a calmness she hadn't known at any other time in her life.

Thinking about it, when had she ever felt safe around another person?

With Patrick, the conversation flowed easily, and his presence was comforting. The waitress asked if they wanted another round, and before

Mae could answer, Patrick said, "We will take two glasses of your finest tap water when you have a chance."

Mae tilted her head. "You're no fun."

"There will be plenty of time for us to share more drinks together. For now, I have to make sure you're sober enough to get back home and not be a liability to yourself when you get there! Plus, I'm afraid I insist on dropping you off at home. No way can you drive like this."

Mae's face flushed with embarrassment. She didn't want Patrick to think she was irresponsible, and suddenly, she felt foolish sitting across from him in a bar.

"Okay, but what about my car?"

He could obviously see the discomfort in her.

He said, "I know it's a nuisance for you, but you don't want to collect a DUI, do you? That would be a worry. Tell you what, I'll drive us both back in your car and get an Uber back here to collect mine afterward. It's only a few minutes away. What do you think?"

She sheepishly nodded. "I can't believe you'd do that for me."

"Just don't make a habit of it," he said and grinned. "Besides, I need to tell you something, and we can chat on the way back ..."

"Oh? What?" Now, Mae looked worried.

"I don't want to cause more trouble for you, Mae." He hesitated. "But if I'm being honest, I haven't stopped thinking about you since the day I met you."

Now, Patrick was the one with a flushed face.

He took the last swig of his beer and wiped his mouth. "Well, tonight sure has been unexpected," he said, trying to lighten the tone after she said nothing.

Mae stared at him, not sure what to say. "Can I see you again? Maybe when things calm down at home, I can figure out what I'm going to do."

She brushed the hair out of her face, trying to compose herself. "I need to take care of my son and make sure that the other day was really just a one-time thing."

"Of course you do," said Patrick. "When the time is right, we will meet again. Come on, let me drive you home ... in your own car!"

The bar was closing, and Mae's buzz had worn off.

Patrick walked her to her car. The air was cool, but the fresh air helped to ensure Mae's sobriety. "Keys, please," he said in a mock stern voice.

She handed him her key and sat in the passenger seat. She guided him on the short drive.

"I feel so silly. What was I thinking of, having all those beers?"

"Happens to us all," said Patrick. "I'm sure you deserved them!" He chuckled.

They parked a few doors down from her house, and he stood awkwardly by the car and quickly dialed for an Uber back to the grill bar to pick up his own vehicle. Neither of them wanted to hang around in case Jacob happened to see them together, though Patrick had been careful to park her car well out of the line of sight.

"Thanks for tonight," she said. "And for the chauffeur service. Really, I'm grateful."

"It was my pleasure," Patrick said, adjusting his shirt.

"I'll be in touch when I can," Mae said as she exited the car. "Like I said, we'll talk about what you told me." She was reluctant to mention it. For one thing, she had a lot on her mind. "I have to go now before he comes outside ... Maybe he saw the car go by the house."

She didn't know what to say to Jacob, worried about his reaction when she finally went inside.

She rarely went out, and he would either be worried sick or angry as hell, maybe both. Either way, what was done was done, and she had no choice but to face him.

Approaching her driveway, the lights downstairs glared out of the front window.

And worse, wasn't that Jacob's voice, hollering…? There seemed to be an argument inside.

Her heart began to quicken, knowing something must have happened while she was gone. She raced into the house as if her life depended on it. She was dreading going in. Couldn't she even get an evening out without some catastrophe happening with Jacob?

Sure enough, Jacob and Trevor stood in the foyer.

Both men were flushed with fury. Mae got between them, facing her husband, demanding, "What's going on here, Jacob?"

He stared into Trevor's eyes, saying, "Ask your son."

Mae turned to face Trevor, who had a look of pure defiance.

"Dad thinks I stole money from him like I'm some kind of thief." Both men, still standing with shoulders straight and chests out, were not moving. "Maybe if you came home once in a while, you would know I don't steal," Trevor snarled as Jacob stared deadpan.

Jacob's eyes widened.

He jolted closer as Mae pushed him back.

"Please explain what happened," Mae pleaded.

"I left a fifty-dollar bill in the top drawer of my dresser, and it isn't there. When I went to get it, Trevor was in our room looking awfully suspicious."

"I was looking for Mom!" howled Trevor.

Without thinking, Mae interrupted. "Jacob, it was me. I had to grab groceries for the boys and couldn't find my wallet. I took your money."

Both men looked at Mae with surprise.

Jacob's eyes narrowed. Looking at Mae, he said, "So you want me to believe that you took money from my top drawer to buy groceries?"

Mae stood straighter, broadening her shoulders. "It's not like I stole it, Jacob. I needed to run out and was in a hurry." Jacob thought he saw Mae's lip quiver.

"Trevor, get out of my sight. And don't you ever talk to your old man like that again!"

Trevor, relieved, nodded as he hurried to his bedroom.

By this time, Jacob was pouring himself a drink, adding extra vodka.

Before Jacob could question her about where she had been that evening, she excused herself to go for a long, hot shower. When she shortly left the bathroom, Jacob had passed out with a drink in hand. She quietly took the glass from his hands and went to bed, grateful for the distraction but concerned about where Jacob's money had really gone. Because of this, he would not give her any housekeeping money this week, and she would be unable to buy necessities.

The next morning, though with a slight hangover, she reflected on Patrick's blue eyes, quick wit, and winning smile. Even more, she'd enjoyed his company, their conversation, and his ability to listen. Now, she felt even more trapped in the nearly two-decades-old marriage.

Trevor splashed water on his face, looking deep into the mirror. He studied his face as he put three clearing eye drops in each eye to mask his dilated pupils.

He knew he'd got lucky when his mother had walked in and prevented his father from finding out it was him who had taken the money. Why had his mother covered for him? But he was grateful for her quick reactions to protect him from his father finding out the truth.

After all, both of his parents had unknowingly led him down the drugs path.

Trevor reached into his pocket and held out the cash. *This should be enough to pay off the dealer,* he thought. Trevor owed the dealer money, and he was growing impatient with the impending debt. He needed to find a job to afford his three-pill-a-day habit.

Many of his friends drank and smoked weed, and he did neither.

So, why should he not enjoy a little fun too, in his own way?

This is just my thing, he reasoned about his Xanax habit. *We all have vices. Look at my dad; he drinks excessively, and I'm positive he has other women on the side.*

Trevor thought back to when his pill habit had started. He'd accidentally overheard a conversation with his father, who thought he was in the house alone.

Jacob had been making plans for dinner at a fancy restaurant two towns away, with someone other than his mother. The woman sounded excited for the evening, and his father had been pleased by her attention. They were meeting at a hotel, and Trevor decided to follow him.

His mother had gone out for a walk, aware only that Jacob had dinner plans with a business associate. She hadn't questioned him about this; it was a regular occurrence.

Trevor wondered if his mother ever had suspicions that his father wasn't faithful. She was always a bit naive and willing to overlook the obvious.

The fact she was covering for him was to his benefit. After all, his father had walked in to find him hovering over the dresser, so it would have been difficult to deny it much longer.

But Trevor, too, had learned the skill of lying. He would have denied it vehemently, never backing down over any accusation, so insistent that the other person eventually questioned themselves. It was the art of manipulation, and he was becoming a pro like his dad.

Trevor followed his father's black BMW as it raced down the streets.

Clearly, he was a man in a hurry, and Trevor struggled to keep up in his older model car. He watched as his father pulled into the valet area, Trevor parking off to the side, seeing a woman thrust herself into Jacob's waiting arms. She looked familiar. Trevor was sure she was Amanda, the family friend his dad had met so many times before.

Her red highlighted hair brushed over Jacob's arm as her red lips landed on his cheek.

She led him into the lobby as Trevor watched.

In her short black dress and with her long legs, she pranced gracefully ahead.

Trevor knew what was going on and he'd suspected this for years.

How his mother had been blinded by Jacob, he would never understand.

He felt a sudden sadness for his mother, which then was overtaken by rage toward his father. It was only a matter of time until his mother found out, and their family would be destroyed.

He tried to process this information and wasn't sure what to do next.

On his drive home, he stopped to play basketball with his friends in the park, which boasted many community assets such as the baseball field, the picnic area, and a glorious walking path. Trevor took the basketball he kept in his trunk and proceeded toward the courts.

He squinted when he saw his mother there, laughing and smiling in a way he almost didn't recognize. She had a lightness and ease about her that he hadn't even known existed.

Trevor watched in shock as she spoke with a man who clearly wasn't a stranger. His head spun like an amusement ride while he desperately tried to understand everything he'd seen.

He would have expected such an act of betrayal from his father, but his mother broke his heart. He'd expected more from her, and her disloyalty shattered any image he'd once had of it.

He watched as they disappeared farther along the path, a dog following close behind.

He exited the car and began shooting hoops. Then, there was a man leaning against a tree, watching him as he took shot after shot. Trevor stopped bouncing the ball.

"What the fuck are you looking at?"

The man approached. He was short and stocky with a full beard and protruding belly.

"From how you are bouncing that ball, it looks like you could use a friend," he said. "You look furious. Or sad. Perhaps even both."

His features were dark, and his voice deep. "Bet I could make your day better."

"I don't think so," Trevor said.

"My name's Tony. Let me give you something to take the edge off."

"No thanks, I'm good."

"Suit yourself," said the man, walking away.

"Wait, what do you have?" Trevor asked as he ran to catch him up.

"This one's on the house. It will take your troubles away. If you want more, you know where to find me."

Trevor looked down at his hand, now holding a small blue pill in a tiny plastic bag. He pushed it deep into his pocket and shot hoops until the sun went down.

Later that night, in bed, he held the tiny bag in his hand, examining the pill.

Trevor heard his mother come in from her errands. She knocked on his door, and Trevor quickly put the bag under the pillow before she entered.

"Trevor, are you okay? You barely said a word at dinner tonight."

"Yeah, Mom, I'm fine."

"I started exercising at the park today. You should go. There's a lot of kids your age that hang around there," she offered.

"I'm sure there are," Trevor said as he stared at his ceiling. *And there are men, too.*

"Well, if you need anything, I'm right in the other room. Goodnight, Trevor."

"Night, Mom."

When she left, Trevor reached for the pill out of the bag and swallowed it.

Before a minute had elapsed, the feeling of ease spread through his mind and then his limbs.

He was flying freely outside his body, watching his movements in slow motion, both numb and elated. Finally, he felt an escape from knowing the truth about his parents' sham of a marriage. His life had been a scam, a lie, a fraud, and all the while, the two people who were supposed to love him most were the ones who had been his deceivers.

He wondered if James knew or even cared.

He wanted to confide in him, to tell what he'd seen, but was afraid James would confront their mother. James had always been closer to Mae and would protect her by finding a reason for what he had seen. Even worse, what if his brother wouldn't believe he was telling the truth?

Either way, it didn't matter; Trevor knew it, and the feeling of lightness helped him forget.

Trevor slept better that night than he had in a long time, and by the time he awoke the following day, he was already thinking about euphoria.

He washed up and went to school, struggling to stay focused.

"Trevor, are you listening?" the teacher scolded.

"Yeah, sorry," Trevor replied.

By the end of the day, depression seemed to have set in.

He felt as though an anchor was weighing him down to the bottom of the sea. He tried to catch his breath, but inhaling the air would get caught in his throat. At practice, he ran laps, trying to flee his thoughts, but he was left feeling like a caged animal. The information was too much to process alone, yet despite his popularity, he had no one to confide in.

After practice, Trevor was the last to leave the locker room, not wanting to go home.

His coach had noticed his unusual quietness. "Trevor, are you all right?"

"Yeah, fine," he muttered. "Just have a lot on my mind."

The coach, assuming, replied, "There are a lot of hard choices to make in senior year. I have confidence you will choose the right college. Don't be so hard on yourself. You'll figure it out."

Trevor just nodded, not correcting his coach. How would he even begin to explain what he'd witnessed? Trevor was embarrassed, shame filling his insides like poison.

Trevor started to drive home when he saw signs to the park. He put on his turn signal to quickly make a U-turn. En route to the park, Trevor began driving slowly.

Was Tony there? After several minutes, he saw the man at the same place where he'd first met him, over near the basketball hoops.

He quickly got out of his car, first looking around to ensure he didn't know anyone who might be at the park. When he was sure he hadn't recognized anyone, he approached Tony.

"Hey, what the fuck did you give me yesterday?" Trevor said, aggrieved and worked up.

"Give you?" Tony said cautiously, not knowing if he was being set up. "What exactly are you looking for, young man?"

Tony wasn't new to this and vetted potential customers before revealing too much. He already had a rap sheet for possession of drugs, and the last thing he needed was more legal trouble.

"You know what I'm talking about. It was great. What do I have to do to get more?"

"Two pills to paradise for thirty dollars. Cash."

"I only have ten," Trevor said, rummaging through his backpack.

Tony looked around, considering the offer.

"This one time, I'll do ten. After that, my fee is thirty bucks."

"Please, man, can you make it twenty? I'm in high school." Trevor held the ten-dollar bill in his hand, desperate to negotiate.

The man snatched it from Trevor's hand and handed him a bag containing two small pills. Trevor nodded and rushed back into his car, making his way home.

Nothing could replicate the first pill he'd ever taken, and Trevor desperately tried to emulate the feeling he'd had during his first experience.

However, even temporarily, the release from reality was worth his spending. Trevor had been saving his birthday money for when he went to college.

With the money dwindling, he had to find another way to get cash. He could get a job, but that would mean not having money temporarily until payday.

The first time he had stolen was from his mother.

Her purse had been left on the counter, and while she was folding laundry, he went into her wallet and took a twenty. Mae never paid mind to the cash she held and probably would never notice it was missing.

The next time, he found a couple of dollars crumpled up next to James' nightstand, and he quickly took them, knowing James would notice but would never suspect his brother.

He would assume he'd misplaced it and soon forget about it. His father was a bit more complicated because he was meticulous with his belongings, especially his money.

Jacob kept petty money in his top drawer to tip the servers at restaurants he frequented. When Trevor entered his father's room, he didn't think he was home. He froze when his father left the main bathroom, and Trevor said, "Oh, I was looking for Mom. I thought I heard her here."

He walked out, and it wasn't until later that night, when his father was getting ready for a business meeting, that he noticed the money had gone missing.

Within weeks, Trevor's need to get high was no longer a desire but a habit. Even if the euphoria was temporary, Trevor was more frequently desperate to escape.

He calculated when he'd take the pill, knowing that if he got caught, he would be forced to stop. With that in mind, Trevor would swallow the pill as he relaxed in his room at night, processing the day's events. It was his way to unwind and forget that both his parents were deceitful, his way of feeling something other than anger.

Trevor had never felt worthy, and now, knowing his parents put their needs before his, it cemented his insecurities. Outwardly, Trevor had a fast mouth, a quick smile, and was uncannily charismatic. Hidden behind his bright eyes, however, lurked a dark side.

He never let people know that behind the tall, handsome boy lay a scared boy feigning attention. Mae did her best to satisfy his appetite for love, but the truth was, it would never be enough. His longing for infinite attention could never be satisfied by anyone, but these little pills did everything he wanted and more. They made him feel protected and powerful.

Anyway, no one would really care; even his mother preferred his older brother.

Trevor didn't think there was room for him in his mother's life.

She would engage with him, but as soon as James walked in the door, the dynamic would change, and Trevor would be left in the background.

He'd often hear tense whispers between his parents behind closed doors. He couldn't always make out what they were saying, but usually, it meant listening to his father calling Mae a bitch.

However, when they emerged from the bedroom, Jacob would smile at his sons and ask who wanted to order a pizza while his mother could be heard quietly sobbing in the shower.

The boys never interfered or asked their mother if she was okay. Instead, she would emerge with swollen eyes and a fake smile, asking if the boys had eaten yet.

Jacob would comment, "Of course they have, Mae. Did you think we were going to wait for you to cook? I took care of it. Like I always do."

Mae never responded to his comments, keeping busy cleaning the kitchen as the men in the house watched the game in the living room, shouting at the television and arguing the plays.

Trevor noticed the sadness in his mother's eyes but didn't know what to do about it.

During their father's rage toward her, Trevor would be kinder and gentler to their mother, knowing she had enough to deal with already.

He suspected it was a one-sided gripe because he never heard his mother raise her voice in return, except in an attempt to keep Jacob quiet. His father berated his mother any chance he got, and no matter how hard she tried, she could never live up to his expectations.

For one thing, she always seemed to be on a diet because of Jacob's cruel comments.

Trevor understood his father in a way the rest of the family couldn't. Although his father was complicated, demanding, relentless, and sometimes cruel, he was also quick-thinking and quick-witted, making him charming and endearing to strangers. Trevor shared many of his father's traits, both good and bad. He could relate to Jacob.

Trevor would watch as James and Mae enjoyed the cool breeze, the smell of blooming flowers, and the way the moon smiled down from the sky.

He admired that the pair was mesmerized by simplicity, but he was also agitated by their lack of focus. Like his father, Trevor wanted to enjoy the same success and all the gusts of life.

The personality differences made an invisible wall between Trevor and his mother, and the feel of the drugs as they ran through his body took away the shame and disappointment.

James woke up still tired from the night before after partying with his new friends from college.

He'd been excited to be included in the rave at one of his friends' dorms, later stopping with them for a late-night snack at the local fast-food restaurant. He was proud of himself for putting himself out there and finding new friends. By nature, he was an introvert.

Finding it impossible to blend in with crowds or groups, he vastly preferred staying in.

But, on this particular night, he'd accepted a party offer and was glad he had.

Now, James looked around for the eight dollars change from the burgers.

Hadn't he shoved them in his blue jeans lying on the floor amongst the other dirty garments? He double-checked his wallet and shirt pocket, but the money had vanished.

"Shit," he said. "I must have dropped my change, walking to the car from Burger Joint!"

This wasn't the first time he'd done this, and he was growing increasingly annoyed with his own irresponsibility. *I must remember to put the money back in my wallet before shoving French fries down my throat*, he thought. "Fucking idiot," he mumbled.

As a last-ditch effort, he looked under his bed to see if the money had fallen beneath it; but he found nothing. Mae walked in to find James down on all fours, frantically searching.

"Maybe it's time to do your laundry, buddy," she said, chuckling.

"There's that and the fact I lost money again," James said, frustrated.

"When else did you lose money?" Mae asked, now with a hint of suspicion in her voice.

"Ugh," James said. "I don't even know. Twice this week, I had change from the money I spent, and I must have dropped it. I could have sworn I put it back in these pockets, though."

Mae studied the room in disarray. She helped sort out the clothing scattered on the floor, but all the time, she was mumbling, "James, you need to look after your money better."

As she sorted everything, she lifted things, shaking them as if thinking the money may drop out. James and Mae even went to the kitchen to check the counter when the money didn't show up. Mae's face brightened; she spotted her purse on the hook between the foyer and kitchen.

"It's not like James to lose money," she mumbled to herself. "I don't want him stressed out over cash, so I guess it's a case of letting him rely on the Bank of Mom. Just this once …"

She reached into her purse and pulled out a ten, a five, and three singles. "That's odd," she said. She looked through the purse pockets, evidently finding nothing.

She stood at the counter for a moment as if retracing her steps.

James returned to his room to recheck his nightstand.

Mae stood for a while, looking a bit perplexed. "But I'm sure I should've had a twenty as well," she shrugged, walking into James' room.

"James, here. Take this. I have an extra fifteen dollars. You can use this until you get paid."

Grateful, James said, "Ah, Mom, thanks. I appreciate it. I'll be more careful next time. I thought I'd put the change in my pocket, but I guess not."

Mae left the room as she patted her son's arm, giving him a small smile.

James carefully folded the money, this time putting it in his wallet.

He was grateful for his mother's generosity.

After Mae left the room, James returned to looking under his bed. There, he found the brochure for the University of Florida that he had hidden a year earlier.

He had almost forgotten that he'd also hidden the acceptance letter and scholarship information. How would life have been if he had gone away to college and pursued his career as an engineer? He'd never revealed to his mother that he'd applied and been accepted, wanting more than anything to be on his own.

If he'd told his parents this news, they would have insisted he take the opportunity.

As the day came and went to accept his admission and scholarship, he felt more obligated to stay home and attend a community school.

His mother had already given up so much for him; she would have been left with a tremendous void. James hated feeling responsible for his mother, but he had to protect her vulnerability. There was also an odd sense of loyalty toward her, perhaps because he had known that he'd started life as an unplanned pregnancy.

Instead of terminating his life, she, in essence, had terminated her own.

James never knew this firsthand; he'd overheard it in an argument between his parents.

"You fucking dote on James more than on me, and you didn't even want him!"

When James heard his father's accusation, his heart sank, not believing it was true.

"For God's sake, Mae, you were so depressed after you had him, we had to put you on medicine for you to even function. So please, don't try to be the doting mother now. You fucking never wanted that kid, and you know it!"

James believed his father was just being cruel until he'd listened to his mother reply, "I never wanted to be a mother at all. You intentionally got me pregnant, and it ruined my life. Chained to the home as a mother, I hated my life so much, I wanted to die. This is all your fault."

There it was. James knew the truth; he'd been unwanted, and his mother had been tricked into this life. The words rang in his ears like a relentless church bell.

He could not deny what he'd heard, and there was no one he could tell. James went to bed that night with gnawing in his stomach and a hole in his heart.

From that moment, his life would never be the same. It brought tears to his eyes every time he saw his mother, shame burning in him.

He was the reason her life had never amounted to what she'd planned.

Instead of becoming cold and despondent, though, James worked hard to please his mother, trying to show her that his life had been worth keeping.

He did well in school, showed her affection, and followed all the rules.

Mae, in return, clearly grew into the role of motherhood. James knew he was loved and adored by his mother despite the fact he hadn't been planned. In her defense, he'd never felt that his mother regretted having him but did get a sense that she was missing a piece of herself.

Mae had talked about college and her aspirations of traveling abroad when she was younger, encouraging James to do the same; she'd said she was excited that his chosen university had a three-week overseas program.

"Look, it's a one-time offer, so go!" she'd said. "It's good to expand your horizons!"

He did not go, preferring to stay close to her.

James was happy when he heard about his mother's interest in real estate; she would study, and to this end, he knew she'd planned to turn a small room into a place to do her college work.

So, it was odd that she changed that space into a home gym. He had meant to ask her about it, but his mother had just disappeared that night, and he simply forgot to inquire further.

The house was tenser than usual when she returned; the apparent coldness between his parents was uncomfortable, and now, Trevor was acting oddly, too. He would usually go into James' room and boast about his football stats or gossip about the recent high school drama.

Lately, though, he'd been all too quiet and had barely spoken to James. His eyes held a haunted, hollow look as if he hated everything around him.

Was Trevor angry at him over something?

But no. It wasn't like Trevor to hold in his emotions. James thought he'd been secretly dating a girl from school that he wanted to keep quiet, but Trevor seemed too insular for even that, locking himself in his bedroom at night and sleeping far too long.

One night, when James knocked on his brother's door and didn't get an answer, he walked in to find him asleep, yet still in all the clothes he had worn to school.

It struck James as odd, and he wondered if he was getting the flu that had been going around. He approached his bed and put his hand on his brother's head, checking for a fever.

He felt cool, and as James turned to leave quietly, he noticed an empty, small plastic bag next to Trevor. He picked up the bag and placed it back down, not considering anything suspicious.

Then he walked out of his brother's room, shutting off the lights and closing the door.

He found his mother in the living room, staring off into space.

"Hey, Mom, what's with Trevor? He's been sleeping a lot."

"Yeah, I've noticed that too," she said quietly.

"Maybe he's coming down with something," offered James.

"Maybe," Mae said, not making eye contact with her eldest son.

James attempted to say something else to his mother but returned to his room, leaving her with her thoughts.

Mae sat on the living room couch, paralyzed by her ruminations. She tried to reconcile the change in her son, the money missing, and Trevor's odd behavior. She tried to understand what was happening but didn't want to be an alarmist. Overall, Trevor was still attending practice, getting good grades, and was almost always accounted for when he went out with friends.

Mae was considering if she was paranoid or overprotective or if there was something more. Her gut was screaming at her, but she had nothing specific to confront Trevor with except for a weird feeling. Knowing Trevor, he would laugh and say casually, "Mom, relax. I'm fine. You don't need to worry about me. I'm good." He would flash her a smile and be off in his room, leaving her feeling foolish. Like his father, Trevor had a way of twisting reality, leaving Mae perplexed and insecure. Mae wanted to talk to someone about her fears.

Someone who would understand and listen, but at times like this, she felt most alone.

Jacob was mainly emotionally and physically unavailable, and she didn't trust him to handle her concerns. She couldn't talk to her mother about it because she would insist that she tell Jacob. The last thing she needed was Jacob's criticism as she sorted out what to do next.

She reached for her cell phone and searched for Patrick's name.

Talking while the boys were in the house wasn't safe. Also, Jacob came home randomly, often with the smell of bourbon on his breath and unsteady on his feet, so Mae didn't want to take the chance to call. In any case, it was half past ten, and it would be difficult to explain a wrong number at that time of night. Instead, she settled on texting Patrick.

'Hi Patrick, it's Mae. Are you up?'

Mae waited to see if he would respond or if he was otherwise occupied. She didn't know whether Patrick was dating or he had a bunch of friends he went out with on Thursday nights.

As Mae thought about it, she didn't know much about Patrick at all, other than what they'd talked about that night at the bar, and she'd done most of the talking.

Suddenly, she felt foolish. A rush of shame came over her, and she instantly felt silly sending a text to a man she barely knew to talk about her family problems.

"What am I thinking?" she grumbled. She threw her phone on the coffee table in the living room and went to the kitchen to pour herself a glass of wine. She rummaged through the pantry for a snack and settled on chips and a handful of almonds.

As Mae walked back through the kitchen to the living room, she caught sight of her reflection in the mirror that hung in the foyer. Her hair was messy, and she had been wearing an old pink sweatshirt from which the logo had worn off long ago. She paused momentarily, staring at herself, and her stomach turned with disgust at the person looking back.

How did I let this become my life?

Mae had felt a deep sense of being unsettled for years, and in recent months, those feelings had overtaken her soul. A pounding in her chest began rising as she entered the living room, placing her wine and snacks beside her phone on the coffee table. She took a long gulp of the wine, feeling the sweet liquid flow down her throat as the essence of grapes filled her senses. She finished the glass and made her way back to the kitchen, this time to bring the rest of the bottle.

As she felt the room slowly move around her, she thought about all she had sacrificed for her family, also about her regrets, and the awful feeling of doom she experienced every day.

Something inside her snapped, and she could no longer stay in the marriage or the life in which she had resided. She was no longer afraid of the finances or the emotional downfall that would eventually happen. Instead, she knew that if she didn't do something, the emotional pain would take hold of her, and she wouldn't ever manage to recover. She thought of the boys, but she had given enough of herself, and it was time to finally put her needs first.

By the time she finished the rest of the wine, her head was spinning, but her decisions were clear. Essentially, she was holding everyone back, especially herself and her peace. She'd seen glimpses of happiness through the years but couldn't recall a time when she'd felt truly content.

She had been going through the motions, getting by each day, slowly dying inside. The young, energetic person she once was had now become a distant memory.

She wanted to feel alive again.

She had fooled herself that she was content in her life after Trevor was born, fearing the cost of her independence. Things were different now. She welcomed independence, even at the price of the demise of the life she had been living. *Was* it even her life she had been living?

Or was it the life designed to keep her small to accommodate Jacob and the boys?

As she thought of her circumstances, it dawned on her that 'her life' wasn't hers at all.

It had been nothing she'd wanted, ever.

In her semi-drunken stupor, reality came crashing down on her like waves against the sand. As her thoughts raced, she saw everything flash before her eyes.

She'd been a young girl when she met Jacob, never expecting much from a relationship. She was having fun and planning for her future, which never entailed marriage. However, as she thought back on that time, slowly, her memory began to zone in.

Her mother had pushed so hard for the relationship with Jacob. She'd encouraged her to allow Jacob to pursue her, even though she'd continually told her mother of her plans to travel abroad.

She even recalled when Jacob and her mother would talk on the phone, having secret conversations. Was her mother charmed by Jacob enough to help him manipulate Mae into this life? She couldn't be sure. However, as she sat and dug deep into her memory, she knew her decision to marry Jacob and have the baby was never based on her wants but on making her mother proud. Her mother wanted Mae to have a stable husband, finances, and family.

Instead, Judy worked hard, scraping by, leaving little time to mother her child.

Mae suspected that her mom wanted more for her daughter. To ensure that, she clung to Jacob, failing to realize that she could make a future on her own. She didn't need Jacob or any man to do that for her, and she wished her mother believed that as well.

It had been drilled into Mae's head to find a stable man since she was a child.

Watching her mother work hard only made Mae crave independence, so she never had to rely on anyone. However, as childhood trauma would go, Mae's internal message was to find safety, not trust herself to make her own future, and therefore, here Mae was, as lost and alone as her mother, only with the comfort of money. More importantly, she was miserable and didn't want to accept these feelings for one more day. Her mother would object to her decision to divorce Jacob. She imagined the hurt and worried look on her face.

It hurt to think of disappointing her, but it terrified her to disappoint herself any longer.

Deep down, the little girl often left home alone because her mother worked so many hours to provide for her; she just wanted to make her mother proud, to make her mother feel that her sacrifices were worth all the hard work she'd poured into her only child.

Mae understood her children felt similarly. She suspected James longed to leave to go away to school, that Trevor was miserable living in the tense-filled house, and that Jacob had emotionally left the marriage long ago. They were all stuck in lives with which none of them was satisfied.

Staying in this cycle wasn't suitable for anyone.

She went to bed that night feeling an unusual peace, knowing that changes were on the horizon and understanding that there had been a profound shift.

Chapter 16

Jacob hadn't arrived home until way past midnight, and Mae was already in a deep sleep. He noticed the empty wine bottle, crumbs from the leftover chips, and the single glass on the living room coffee table. He found it odd, as it wasn't like Mae to leave dirty dishes around, but he headed to bed himself after a night of drinking and entertaining his not-so-secret girlfriend.

Jacob had no idea that night that his life would inevitably change. He probably would have been happy going through life as it was. He'd got the best of both worlds. He had a wife, two kids, little responsibility to care for them, and an entirely separate life outside his marriage. It was a win-win for Jacob, but his image and living arrangements would soon be altered.

He'd married Mae to escape the control of his mother, knowing they weren't suited for one another. His resentment toward his mother's controlling ways was buried deep inside of him, and his anger was taken out on Mae. She'd never wanted any of this, feeding into his insecurities.

When Mae woke up the following morning, her head felt as if a hammer pounded from the inside out. She was foggy from the night before but clear what she had decided. Instead of second-guessing her decision and allowing the excuse of alcohol to hold her back, she was more committed than ever to divorcing Jacob and starting to live her life. She reached for her phone to check her emails, and there was the text she had sent Patrick the previous night. Mae had carelessly forgotten to check her phone after reaching out to him, distracted by her thoughts.

Her heart skipped a beat when she read the response:

'Mae, Hi. How are you? I'm up. Call me.'

Consequently, when Mae didn't respond after an hour, he sent another message:

'I guess I missed you. I'm around if you want to talk.'

And then, an hour after that, there was one last message.

'I guess you fell asleep. Sweet dreams. I hope to hear from you again soon.'

Mae's heart whirled with excitement.

She wanted to text him back and see him again, but right now, she needed to keep her focus on her life. Mae vowed to heal and get her life in order before contacting him again.

She took a quick shower and searched the internet for divorce lawyers providing free consultations, wanting a female attorney. When she stumbled upon the name Linda Steer, she strongly wanted to call. With her hands shaky, she dialed the number on her cell phone, reminding herself to delete the call log.

That midmorning, on a brisk day as the sun shone, Mae took the first brave step to file for divorce. Her consultation wouldn't be until the following week, and under the receptionist's recommendation, she would take that time to collect financial paperwork lying around the house.

Mae didn't know where to start, but she needed to be discreet.

She didn't want Jacob to know her plan, fearing he would destroy documents, transfer funds, or worse, cause harm to her or the boys. She had no choice but to blindside him for her safety and future security. She quickly went through their files, making photocopies of bank statements and searching through papers for any documents that might be useful.

These were the times when she wished she'd paid more attention to their finances.

Jacob took care of those issues, insisting it was easier for him to manage the finances and Mae to handle the home. When it was time to sign tax documents, she would briefly flip through them, but Jacob would immediately insist she just sign them so he could mail them back.

Now, though, she was determined to uncover their financial status along with the information she could gather to help her case during the divorce.

While looking through the files, it appeared some papers were missing.

She had heard Jacob in the office the night before and wondered what he was doing so late at night, looking through documents. She didn't think he was aware of her meeting with the lawyer; there was no way he could have known.

Before lamenting that possibility, she continued her search through the paperwork.

She didn't have much time before the boys returned from school, so she wanted to be sure she could calm down her already overactive nervous system.

Mae had a little time before her meeting and intended to spend the next few days sifting through the paperwork. By the end of the day, she was exhausted but spent time researching her rights. There still wasn't as much financial information as she had hoped to find.

Maybe Jacob keeps the papers elsewhere, she thought. She looked in his closet and under the bed, but there was nothing. Although frustrated, she smiled, knowing she was slowly regaining her power, and each day, she felt the weight of the last years lifting off her shoulders.

In the following days, a new energy emerged for Mae. She found herself waking up, changing into her workout clothes, entering the now family gym, and spending over an hour working out. Afterward, she would shower, allowing the water to wash away the sweat and any hesitation that might be creeping in about her decision to divorce. Mae would wear jeans instead of her usual leggings, apply make-up, and even squirt a spray of her favorite perfume. Within days, her confidence was growing, as her waistline was ever so slowly getting slimmer. She no longer ate generous portions but instead chose vegetables and drank excessive water.

In the past, she would drown her lonely feelings in a bag of chips. Now, she went on the treadmill and walked two miles in the evenings.

Her boys were impressed with her transformation and attitude.

"I guess the home gym has been useful," said James.

"I'm so glad your father insisted on it," Mae said breathlessly as her speed increased, walking now on an incline. Mae was, of course, being sarcastic, but she didn't know if James had picked up on it. She gave him a wink and started a light jog as he left to finish homework.

Trevor had already gone to sleep for the night, and she had been seeing him less and less.

She tried to catch him in the mornings before school, but lately, he had been oversleeping and running late. After practice, he texted Mae that he wouldn't be home for dinner and would stroll in by eight. It was early enough not to raise red flags but different enough that Mae noticed.

Later that evening, Mae asked James, "Does your brother have a girlfriend he's hiding from the rest of us?"

James fidgeted with his hands, nervous.

"I was wondering the same thing," James said. "If he does, he hasn't shared details with me."

The cadence in James' tone made Mae suspect he knew more than he was saying.

Mae dismissed it as a brotherly bond and figured that if Trevor wanted her to know about a girl he was seeing, he would eventually tell her.

She thought back to months prior when Trevor had experimented with drugs; she was grateful it had been a fleeting teenage moment. Now he was out with a secret girlfriend, home by eight, and still at practice after school, she breathed easier. All the worry about the situation was gone.

The nagging feeling that something was off about her youngest son still haunted her, but she shrugged it off as the insecurity of a mother. She reflected on her teenage years and the irresponsible things she'd experienced, grateful that her boys got into very little trouble. With the exception of Trevor, they had given her extraordinarily little to worry about.

Mae tried not to think about her son's unhappiness. It made her feel like a failure as a mother, and all of the sacrifices would be for nothing. Her boys had just about grown up, and it was time they became more independent, and Mae found an identity of her own. She understood how her mother felt, wanting an easier road for her children.

As the days passed, Mae continued her endeavor. She collected piles of tax returns and banking statements and even found an overseas account. She made copies of everything, meticulously labeling each year in its appropriate folder. Mae hid the file under the mattress, secretly proud of herself for being so successfully deceptive. *He sleeps at night on his own demise,* she thought as she placed the now-expanding folder back in its hiding place.

While going through the papers, she found a folder with a large manila envelope inside. The years of it being stuffed in the file cabinet were evident by the creases and the ink that once had said in purple letters, 'Jill & Mae's Adventures,' now faded. Inside were pictures of her college days with Jill. She studied one photo of the two sitting side by side, laughing. Jill's red hair glistened under the sun, and Mae wore a large smile as the two drank beers by the river.

She missed Jill and realized that Jacob had ruined that friendship, and she had allowed it.

So many years had passed, and Mae wondered where Jill was now.

She picked up her phone, searched her blocked callers, and recovered Jill's number. Mae dialed the digits she'd once known by heart, hoping Jill still had the same phone number.

On the third ring, her voicemail picked up. "Hi, Jill. It's Mae. I came across some pictures of us from college, and I just wanted to tell you I've been thinking about you." Mae hung up the phone, surprised at her vulnerability, hoping Jill would receive the unexpected call well.

As she rifled through more of her college memories, her phone rang.

"Jill, hi. Oh good, you got my message."

There was a brief silence on the other end. "I've been waiting for this call, hoping one day it would come."

They talked for hours, Mae telling her all that had transpired through the years. Mae said at the end of the call, "I miss you. I want to see you."

"That would be nice," Jill responded.

They made plans to get back in touch in the coming month once Mae was more settled with the divorce proceedings. For now, the call gave Mae the confidence to go through with filing for divorce. She looked forward to her appointment with the divorce attorney, though she had trouble sleeping the night before, filled with nerves and anticipated excitement.

When Jacob left early the following morning, he commented, "Why are you up so early?" with a hint of suspicion in his voice.

"I want to get a head start on the day. I've been working out a lot. I know you mentioned last month that I was starting to look like a—"

She searched her memory for the word. "What was it again? Oh, right, a heifer."

Jacob looked at his wife with a moment of regret but said nothing. He then gathered the rest of his belongings and hurried out the door.

Before closing it, Mae said, "By the way, love the home gym. Nice call. It's the best thing!"

Jacob looked over his shoulder and shook his head in disbelief before starting his engine. He drove off as she waved at the front door, noticing him looking perplexed as he stared in his rearview mirror. Mae chuckled as she closed the door of their house. She made all the beds as the boys slowly began to wake, hearing the shower go on and the bathroom door close.

She fixed them breakfast, a task she had done their entire lives. As she was buttering their toast, she decided that would be the last time she made breakfast regularly for her adult sons.

She watched the two young men shove toast in their mouths as they hurried out the door for the day. As Mae watched the boys leave for school, she leaned against the door, relieved.

Then she dressed quickly, gathering the papers that sat neatly in a folder.

On her way to the attorney, her mind raced with anticipation and fear. She was unsure what to expect or how the attorney would receive her. While she had gathered information and researched her rights, she was still uncertain whether she could manage financially. Would the attorney judge her for not working outside the home or view her as weak and pathetic?

Mae felt inferior to most women because she'd allowed herself to be controlled by a man, and she'd given up her financial power to stay home with her children. Thus, she had forfeited her career, now deemed less than in the eyes of society. Mae's perception might have been skewed, but she still couldn't help but feel humiliated by her circumstances. Trying to remove her negative thinking, she opened the windows and put the radio on to drown her thoughts.

Once parked and after entering the law office, she was impressed by the large plants and the fragrant smell of vanilla from a candle burning on the receptionist's desk.

"Good morning," the woman greeted. She had dark brown hair and green eyes and wore large glasses. She was friendly, smiling at Mae shuffling her feet while being handed paperwork.

"I know this must be a stressful time," she continued. "One of the reasons I burn candles is to make our clients feel more comfortable. If you would like, there are donuts and coffee at the table over there," she said, pointing behind her desk.

This was different from what Mae was expecting. She'd thought the office would be cold and intimidating, but instead, she felt calm and welcomed.

When Mae was escorted to the conference room to meet Linda, she held her coffee cup in one hand and greeted Linda with the other.

Linda motioned for her to have a seat, clasping her hands together.

"It's very lovely to meet you. I'm sure you're apprehensive about our meeting. At Steer, we strive to make our clients feel comfortable. But don't let us fool you. I'm an aggressive attorney who specializes in divorce cases. Upon your call, I've reviewed my assistant's notes, and I want you to know that you're not alone. I've represented many women who chose to raise their children only later in life to find themselves in the same situation you are now."

Linda's eyes were warm as she spoke, but her voice was stern.

She wore a black suit with a soft pink blouse, matching shoes, and earrings. She carried herself more like a grandmother than a high-powered attorney. Still, Mae felt at ease in her presence, knowing she would take care of her case.

"So far, any questions?" Linda asked.

Mae was overwhelmed.

Her voice shook as she pulled out a list of questions she had written. "I guess, firstly, how will I pay you? Jacob has control of all the money. He gives me an allowance."

Linda put her hands on the table. Her nail polish matched her blouse, too, which Mae noted because it reminded her of the way Jill always matched impeccably.

"Once I file a financial restraining order, the court will enforce that Jacob cannot withhold or transfer funds," Linda said.

Mae felt a wash of relief. "Once you file the divorce papers and he is served, how will I ensure my safety? What if he doesn't leave the house? What if he retaliates? What—"

Mae's voice was quivering as she continued firing questions at Linda. She was visibly distraught, and Linda instructed her to take a breath.

"Okay. I know this is a lot to process. Are you afraid for your safety? Has your husband ever done anything to harm you prior?"

Mae thought back to the intimidation, the verbal abuse, the sexual aggression, and, on occasion, the physical abuse. She couldn't prove anything. "Not recently, but in the past, yes," she said quietly. "A couple of times, he got aggressive, once slamming my head on a counter and some other stuff." Mae didn't want to talk about it. She'd avoided thinking about the years of abuse for fear that the memories would break her steadfast focus.

"Do you want to get a restraining order?" Linda asked.

"I don't think that's necessary. It may just make matters worse."

Linda exhaled, studying Mae. "If you change your mind, it is an option."

Mae left the meeting more terrified than she had expected.

While she felt legally protected, there was no way to ensure Jacob wouldn't do something insane. He did, after all, have a lot to lose. So did she.

Although Linda assured Mae that the court would work in her favor, she feared Jacob would find a way around it.

She had heard of women left financially drained after divorce, and she worried that her lack of employment would disadvantage her, even though Linda said it would be the opposite.

Mae stared out the window as she turned the car engine, watching from afar as two squirrels chased each other up a tree. One attempted to escape while the other, a bigger one, would not give up. Mae chuckled at the irony, feeling trapped yet desperately trying to break free. A part of her wondered if Jacob would be relieved by the divorce.

They hadn't had sex in years, barely spoke, and essentially lived different lives.

She knew Jacob had extramarital affairs and preferred the company of anyone other than her. It was apparent to both of them and their kids that their marriage was nowadays a formality, not a commitment of love. He must surely feel the same, and the divorce would unshackle him.

As she was preparing dinner, she looked around her house. It had served her well, and she reminisced about the years spent raising the boys within these four walls. She had grown to love this house and wondered if she could stay there, at least for a while.

She thought of the holidays spent in the kitchen, preparing meals, listening to the boys bickering, and later discussing their plans. As much as it pained Mae to think of the change that would soon occur, she knew it was the best decision.

But what she called 'the beginning of her life's end era' also made her melancholy. She wished it had turned out differently but accepted that she could no longer continue this way.

The hardest part would be telling her mother. Judy was bound to suggest marriage counseling, prayer, and maybe even some time apart. Little did she know that nothing would fix two people who simply didn't love one another anymore. Her mother would never understand this, for her marriage was her security. Love had little place in her mother's life.

Mae had resisted this kind of shallow thinking throughout her adolescence, wanting to be independent somehow. However, the seeping childhood feeling had nevertheless led her to fall prey to a controlling man, one who had led with the promise of financial security.

She shook her head, trying to get the thoughts out of her mind.

She could no longer worry about her mother, her children, or Jacob.

It had been two weeks, and Linda had yet to contact Mae to give her an update. When she finally made the call, Mae was growing impatient.

"Oh, Mae, I'm sorry! I've been stuck in a trial. I was going to contact you sooner, but things are hectic."

Mae was disappointed. She'd thought Linda would be more attentive to her case and was expecting results sooner. "So, what is the status? Have you filed with the court yet?"

"I have. They're backed up at the moment. We should hear something by next week."

Mae hung up the phone, defeated. She had made the decision and was afraid that the more time passed, the more likely she would lose her nerve.

She tried to stay steadfast, remembering why she needed to get out of this marriage.

She was lost in her thoughts when the phone rang again. This time, it was a familiar number: Trevor's high school.

"This is Mr. Plumber. I have Trevor here in my office. It is best if you get down here right away."

Mae was shocked. "Is he okay? What's going on?"

"Can you be here in the next ten minutes?" he said sternly.

"Yes, sure, I'm on my way," said Mae as she gathered her keys and coat and ran out the door.

Frantic, she rushed to her car, fumbling to put her keys in the ignition. The tires screeched as Mae hastily pulled out of the driveway, causing the neighbor from three doors down—who was walking her miniature poodle—to look at her with concern.

"Dammit," she grumbled as she met eyes with Mrs. Shadow. "Fuck," Mae gasped under her breath, annoyed at the attention she had drawn.

She slowed down to pass Mrs. Shadow, waving with a soft smile, trying to keep composed. But all the time, her insides roiled. The last thing she needed was the neighbors talking about her. Gossip got around quickly in this neighborhood, primarily thanks to this same woman.

She had a knack for observing, judging, and spreading malicious talk.

Two weeks prior, when Mae had been collecting her mail from the bottom of the driveway, Mrs. Shadow caught her eye as she closed the mailbox.

She appeared out of nowhere, startling her.

Mrs. Shadow was out for her evening walk, though Mae felt sure she used her nightly stroll as a guise; it was how she surveyed the neighborhood for the weekly comings and goings of the other neighbors.

"You did hear they are divorcing, didn't you?" she said during their last encounter. "I believe she was cheating. And now their poor daughter is in pieces over it. I saw her the other day, and she looked like she'd started hanging out with the wrong crowd. She was wearing some sort of outfit that showed way too much skin if you ask me."

Without missing a beat, Mrs. Shadow continued, "But what do I know? I try to mind my own business." Mae stared at the older woman, unsure what to say next.

She quickly excused herself as she gathered the rest of the mail and waved goodbye to the woman. As she entered her house, she looked over her shoulder, watching as the gray-haired lady adjusted her glasses, peering into the open crack of the door.

Mae focused back on the road, hoping her rapid departure did not raise eyebrows.

Once she reached the main road, she picked up speed and quickly turned onto the school property. There, she parked in the visitor area, watching the high school seniors mill around their cars, taking advantage of the senior privilege of leaving school grounds during their lunch hour.

She recognized some of the boys from the football team.

Eddie, Trevor's friend, met Mae's eyes as he walked toward the building with the leftover remnants of a fast-food burger. Eddie froze as he watched Mae recognize him.

Then, he quickly put his head down, walking faster to catch up to the other boys.

Mae felt a sudden surge of embarrassment as her breath became shallow and her teeth clenched tightly. She felt the eyes of teenagers staring her down with concern and entertainment.

The high school thrived on gossip, and whatever this meeting was about, the student body had already been made aware. She felt her face burn with embarrassment from her ignorance as she rushed past the gaggle of girls applying makeup in the reflection of the car door.

Once inside, the Vice Principal, Hannah Goharp, greeted her, looking at Mae with compassion. "This way," she whispered. Mae walked past classrooms of teachers instructing their students on the day's lesson. The smell of teenage sweat, cafeteria food, and the faint aroma of the bake shop's class-burnt brownies overwhelmed her senses.

There was a knot of tension in her stomach as she struggled with the overstimulation of high school. It had been years since Mae had been in a school in session; how had she managed?

The chaos of teenage clamor made her head spin, and her heart raced as she rushed toward the principal's office.

At the doors, Ms. Goharp offered Mae water as she sat at the long wooden conference table. The secretary peeked her head inside, saying with a stern voice, "They will be here shortly."

Mae could have sworn that the woman, short in stature, plump, and close to retirement age, must have had many similar situations in her years as the principal's secretary.

Mae remained still, staring down at her hands, attempting to swallow the sharp dryness in her throat. She should have taken them up on the water and wished she hadn't declined.

Before she could request water, the doors burst open, and Mr. Plumber entered with authority. He wore a blue shirt with a black tie, his gray hair lying matted against his skull.

He ran his fingers against his beard as he took a long exhale. Mae could tell that whatever had transpired with Trevor had startled him enough that his tired eyes begged for a drink.

"Where's Trevor?" asked Mae.

"He is fine. An officer is with him in the bathroom."

"An officer? Why is there an off—"

Mae was cut off when a young officer entered the room with Trevor.

He kept Trevor close by, watching him as he stumbled into the room.

"We didn't want to take him into custody until you were notified and had a chance to see him. We don't believe he's a threat, but protocol required us to call the police."

Mr. Plumber spoke slowly, ensuring Mae could follow what he was telling her. Mae's eyes were wide, and the sting of tears began to rush down her cheeks.

"What happened?" Mae demanded. "What did he do that there's an officer ready to take my son into custody?"

Mae looked over at Trevor, who was pale and his lips slightly blue.

She hadn't noticed how skinny he had become, as his red t-shirt loosely fell off his shoulders. His eyes were distant as he surveyed the room, finally making eye contact with his mother. She looked at him in disbelief, willing him to have an explanation. Trevor's eyes pleaded with his mother to get him out of this trouble, but their vacancy made Mae hesitate to speak.

"Ma'am," the officer began, "Your son had two opioids in his gym bag that we believe he has been receiving from a local drug dealer with the intent to sell. We want your son to cooperate so we can get this man off the street and bust the operation. This is increasingly becoming a problem in this neighborhood, and with Trevor's help, we can eliminate the source."

Mae was processing what the officer, who wasn't much older than her eldest son James, said. The attempt to remain calm was difficult as all the blood seemed to drain from her body.

She hadn't gotten past the fact that Trevor had drugs on him at school. Making matters worse, they wanted his help in arresting a drug dealer. This was too much for her to comprehend.

Mae knew to contact a lawyer, but first, she needed to call Jacob. It was happening all too quickly, and she needed time to think. For the first time, Trevor began to speak.

"Mom, this isn't what it looks like. I promise. I'm being set up. The drugs aren't mine, and I don't even know a drug dealer." She looked into her son's eyes and knew that whatever the officer suspected was true. Trevor was clearly under the influence of some drug, and there was no denying it. Mae's mothering instinct snapped into place.

"Trevor shut up. Do not say another word. Do you understand me?"

Her effort to keep the damage down was useless.

Her voice was stern, though her lips were quivering.

Trevor looked at his mother.

"Don't tell me you think I do drugs. This is horseshit."

Mae's head whipped around as she got out of her chair.

"Trevor, I mean it, shut the fuck up, right now."

Trevor looked down, clearly embarrassed and surprised by his mother's reaction. He had expected her to take his side and walk him out of the office, demanding an apology.

He could always count on his mother to help him out of a situation, but he didn't know why she was cooperating with the authorities this time.

However, Mae had more significant problems than helping the authorities. She had to deal with the fact her son was taking illegal substances, and she hoped she wasn't too late.

She steadied herself against the large walnut bookcase adjacent to the conference room table. "I need to contact my lawyer. Trevor will not be speaking with any of you. Unless you are arresting him, then you have no reason to detain my son." Mae was uncharacteristically aggressive, her protective nature the force behind her words.

"It will be easier on all of us if Trevor cooperates. He would be doing something good for the community and getting himself out of trouble if he gave us a name. The sting operation—"

"Sting operation? Do you want my teenage son involved in a sting operation? Have you lost your minds? The only evidence you have against Trevor is there were pills found, not even on his person. Pills that he claims were not his, nor does he know how they got in his gym bag." Mae's voice was growing increasingly loud. "Furthermore, you have no proof that someone didn't plant these pills. Aren't the lockers kept open for all athletes?

"Wouldn't it be possible for another student to plant the drugs in Trevor's locker for safekeeping and would retrieve them later?"

Trevor looked across the room, obviously impressed by his mother's tenacity.

She would always protect him when it was time. Mae took a moment to catch her breath as she studied the officer's face. Knowing that Mae was correct in her assessment, the principal would be no further help to the police department.

"If nothing else, gentlemen, I'll take my son home. This has been overwhelming for all of us."

Trevor followed his mother out of the building toward her car. "Mom, wow, you were amazing." Trevor was now more alert than previously. "I didn't know you could—"

"Trevor, I mean it. Shut the fuck up."

Mae's tone was so unusual that Trevor looked concerned. "Mom, are you okay? You need to chill. This isn't a big deal. You handled it."

Mae's eyes darted toward Trevor and then back to the road. She said nothing for the rest of the drive, and the two of them drove home in silence.

Chapter 17

The wind was causing the big oak trees at the front of their home to sway. Winter was approaching, and the last of the leaves clung onto the branches.

As much as she wanted to believe the habitual lies Trevor had told, it was now time to face the fact that he was using drugs. The excessive excuses, the times when he could not be accounted for, the money missing from the house, and the looks of vacancy in his eyes were the clues she'd chosen not to see over the past months.

Whatever delusion Mae had been holding on to was gone. She recognized she had a situation on her hands and needed to take control of it before it was too late.

Whatever Trevor had taken had worn off, and now he stared out the window, looking vindicated. When they approached a red light, Mae studied her son, observing his mannerisms.

There were more secrets he kept than she realized.

She assumed the previous time she'd found him high was an act of teenage curiosity, but now she considered he had become better at hiding it. Internally, she was terrified of what she had seen just an hour prior; Trevor had been taking drugs, and she needed to find out to what extent.

Mae glanced in the rearview mirror, enjoying a sense of empowerment.

Her experience in law had served her well, and she was proud that she'd held her own.

It satisfied her that she'd remembered her legal rights and expressed herself with authority.

Now, though, she needed to exert her power and take charge of her son's well-being.

Mae pulled into their driveway and walked briskly inside, Trevor trailing behind. She looked through a notebook to his doctor and began dialing a number.

Trevor, who stood in the foyer dumbfounded, stared, waiting to find out his mother's plan for him. After the third ring, the receptionist picked up.

"Hello, this is Mae Greene. I'm Trevor Greene's mother, and I would like him to come in for blood tests. I believe Trevor has been using drugs, and I would like to have a full panel screening done to see what we are dealing with."

Mae spoke with authority.

Trevor watched in horror until he saw his mother's shoulders slump.

"How can that be? He's under my care and insurance, and I should have the right to all information pertaining to my teenage son." There was a brief silence when Mae conceded, "I understand. We will be at the appointment, and I will speak to Trevor about the situation."

Mae slammed the phone down, infuriated.

Exasperated, she screamed, "Fuck!"

Trevor felt a pang of guilt over his mother's distress and approached her gingerly. "Mom, please, calm down. I'm good. I promise."

Tears sprang from Mae's eyes, unable to control herself any longer, no longer interested in controlling their rapid fall. Her head was down as she sobbed into her hands.

"Mom, you're overreacting. I'm fine. I promise."

There were those words again: "I promise." How many times had Mae heard them, and they'd never been true? Trevor didn't know what a promise meant; they were just words to get him out of something and make the other person feel better.

"I'm tired of your promises, Trevor. You have a drug problem. I'm no longer willing to keep my head in the sand just because I don't want to believe it's true."

Trevor's eyes grew wide as his mouth fell open. For the first time, Mae challenged him, and he didn't quite know how to react. "What? Mom, what? You're crazy. Dad's right. He thinks you overreact to everything, and now I see what he means. You need help." Trevor sloped off to his room, slamming the door behind him as the pictures on the walk shook.

Mae's suspicions had been correct. Jacob did talk poorly about her to the boys.

She'd noticed the shift in her boys' behavior when Jacob was around.

Boys usually have a unique relationship with their fathers, and Mae wondered where their allegiance would be once the divorce was underway.

She had to discuss this with Jacob and wait for him to come home. She called, asking to meet him after work out of the house because she had something important to discuss.

"Can't it wait until I get home? I have an important event after work that I can't miss."

Jacob always referred to his affairs as events to make them sound more important, with the assumption that Mae was too stupid to know what he was doing.

"No, Jacob. I can't wait. Today, your fuck fest is going to have to wait."

Mae heard the call end abruptly and immediately dialed Jacob's number again.

She was about to hang up by the third ring when she heard his voice. "Listen, you bitch, don't you ever question my work schedule again. You would be starving on the street if it weren't for me. And if you keep this up, I'll ensure you will be!"

He hung up again this time, Mae hearing a woman's voice in the background, giggling.

He was already with someone for the day and putting on the show to prove that this marriage meant nothing. The burn on Mae's face felt like lava from a volcano. She could feel the rage burgeoning inside her as if an explosion was about to cause havoc and destruction to everyone around. She called once more, this time out of spite rather than desperation.

This time, on the first ring, he answered,

"What now? Don't you have some laundry to take care of?"

Before Jacob could say another word, Mae responded with ice in her voice but calmness in her breath, "Listen, you stupid cheating fucker. Your son is on drugs, and I strongly suggest you get your sorry ass home because I will be sending him away to rehab this evening."

There was silence on the phone, though Mae could hear the noise of patrons in the background. "Oh, Mae, you are so pathetic. Making up stories about your son for attention. Truly darling, get a life."

The phone went dead, and Mae decided she no longer needed his approval to save her son or make decisions. She could do it without him, and he would be sorry if he tried to stop her.

After numerous calls, Mae found an outpatient rehabilitation center forty minutes from the house, close enough to commute back and forth but far enough away that the neighbors would not know her business. It took two days to convince the administration of Healing Hands to speak with her about patient intake. She needed Trevor's permission but wanted to present all the facts to him before making the move. She was nervous to approach this, knowing he could easily refuse. Trevor didn't think he had a problem, James wasn't willing to betray his brother, and Jacob was in complete denial. Mae was alone in the fight to save her son.

Trevor wasn't what a typical drug addict user appeared to be, and it was a challenge to get people to understand he was smart enough to hide it.

Trevor was an athlete, a good student, dressed well, and friendly. However, behind closed doors, he slept often, didn't engage with his friends, and was often moody.

He had lost weight and hid it behind baggy sweatshirts. Mae knew something was happening, however, and he couldn't fool her anymore. She stayed oblivious for far too long, terrified to face the truth, but was no longer willing to continue with her delusional hopefulness.

Three days later, with much tension throughout the house, Mae finally made her plea to Trevor. She waited by the front door for him to come home, pacing the foyer until she heard the sound of the engine pulling into the driveway. When he arrived, he was wearing a black sweatshirt hoodie, his eyes sunken in, and he sported a beard from not shaving.

His hair was greasy from not showering, and he appeared disheveled.

Mae wondered, *where has he been after practice? It's nearing eight o'clock!*

She didn't bother to ask, already knowing the answer, and she instead took the advice of the Helping Hands counselors about how to approach her son so that he would agree to get help.

She quickly raced into the kitchen, so Trevor didn't suspect the intervention and return to his car to leave again. When he walked through the door, Mae escorted him into the kitchen.

Thankfully, James had plans that evening, and Jacob was out on another one of his 'events.'

"Trevor, please come sit with me. I need to talk to you about something,"

Mae noticed his face drooping on one side, and his eyes appeared narrow and glassy. She knew just by his appearance that he'd been using drugs that evening and had driven home high.

"Trevor, I love you. I'm worried. You need help, and I'm here to support you."

Before Trevor could interrupt, she continued, "I've found a place where you can go to get help with your substance abuse issue; I'm worried about the consequences if you don't. On the news daily, kids your age are dying from fentanyl laced in the pills ingested. I don't want you to become another death statistic, and I'm asking you to allow me to help you get sober."

Mae slid the pamphlets across the table to her son, who looked at them incredulously.

"Is this about the other day at school? Mom, it was nothing. They're lying. I promise this is just a misunderstanding. I'd never lie to you, Mom."

He was babbling now, quickly saying any excuse to distract Mae. "Even Dad thinks you're overreacting. He says you're going through something, and I shouldn't worry about what you say. Mom, I love you, but I'm good. Really. I promise."

It was challenging to hear Trevor deny the undeniable, but it was also infuriating to know how much damage Jacob was causing to her relationship with Trevor.

He would do anything to undermine her and stop at nothing to make her look crazy.

These last years had finally taught Mae to stand up for herself. She couldn't believe she'd allowed Jacob to have so much control over her life while she'd been too distracted raising her boys. She kicked herself for being weak and ignoring her instincts. She could no longer live this life; like an epiphany, she grasped that this relationship no longer served her needs.

Dealing with Trevor was first on her list of priorities. Her son's health meant more to her than anything, and she was determined to help him get well. The marriage was over, and she was tired of being made a fool. *When you hurt hard enough, you make changes,* she decided.

Mae continued, "Trevor, I love you, but we can't keep doing this dance. The promises, the lies, the money missing, the times you disappear for hours and reappear looking like this." She motioned her hand at him. "Please just come with me and meet the staff. They're expecting us. Let's check it out, and you can consider it with all the necessary information."

Trevor looked deep into his mother's eyes. For the first time, she saw her son, the boy with a lot of personality. His beautiful blue eyes melted her heart. She struggled to hold the tears back, as it was the first time he had made eye contact with her in a long time.

"Please," Mae begged.

"I don't need this, but I'll go for you. I promise, Mom, I'm good. You'll see for yourself."

Mae felt instant gratification, and before he could change his mind, she grabbed her keys and Trevor and drove off to Helping Hands.

The admitting counselor was waiting for their arrival and guided them into a room to fill out paperwork. The fact that Trevor had just turned eighteen left little authority for Mae to interject on his treatment. Mae's frustration over the law caused her to feel useless in the process, but she kept her focus on the fact she'd at least got Trevor this far.

Mae waited in the lobby as the counselor asked Trevor questions and took blood tests. She looked around her as other loved ones stared into space, in despair. Mae had no experience with this process and let her gut guide her through, hoping she was making the right decisions.

The person to her left sat with her distraught daughter, who was shaking from withdrawal.

Her eyes red from crying, Mae nodded at the mother, showing support.

How many other parents were going through this terrible disease with their children?

She only hoped that Trevor would adhere to the program and get clean. She had spent hours researching, trying to understand, but she still could not believe she was in this situation. It was hours before Trevor reappeared, and Mae stood up and hugged her son, who looked shell-shocked. She embraced him but was met with a weak hug. She had many questions, but the counselor could not give her the information since Trevor would not sign a release form.

"Trevor, please let me talk to them. I can help you, but I need to know what I'm dealing with," she pleaded.

Trevor wouldn't make eye contact with his mother. He just said, "Mom, I'm good. I'm eighteen, and you have no right to intrude on my medical issues."

His voice was defiant.

"I'm your mother. You live in my home. Please, Trevor—"

Trevor walked to the door, indicating the conversation was over.

Mae tried again to reach her son. "Trevor, will you attend the meetings?"

"Yes. I'll go."

He was short with his answer and kept walking. Mae wondered what her son was thinking and if the counselor had convinced him that he did have a problem and that there was a solution.

"From now on, Trevor, I need you to be honest. If you are struggling, please come to me, and let me know. We can figure this out together," she said, reaching for his hand.

"Mom, I've dabbled with pills, but you're overreacting."

Mae considered his statement, knowing she wasn't overreacting, and he was gaslighting her into thinking that his use of illegal drugs was not an issue.

"I'm not here to judge you, Trevor. I just don't want you to go down a road where there is danger and no way back. You aren't prepared."

Later that night, when Jacob heard of what had transpired, he came home with his usual whisky on his breath and the slurring of his words.

"Dammit, Mae, you're such a fucking drama queen."

Mae ignored his insults and simply walked past him with little regard.

When he wouldn't let up, she finally bravely confronted him, face to face. She could smell the sour odor of alcohol and the faint scent of a woman's perfume on him.

She ignored it and said, "Leave my kids to me. You are useless to all of us." As she walked away with arrogance, she turned and said, "By the way, I'm filing for divorce."

The words slipped out unintentionally, but she could no longer hold back.

"I dare you, bitch. Without me, you're nothing. And I'm not giving you any financial stuff."

The words spit out of his mouth like poison. But she wasn't even fazed this time.

"Well, we'll see," she said. "I'm also made to feel like nothing when I'm with you!"

She straightened her shoulders confidently. "And besides, I have all the financial records I need, which are safe with my attorney. We already know about the shady dealings within your firm. I'm sure the IRS will love to hear about that if you don't cooperate."

She laughed sarcastically. "We have quite a nice nest egg,"

Jacob stared at her with disgust. He knew she was right. He had done some illegal dealings in the stock market, and she now had the proof. There would be mounds of legal trouble if it were uncovered. He had to play his cards right to minimize the damage and surrender to her demands.

She had beaten him at his own game.

"Now get out," she demanded. "Until we go to court to sort out who lives where, I hope you'll agree I stay here, in the boys' home. I can't really go anywhere else right now, and anyway, your days of manipulating me are over. This is your mess, so you need to be the one to go."

Mae stared down Jacob until he finally retreated into their bedroom. It was all too clear she wasn't going anywhere.

She heard him rumbling through the closet for a suitcase as she poured herself a much-needed glass of wine. She took large gulps, feeling a new sense of power. His illegal dealings had left him no choice but to succumb to her demands and leave the house quietly.

Her shoulders relaxed as he walked out with two large suitcases, slamming the door behind him, turning around only once to say a final "Fuck you." His engine roared, tires screeching as she heard the car leave the driveway. Knowing he had been drinking, she considered calling the police and getting him busted with an anonymous tip for DUI.

She decided against it; he knew half of the police department and would escape it anyway. Feeling so self-important, he'd made sure he introduced himself to just about every officer he'd ever seen, ingratiating himself. He'd even been out for drinks with a few.

Mae went to bed that night with a feeling of peace she hadn't known in a long time.

She felt empowered by recognizing her son's addiction, taking action, and finally ridding herself of the toxicity of Jacob.

In the quiet of the night, she picked up her phone, feeling the effects of the wine.

She hadn't forgotten about Patrick. In fact, he was her motivation for finding a meaningful life. She texted him. 'Hey. I know it's been a while, and a lot's happened, but I was wondering if we could meet for a drink tomorrow night. I could use a friend.'

Immediately, Mae saw white bubbles across her screen, indicating that he was responding. "Yes. Please," was all it said.

Mae responded, "Our usual?" though they had only met there once before. "Seven?"

A heart emoji showed instantly, and Mae's mood lifted.

Chapter 18

SHE WORE A TIGHTER than usual red blouse and black pants that she had bought earlier that day. Her red lipstick, earrings, and bracelet all matched and made her feel elegant and sexy.

She glanced in the mirror, smiling at her reflection, something she couldn't recall doing in years. Mae wondered how this transformation had happened.

How quickly she'd evolved from being a sullen woman controlled by an egotistical husband to wearing red lipstick with matching heels.

Mae gathered her purse and headed out early to calm her nerves with a drink before meeting Patrick. She tried distracting herself with music, but she noticed the race of her heart and the feel of her sweaty palms gripping the steering wheel.

She lowered the heat as perspiration gathered under her armpits, mostly due to nerves—something no man had ever made her feel. She lowered the windows for fresh air, hoping it would provide some relief. The refreshing, cool breeze hit her face as she headed toward the parking lot. As she pulled in, she looked at the black Toyota parked in the spot closest to her.

An instant smile crossed her face.

Patrick looked nervous, too, sitting with the windows down and taking deep breaths. He glanced over, and he, too, began to smile.

They had both arrived early, filled with nerves. When he stepped out of his car, Mae did the same, and they met halfway for an embrace. It was the first time she'd felt the warmth of his skin against hers, and it left her breathless. They stared at one another, void of words until he finally broke the silence. "I guess we were thinking the same thing."

She smiled coyly. "Nervous too?" she asked weakly.

"I'm dying. I don't think I've ever been this nervous for a date in my life."

"Date?" Mae asked. "Is that what this is?"

"Well, you know, maybe not a date. Is this a date? It's okay if it is. But if it isn't, that's cool too." Patrick was rambling.

Mae covered her mouth with her hand to hide her laughter.

"Anyway, shall we go in?" Patrick said, evidently embarrassed.

Mae looked at him as they walked into the bar, mesmerized by the swagger of his body and the ease of his walk. He appeared taller than he was and held a quiet and humble confidence.

He was also more handsome than she remembered.

This was the first time she'd seen him dressed in a button-down shirt and dark blue jeans. The last couple of times they'd met, he had worn more casual clothes and a baseball cap. There was something about how he held himself: Mae felt safe in his presence. He walked beside her proudly, holding open the door as they entered the bar. The smell of his aftershave had her reeling with desire, and she moved closer as they sat beside one another in a booth.

At first, he went to sit across the table from her but said, "Do you mind? I just want to be close to you." Mae's cheeks burned as her eyes said she didn't mind.

They ordered burgers and beers and ate, pausing to discuss what had happened in her life.

"I was nervous to call you, but if I'm being honest, I've spent months thinking about you. I was trying to do the right thing, but the truth is, my marriage has been over for a long time. I've already contacted an attorney, and Jacob knows my plans to divorce."

Patrick looked down at his hands, fidgeting with his fingernails.

When their eyes met, Mae detected a tear forming.

He said, "Mae, you have no idea how much I've longed to hear those words from you. I've spent countless hours walking the path, hoping to see you again. I looked you up on Facebook and stared at your profile, hoping you'd reach out. I know you have had a lot going on with your family issues, but I want to be beside you and go through them with you."

This time, Mae's eyes filled with tears. She took her glass and raised it in the air. "To new beginnings," she said with a smile.

"To finding my soulmate," he responded.

The waitress offered another round of drinks.

They said an emphatic "Yes, please," in unison.

"Okay then," the waitress replied. "Coming right up."

As she walked away, Mae said, "I'm having a great time. Thanks for meeting me."

Patrick took her hand, and Mae winced excitedly as this was the first time he had ever held it.

"I hope I get to see a lot more of you. I understand this will be a challenging time, but anytime I can see you, I'd love it. Just drop a message the same way you did yesterday."

"Okay, I will." Mae looked down at his hand, noticing how well it fit in hers.

She saw that she was still wearing her wedding band. She spun her ring around with her thumb, feeling its invasion upon her finger. "I guess I should take this off now," she said.

Patrick whispered, "When it's time, and you're ready, you will know it."

The lighthearted conversation slowly became more serious.

They discussed the future and how they fit into one another's lives, knowing neither wanted to rush things. Holding a conversation where Mae could be vulnerable, and Patrick could be honest was comforting. They discussed what was important and how they yearned for an equal and genuine relationship. Patrick explained that his first wife had left him heartbroken.

It had taken him years to recover. When he finally had, he'd started to date and realized how many damaged people were out looking for love but hadn't yet learned to love themselves.

"It was brutal. I didn't think I'd ever meet anyone compatible again until I met you. My friends tried to set me up with people. I tried online dating but couldn't connect with anyone."

Patrick shook his head in disbelief at his dating life.

"I know this sounds crazy, Mae, I do, but when I saw you for the first time at the park, something inside of me felt alive again. When I saw the wedding band on your finger, I was disappointed, but I just knew somehow, one day, we were meant to be together." Patrick gazed at Mae, hoping she believed his words. "Trust me, I was never a believer in love at first sight."

He took another gulp of his beer. "But I am now."

"I have to admit, I'm shocked. I kind of thought you'd forgotten about me. I haven't reached out in months and was worried you wouldn't remember me."

She looked at Patrick, feeling vulnerable as she waited for a response,

"Oh, I remember you, Mae," he said as he moved closer, touching his lips against hers. The smell of beer and burgers emerged as they kissed slowly, not caring that they were not alone.

The waitress reappeared with the beer, clearing her throat as she approached.

Patrick got up to use the restroom, and when he returned, the song "Don't Stop Believin" played from the speakers above. "I'd say this is an appropriate song," he said as he held out his hand, "Shall we?" he said as he invited her onto the dance floor. He twirled her around until she was dizzy, laughing throughout the song. When it ended, they finished their beers and paid the bill. He took her hand protectively as they left.

"So, I guess this is it?" Mae said.

"When can I see you again? Patrick said, eager.

"I'm meeting with my lawyer this week and will be in touch soon."

"I understand," Patrick said. "Don't worry about me. I'll be here waiting. I finally found you, and I'll wait while you handle your divorce."

"Thank you," said Mae. "I mean, thank you for being so great. For being everything, I always wanted."

Before Mae could finish, Patrick put his hands on the small of her back and pulled her close. Their lips locked as his tongue gently touched hers, both breathing heavily.

A car's headlights coming into the parking lot pulled them away.

"I guess I should be going now," Mae said.

As she pulled out of the parking lot, she watched in her rearview mirror as Patrick stood smiling. Once driving down the road, she let out a gasp of excitement.

The feelings she was having, she didn't even know existed. Exhilarated, she drove home in silence, taking in the night's events and replaying them in her mind.

Mae was grateful that Patrick made no demands on her or her timeline to commit to the relationship entirely. She knew her marriage was over, and divorce was imminent.

But she feared that Jacob would retaliate and make her life difficult. She wanted to protect Patrick from his endless threats and the long road she was certain he would have to travel.

Still, the thought of Patrick waiting on the other side gave Mae solace.

She hoped her boys would be happy for her, for finding someone who would be kind, but that was a long way away. She wouldn't entertain any meeting, especially since Trevor had recently agreed to get help for his addiction.

Two days later, she met Patrick for a short walk. She had already missed him and wanted them to spend time together. As they walked, she was initially hesitant to tell Patrick about her son's problems, but instead of being scared off by them, he was emphatic and encouraging.

"I thought it was just a phase the first time," she explained. "I feel so foolish; it just happened so quickly." Her voice cracked.

"Mae, it happens to many families. Kids experiment. You didn't know, but you do now and have gotten him the help he needs. This is beyond your experience. You're not a drug counselor." His voice was soft, with empathy, and his eyes showed compassion.

"It's just that—" Mae continued. "I am, if this makes sense, ashamed."

Patrick wiped her tears, cupping her face a bit longer. "Don't be hard on yourself. This isn't your fault. Addiction is rampant, especially among teens."

The struggle to not take it personally weighed heavily on her.

"I know your words are true, but as his mother," Mae said, looking off into the distance. "It is hard to reconcile." Patrick took her hand, rubbing it softly.

"We will get through this."

"We?" Mae said.

"Yes, I'm here for you and will do whatever you need, even if it's just being a listening ear."

She confided in Patrick more than she'd confided in anyone before, except for Jill.

It felt good to trust him with her feelings, without guilt.

Patrick was interested in her and offered feasible solutions.

While Mae was grateful for their budding relationship, she had to be cautious with her heart.

She didn't want to rush into anything, but a calm came over her, one that had been absent throughout her marriage. Healing from her relationship with Jacob would take time, but her priority for the time being was ensuring Travis received help.

Chapter 19

Walking into the house, there was silence accompanied by a profound loneliness.

As Mae was getting ready for bed, the quietness was especially intimidating. Both boys had gone to dinner with their father, and she wasn't sure when they would be home.

Not having Jacob home was unfamiliar but peaceful. It wasn't so much that he was physically not there; she was used to that, but his shoes were no longer at the front door, his dirty wine glass wasn't on the kitchen counter, and his toothbrush was missing.

These things were unusual.

It would take her a while to reconcile her new life, but she felt the weight of his unpredictable behavior wash away. Mae was comfortable, feeling at peace. Used to living with the anxiety of Jacob's mood swings, she now relished the emotions and sanctuary of quiet.

Jacob was staying in a hotel a few miles away and would likely find a permanent residence far away from their home. Sometimes, Mae worried that he would come in and harm her; she even considered calling a security company to fit cameras and an alarm.

The feeling of independence frightened and invigorated Mae.

Though her heart ached at the massive change within the home, she was excited about her new beginnings but needed to organize her life to prepare for whatever would follow.

Gone were the days when her boys needed her, or she was busy with practices and sitting on the bleachers watching their games. They had grown up, leaving their mother to forge ahead with her life, creating new experiences. She longed for a time when she could finally live with her own suppressed ambitions in mind, and now that it was finally happening, she was scared.

It was uncomfortable knowing she was on her own. She hadn't been alone since college, since before she'd met Jacob. She thought about that time in her life and about how he'd so easily manipulated her. She regretted losing herself for the sake of her mother's need to see her secure.

As a mother herself now, Mae knew her mother's intentions had been pure; she just wished she had followed her path and allowed herself to live the life she had intended. There was no point in lamenting the past, though the ache in her heart told her differently. She sat on the couch for a long while, thinking about the last twenty-two years, trying to reconcile the time.

It had gone by quickly. She pondered at what point she had had enough of being a domestic doormat, not being respected, and Jacob's condescending words. There were many instances when she'd longed to walk away from her marriage, including the day of her wedding itself.

She held on to the façade; breaking her mother's heart seemed cruel at the time.

Now, though, with age, wisdom, and less tolerance for bullshit, Mae didn't care what anyone thought. She had to let go of her past choices with the knowledge to make better ones.

Mae reflected on the home gym Jacob had built, knowing he was spoiling her plans to make it an office for her real estate practice. That had been her last straw, the moment she'd decided she no longer would stay in the toxicity of the marriage.

Exactly how she would finally flee emotionally and physically was yet to be known. But at least she had the beginnings of an escape, and she was doing it in the right way, the legal way.

Perhaps it was the wine, or the confidence Patrick promoted, but Mae was ready for massive changes. Getting her real estate license was still tempting; being a real estate agent would be convenient for her family. Yet her heart's desire had always been law. It'd been her intention so many years before, and now, without the berating of Jacob, she was ready to take the plunge. Mae had enrolled in law school and was thriving.

Mae had enrolled in law school and was thriving. It had taken her six months, but she finally called her mother, asking to visit her at her home. It had been a long time since Mae had set eyes on her; Judy usually came to see Mae so that she could also spend time with her grandsons.

Mae never disclosed that Jacob would not have allowed her to take the long trek to her mother anyway, and it was easier that Judy was willing to visit Mae at her home.

When Judy opened the door, she looked so much older. Her hair had turned completely gray now, and the lines on her face were more distinguished.

She moved about slower and more carefully but still had the warmth Mae remembered.

"Hi, Mom." Judy was ecstatic about the visit and held on to her daughter for a long time. Her embrace brought tears to both of their eyes as Mae absorbed her mother's essence.

"Dear, what brings you here? I told you I'd come to visit over the holidays."

Mae studied her mother's sweet face, thinking she had no clue how hard her life with Jacob had been. Mae was good at keeping secrets and putting on a brave face, but had her mother never sensed her daughter was so deeply unhappy?

"Mom, I need to talk to you. There is no easy way for me to say this." Mae hesitated as she watched her mother's eyes grow concerned.

"Come in. Let's sit down. Can I get you anything?" Judy asked.

Before she could speak, Mae felt a rush of tears.

Before being able to compose herself, they flooded her cheeks uncontrollably. Judy balanced herself against the kitchen table, slowly sitting down and instructing Mae to do the same.

"Mom, I'm getting divorced. I know this will be shocking and disappointing, but I can't keep living a lie."

Judy's hand touched her chin as she considered the words that her daughter was spewing.

Mae watched as her mother processed the declaration and began to nod. She waited for her to say something, and when she didn't, Mae bowed her head in defeat. "I'm sorry. I know how much you like Jacob and how badly you wanted a different life for me."

Judy let out a sigh, which sounded almost like a laugh.

"Oh, honey. I've been praying for this day. I've prayed for you weekly, hoping you'd find the courage to leave that man."

Mae gasped at the words.

"What, Mom? Why didn't you say anything?"

Now, Mae was angry that her mother had kept quiet, knowing that her daughter was unhappy and had never confronted her about it once in all of these years.

"Why did you think I'd come and visit you all the time? I was waiting for you to say something to me. It's not my place to interfere in your life. Whenever I'd come for a visit, you would have a big smile and act like you were okay. Darling daughter don't be fooled.

"I knew. I saw the sadness in your eyes and tried to give you the space you needed to tell me, and when I thought you would, Jacob continually interrupted.

"He watched our every move, and when you didn't say anything..." Her voice trailed off.

Mae felt rage overcome her as she stood from her seat.

"So, you did nothing? You are my mother! You could have said something, giving me space to tell you how I felt. Instead, you showed up at my house, making small talk with Jacob, pretending to be there for a nice visit."

Mae's face flushed as she felt a gentle shake of her hands.

Judy's eyes were begging her daughter for forgiveness and understanding.

"Mae, I tried many times to reach you. I wrote letters and left messages, and you never replied."

"What letters? What calls?" Mae hadn't received anything from her mother.

She'd only spoken to her mother when she called her on Sunday afternoons.

"Jacob gave me your private number and PO box."

"Mother, what are you talking about? I have neither." In an instant, both women understood what had happened. Jacob somehow had the calls from her mother blocked from Mae's phone and had given her a mailing address to his office.

By the end of the visit, the women understood that Jacob had manipulated them both.

Mae realized her phone had been cloned, and Jacob knew every call she had made, every place she had visited, and every move she had made. It made sense now why he'd been unsurprised about the divorce papers and how he could filter most of the money out of the accounts before the court ordered him to stop. Luckily, she was able to secure some of the funds prior, but she suspected there was money missing from the accounts.

Jacob was more sly than Mae had given him credit for.

She shook her head in disbelief at the ruses he'd used simply to keep control of her. Mae was mostly angry at herself for allowing it and not being wiser.

She knew he was scrupulous but didn't realize how closely she was being watched.

"All of this time, I thought no one cared. That no one noticed and that I was alone and miserable," Mae said through tears.

"I'm here now, love. It's time to make a change. It's time to let go of the past and look to the future. You can't keep living life like this. You have too much to offer this world."

Mae was grateful for the honest conversation with Judy.

In an afternoon, the invisible wall between them disappeared. She assured her mother she would be okay and would be in touch soon.

On the way home, Judy's words echoed in her ear. *You have too much to offer this world.* Mae put her hand on her heart, knowing her mother was right.

Mae had more to settle now that the information she'd gathered with Judy put her on high alert. She immediately bought a new phone, hired someone to check for bugs in her house and car, and realized how incredibly dire the situation was.

A tall man with thick glasses showed up and surveyed the house.

As expected, Mae's car had a GPS tracker, and the house was bugged in three areas.

What angered Mae most was that Jacob must have been aware of Trevor's struggles, yet he had done nothing to stop his son or help him recover. In retrospect, Jacob always knew what was happening despite being rarely home, and she hardly told him any details.

"How could I be so stupid?" she told the security man.

"Ms., if you don't mind me saying so, I see a lot of stuff in my line of work. Many women are fooled by their spouses, and you wouldn't believe how many cases like this I see weekly."

His gaze softened as she signed the receipt, and he went to the door.

Before leaving, he glanced back. "If your husband goes to this much trouble to monitor you, I suggest you consider protecting yourself."

Mae nodded as he left, letting out a cry as she leaned against the locked door. She had changed the locks throughout the house, but she still did not feel safe.

She would have to move from her home, but for the time being, it gave her relief knowing he didn't have keys to the house. Mae remained unexpectedly calm during this time, though she would panic if she spent too much time reflecting on it.

Jacob would try intimidation with Mae, and sometimes it worked, but most of the time, she would hang up on him, not allowing herself to be roped into his abuse.

"Listen to me. I'll take you down. If it weren't for me, you would be overseas, making pennies to help a third-world country."

It seemed Jacob thought he had saved her by stopping her from pursuing her dreams of going to Guatemala to help underprivileged people.

He always thought he knew better, despite Mae knowing precisely what she wanted and why. Mae desperately tried not to continue to think about the past and all that she had given up.

When Mae wouldn't react to his threats, Jacob would cut off the family credit cards or change the passcode to the mutual bank accounts. Mae would have to contact her attorney, who would then file a motion to stop Jacob from doing these obstructive things, but much of the time, it was too late. Her attorney fees were piling up, and Jacob found satisfaction in making Mae miserable.

Jacob didn't miss Mae.

He missed controlling her and resented that she was finally fighting back. He would tell the boys that she'd left the family to be with another man, which only confused the boys.

"Is it true?" James asked her one night as she was sitting on the couch.

"Is what true, James?" Mae said.

"Have you been cheating on Dad for years, and that's why you filed for divorce?"

Mae tried to stay calm but became agitated. Jacob would stop at nothing to bury her and make her look bad to their sons.

"James, no, of course not," she explained.

She didn't want to provide too many details or stoop as low as Jacob had, but she was growing tired of being portrayed as the bad guy. On the advice of her lawyer, she took the high road, keeping the children, though adults now, out of the drama of their divorce. The truth would come out in time, but for now, she focused on finalizing the divorce and moving on with her life.

"I didn't think so," James said quietly. "It's just that Dad keeps saying these awful things about you. I don't know what to think."

"I know this is all so confusing, James. But in the end, it will work out."

"I'm also worried about Trevor, Mom. I know he's getting help, but what if he starts using again?"

"We just have to support him and pray that he doesn't. As much as I want to see him healthy, Trevor has to choose not to take those pills. No one can do it for him. Honestly, I think he just got off track for a bit. I have faith he will find his way back."

"Me too," said James.

James looked around, taking in his surroundings.

"Tomorrow's a big day." There was a sadness in his voice, holding on to the last moments in the house with his mother.

"It sure is. I'm sad. But this house has served us well, and now it's time for change and for a new family to make their memories here."

They sat on the couch together, boxes surrounding their feet.

"I'm going to head out to Dad's now. Mom, I love you. And I had a great childhood here."

When Mae heard the door click and James' car started, she melted into the couch, weeping. The emotions of the past and the uncertainty of the future were too much. She slept on the couch that night, taking in the last of the house's many memories. Tomorrow would be a new day, and it would be time to say goodbye to the house where she'd shared many laughs and tears.

It was almost time to let go. Mae looked around the empty house one last time.

She gazed at each room, absorbing the memories in her mind, remembering the details of the house where she'd raised her children. She brushed her hand against the banister, recalling her young boys chasing one another down the stairs on Christmas morning.

She glanced at the kitchen, smiling at the once-busy school mornings when frozen waffles and orange juice had been consumed. She let herself feel the loss of her old life, holding on to the memories of the past. It was evident to Mae how life changed: children grew up, parents grew old, and the sun still rose each day, no matter what. Life went on. She just hadn't thought it would be so difficult to let it go, also never considering how quickly time passed.

She walked through the kitchen to the back window, noticing her reflection in the bay window. Her face was older now, her soul aging, and her body more tired, and she thought, *"This has been a good life. Even with my marriage never being whole, raising my boys was a happy time."*

Before she allowed herself to shed another tear, she walked to the front of the house, opened the door, glanced one last time at her home, and strode out.

Mae moved into a small apartment above a storefront in the center of town. The rent was cheap, the quarters were quaint, and Mae was happy to have a place of her own. The boys came for an occasional visit, but mostly, they met for a bite to eat.

The last time she'd seen them had been months prior. Their father still had control over them, and as much as it pained her, she didn't want to add to their stress by bringing it up.

They met at their favorite Italian restaurant. From their window seat, Mae watched as her two boys, now grown men, walked together toward the front entrance.

"There are my boys."

"Mom, when are you going to stop calling us boys?" James said with a quick smirk as they hugged.

Trevor hugged his mother tightly too. "Mom, looking as beautiful as ever."

"You will always be my boys despite the fact you tower over me," Mae said, smiling. So, how are you two?"

Mae's eyes met Trevor's.

She knew he was still struggling with addiction and had recently relapsed.

"I'm good," he said and sighed. "It's hard sometimes. I'm learning the tools I need to move forward with my life. I just accepted a job as an assistant counselor. I need to be clean for another year before I get moved up, but it gives me a goal. In the meantime, I'm still taking classes and hope to graduate within two years."

"Are you still studying social work?" Mae asked.

"Yeah, I have a passion for helping people. My experience can be valuable to others; hopefully, they won't take the same path I did. I'm just lucky I had you there for me, Mom."

Mae's eyes looked deep into Trevor's, seeing for the first time that he was now a man.

He showed no more irresponsible outbursts, poor choices, or blame. That was all in the past. Before her stood a six-foot burly man with a beard and a plan for his future.

Mae was hopeful of his success and proud of his determination.

An awkward silence surrounded the table.

James interrupted. "Yeah, well, now that my brother here and I are roommates, I keep a close eye on him." He patted Trevor's shoulders.

"How's law school?" Trevor said.

Mae was touched that he cared.

"It's great. I graduate in the spring, and I was hoping you'd come to my graduation and maybe even meet Patrick."

The room became still.

Mae nervously waited for a reply, and the boys stared at their half-eaten pasta dishes.

"Mom," James said. "We want to be there. Dad will stop helping us with rent if we have any contact with Patrick though. He's still hellbent on the notion that he ruined your marriage."

Mae knew this, of course. She had hoped that Jacob had let it go by now.

No matter how often Mae insisted this wasn't true, Jacob convinced the boys of the narrative, leaving them to choose sides. She knew how much they loved her, but their father used money as power, and Mae couldn't financially compete. As complex as the years had been for Mae economically and emotionally, she was proud of the life she'd created.

She was finally free to live life on her terms, letting go of the past and looking to her future. However, she was aware that it came at a price. Jacob could continue to control the boys through finances, but she knew she had their hearts. Jacob's control put them in a terrible position; they were just now finding their way and still relying on their father for money.

Mae tried to hide her disappointment. "I know. It's disgusting what he does to manipulate. When I finally start working as an attorney, you won't have to rely on your father's wallet."

"Mom, as soon as I graduate and get a job, I'm going to tell him to stick his money up his ass," Trevor said, chuckling.

James nodded in agreement.

She took her boys' hands in hers. "I love you both so much."

As they said goodbye, she hoped they could consider attending her graduation. She had worked hard and wanted them there to celebrate but knew Jacob held them hostage through their financial dependence.

Chapter 20

Spring had arrived as Mae walked across the stage, beaming when she heard her name called. The sun was hot, and perspiration was gathering at the top of her head. The past years had been difficult for Mae, with the divorce, taking out loans for law school, and dealing with the emotional wreckage it had caused. She looked out to the crowd and found Patrick standing and waving proudly as she smiled. Mae had done it.

She'd graduated from law school with a focus on international law.

She had already secured a job with the United States Embassy, where she would help immigrants obtain their papers to become citizens.

Mae thought about how far she had come.

The invisible scars that the years of abuse had left empowered her instead of defeating her. She had found her voice and purpose and no longer allowed her past to dictate her future.

"I'm so proud of you," Judy said, hugging Mae. "You did it. All on your own."

"I sure did. It wasn't easy, but I was determined," Mae said. She looked through the crowds, her eyes darting to unfamiliar faces, hoping her boys would be amongst the mobs of people.

"Sweetie, you did this for you. I'm sure the boys are proud of you, too," Judy said.

"I know, I just hoped by now they would be more ... I don't know, more accepting. Less influenced by their father."

"Eventually, they'll come around. We all do," Judy said with a chuckle.

Patrick waited for Mae and Judy to finish their conversation, giving them a private moment before opening his arms to hug Mae tightly.

"Babe, you did it! I knew you would! You should be proud. I made a reservation at a restaurant down the block. Let's go celebrate."

Mae felt a sudden sadness in her chest. She had hoped the boys would come to see her graduate. Judy and Patrick locked eyes, noticing Mae's demeanor.

"C'mon love, I can use a drink," Judy said, grasping her arm.

Suddenly, James and Trevor unexpectedly grabbed their mother from behind, screaming, "Mom, you did it! Congratulations."

Mae was speechless. She had assumed they hadn't shown up, and that the cheers in the crowd only came from Patrick and Judy.

"Surprise," said Patrick.

"Wait, you knew about this?"

"You have some great kids here, Mae. The boys and I met last week for dinner and planned to surprise you."

"Dad's money will never keep us from celebrating our mother," Trevor said.

Mae was overjoyed and emotional.

"Thank you," she sobbed.

"Just don't tell Dad. He thinks we're on a skiing trip."

"When are two going to stand up to your father?"

"When we don't need him to pay our rent," teased Trevor.

James, more serious, said, "Actually, we were thinking about that. Trevor's graduating soon, and we will let him know by summer that we can manage on our own now."

"We've been working and saving money. It just doesn't feel right taking money from him anymore," James added.

"Maybe he'll finally realize that money isn't everything," offered Mae.

James shrugged, knowing it wasn't their journey to teach Jacob a kinder way of living. He would have to find that out on his own.

Finally, having time to approach their grandmother, Jacob and James took turns and embraced her tightly. "Grandma," shouted James. I've missed you."

"You two are great sons," Judy said, clasping onto their waists.

After the tears and continual hugs, they packed into their cars and drove to the restaurant.

During the short ride, Mae was quiet, taking in the scenery and reflecting on finally pursuing the life she had sought many years before. She thought about the young girl in college, with all her big dreams, and thanked her silently for achieving the goals she'd set long ago.

Mae had given up many things for motherhood, things she shouldn't have, but she felt pressure to do so. Now, she realized what Judy had also given up and felt deep respect. She could not expect her children to understand the strife of parenthood until they, too, were older.

Realizing the expectations placed on mothers was not only unreasonable but unattainable. Many women started to live their lives when reality set in. Children would always grow, begin making decisions, and eventually no longer accept the parent as the main authority.

It had taken Mae until later in life to get this, staying married to a man she despised so as not to disappoint other people.

Next, she thought back to Jane and her relationship with Jacob.

He, too, had succumbed to pleasing his mother.

He had even once admitted that he'd never wanted to go into finance. Still, his great-grandfather, grandfather, father, and brother were bankers, and he'd felt pressured to uphold the family tradition. The toxicity of people-pleasing had gone on long enough, and Mae was determined to break the cycle. She appreciated her mother's support, but how many years of her life had been wasted doing what she thought she should rather than what she'd wanted?

She needed to cut the cycle, so that her boys did not fall victim to the same fate.

Thinking back on James, she remembered his desire to go away to school, but at the last minute, he'd changed his mind. In how many more ways had she held her children back by not letting go? From this point on, she'd live differently, vowing to allow herself the grace and freedom to explore life without worrying about how others perceived her choices.

She committed to doing the same with those in her life, starting with herself, then the boys, and even Jacob. Letting go was one of the hardest and best lessons she had learned in life, and she was grateful for the hard but necessary tools to uncover her strength.

As they parted ways later that evening, Judy held Mae's hand tight.

Tears came to her eyes, causing Mae to have the same fate.

Judy placed her now old, wrinkled hands on her daughter's face. Looking deep into her eyes, she proclaimed, "My daughter, you have made me so proud, not by your success but by your willingness to fail authentically. You have chosen to live your life now as you had initially intended. I'm sorry if I've held you back. But daughter, you have now arrived. Be present, live your life, find true happiness, and know I'm forever grateful to have you as my daughter. My heart beams with pride, and I couldn't be more grateful to have watched your life unfold to where you are now." She took her now sobbing daughter into her arms, cradling her head, and gently rubbing her long brown hair. "Thank you, Mom. I love you."

Three days later, Judy died peacefully in her sleep.

Mae stared at a hummingbird as it made its way through the garden. She watched as it aimlessly skirted around the flowers, yet careful to admire its surroundings. She wished to be more like a hummingbird, appreciative of the beauty but particular in its efforts.

Mae settled next to Patrick, putting her head on his shoulder.

He leaned in and kissed her cheek, something that Mae loved most.

In the years she had spent with Patrick, there wasn't a time he didn't show her affection.

His adoration took time to get used to, but eventually, she began to do something she'd never intended again. She began to trust.

Patrick stayed consistent, and Mae's heart eventually opened up again in a way she hadn't known possible. She'd known from the day she met him that there was a special connection.

With time, Mae could love Patrick because she loved herself fully.

She was able to trust in him too, solely because she trusted herself, no longer allowing her desires to be diminished. She lived fully. Patrick never failed to see the best in Mae, and in return, Mae brought the best of herself to their relationship.

Occasionally, she would see Jacob at an event for one of the boys, where he would nod in her direction, and she would give him a weak wave as she walked by.

Since a bout with cancer, Jacob had become softer, kinder, and humbler.

If he had learned a valuable lesson through cancer, Mae wasn't sure, but the boys reported how much their father had changed in the last years.

He no longer intimidated her either; she'd regained her control, and he was a stranger.

"It's funny how that happens," Mae lamented. "I'd never have believed that the man who had control over me for so much of my life would one day be a stranger I barely recognize."

It was as though she'd never had a life with him at all.

"What do you mean?" Patrick asked curiously.

Mae pondered her response. "All of the years I spent with Jacob ... Honestly, we barely really knew one another. We just kind of coexisted."

"I reckon that happens more than you think," Patrick said thoughtfully.

"It's sad. I wish my younger self had known what I know now."

"You need to let it go, Mae. Isn't that what you always say?"

Mae smiled at Patrick, knowing he was right.

Despite her past and the efforts injected by Jacob to keep her small, Mae rose above, knowing she had been capable all along.

Acknowledgments

Letting Go is a tribute to all those women who find themselves in uncomfortable situations based on societal expectations. Often, it is only when we become a shadow of who we once were before we are ready to make a change.

I want to give special thanks to my mother, Franny Parisi, my biggest supporter and champion. I am forever in awe of your love and example. Thank you for guiding me through the most difficult journeys and believing there would be light on the other side. I know now I am enough.

Thank you, Joe, for always being so good to us. You hold a special place in our hearts.

Thank you to my siblings and best friends, James, Marissa, Phyllis, Andrew, Victoria, and Tim. Family will forever be an important part of my life, and I am grateful to share it surrounded by love.

Thank you to my aunts, uncles, and cousins near and far. There are far too many to name, but your continued support means the world to me.

Thank you to Suzanne, Aimee, Christine, and Helen, who continually inspire me to be my best self. Our friendship is forever, near or far.

Thanks to Sophia, Rocco, Gloria, and Jim, I am honored to be part of the family.

Thank you to my editor, Annie Jenkinson, and her team for the incredible transformation, brilliance, and patience.

To my beautiful children, William, Emma, Benjamin, and Matthew, watching you grow has been my biggest blessing. I will forever hold the Fab4 as my biggest accomplishment. As I say all the time: it all works out. It always does... So, believe in the magic of life.

Marc Ferolito, there aren't enough words to articulate my gratitude for your love, support, patience, and dedication. The life we are building is more than I could have imagined. Having you by my side brings me immense joy and pride. You have given me the courage to live my most authentic life, knowing I am fully loved for who I am. I choose you today, tomorrow, and always.

About the Author

Donna Lynn Lito received her master's in creative writing in May 2024. She currently creates podcasts and blogs on her website, Donnalynnbooks.com.

In addition to her latest novel, Letting Go, she is the author of 4FCKS SAKE and Securely Insecure.

Be on the watch for her book The Mixing Bowl, which is due out later in 2025.

Donna Lynn enjoys spending time in South Carolina, creating her authentic life while "letting go" of the past and focusing on the future.

www.ingramcontent.com/pod-product-compliance
Lightning Source LLC
Chambersburg PA
CBHW071410300726
48976CB00006B/2044